Also from Mickey Hoffman
& Indigo Sea Press

Deadly Traffic

www.indigoseapress.com

SCHOOL OF LIES

BY

MICKEY HOFFMAN

Stiletto Books
Published by Indigo Sea Press
Winston-Salem

Stiletto Books
Indigo Sea Press
302 Ricks Drive
Winston-Salem, NC 27103

For information regarding bulk purchases of this book,
digital purchase and special discounts, please contact the publisher
at indigoseapress@gmail.com

Cover Concept by Maribeth Shanley
Cover design by Pan Morelli
Manufactured in the United States of America
ISBN 978-1-63066-358-2

For Myles, who is the best part of my life. Without your patience, emotional support and ability to mind read this book would not exist.

Heartfelt thanks to Roanne, Margalit and Dan, for their invaluable help.

And for my ex-students who could not speak up for themselves, this one's for you.

—Mickey Hoffman

Indigo Sea Press,
your literary home
for all genre publications,
including suspense, thrillers,
mysteries, espionage and mysteries
from Mickey Hoffman
and other fine authors.

1.

Monday morning

Vice Principal Zant's enraged voice easily penetrated the office's thin walls, which provided only a token sense of privacy. Kendra inched closer to the windowed partition and took in the unfolding drama through the dusty blinds.

The setting and script were familiar, as were the lead protagonists. The boy's black hair and matching attire made a bold silhouette against the dingy beige walls. From her vantage point she could just see the glass tank that housed the VP's pet tarantula.

This would be the umpteenth student rescue operation she had mounted since the newly promoted Zant had arrived at Standard High, vacating his previous niche as the worst English teacher in the district. Upon hearing a hall monitor make reference to a skirmish in Zant's office, Kendra had detoured from her path to the teachers' lounge.

"Empty your pockets, son!" The Vice Principal slammed the behavior slip to his desktop.

"I ain't your son. Your son's in a cage at the zoo."

Mr. Zant reared from his chair, affronted at the student's impertinence, although he couldn't have been surprised. "I've heard enough!"

His bulk poised to move in on the gangly teenager seated before him. Then, for once realizing he was showing a lack of self-control, he retook his seat and conjured up a frosty and very fake paternal smile.

Kendra froze. Although she'd chalked up a moderate success rate in her duels with Zant, the encounters stretched her courage to the limits and she knew hours would pass before she'd recover from what was to come. Mr. Zant thought to cover his ineptitude by attacking anyone who questioned him. Kendra braced herself, turned the doorknob, and stepped in. The Vice Principal's chair squeaked at the intrusion.

"Ah, look who's here. It's Ms. Desola. But I don't recall asking you to come down. Really, there's no need for you to be here. I'm sure you have plenty of your own work."

Kendra made a show of setting down her load of books and lunch bag while she frantically worked up a fitting reply. Sensing that the heat was momentarily blowing in another direction, her student assumed the facial expression of an orphaned puppy.

"Ms. D., I ain't done nothin'." Jon shuffled his feet, or what could be seen of them under his voluminous jeans.

The VP countered. "The only place where I'm sure you haven't done anything is inside a classroom." Zant smiled at his riposte.

Jon blinked and offered, "At least I ain't been inside my sister."

Mr. Zant bridged the desk with his hands as he stood. "For that, I'm adding two more days to your suspension!"

In spite of the closed quarters, the office temperature dropped very low. Kendra prayed that Mr. Zant's lips would be frozen shut before he traded another insult.

She moved closer to the boy, hoping that her proximity might silence him. The telltale odor of adolescent sweat made a lie of his posturing. Jon was one of the "at risk" students, dyslexic and below norms in both achievement and emotional growth. If he was expelled from Standard High, he'd totally give up on school and his life would unlikely proceed in a positive direction.

"Mr. Zant, can you please tell me what happened?"

Zant appeared to be on the verge of dismissing her, but then sighed and settled himself into his chair, fingering his silk tie into alignment. "Jon was chasing after Anita Hodges, and tried to set fire to her bandana with a lighter. When the hall monitors asked him to come to the office, he took off. They ran him down near the cafeteria. That's how you found out, I assume?"

"I didn't do anything to her stupid do-rag! That bitch is lying," yelled Jon, unhelpfully.

For once, Zant ignored the kid's profanity. "We have a witness, Anita's girlfriend."

"Why do you want him to empty his pockets?"

"Why do you always question every move I make, Ms. Desola?"

This complaint was one with which she was familiar, but she preferred to regard her character trait as "attention to detail." She

2

stood her ground. "Why the search?"

"Anita told the hall monitors that Jon put the lighter in his pocket. We'll get it from him one way or another."

Jon burst out, "I don't have a lighter. You wanna strip me, you perv?"

Zant yanked open a drawer and brought out a pair of latex gloves. He set this 21st century gauntlet on his desk with practiced stagecraft. Kendra recognized the VP was enjoying this a great deal. It wasn't out of the ordinary for staff to use the gloves when handling student clothing, but she was certain Zant meant something more invasive.

She said, "Jon, if you haven't got the lighter, then show us you don't have it, okay? Please, let's get this over with." She sat next to him and nodded in encouragement.

Jon glanced at Kendra and then at Mr. Zant. Slowly, the boy emptied out all five pockets of his cargo pants. He put each object down on the seat next to him, one by one, with quite a bit of what Mr. Zant was sure to label as "attitude." What appeared was the usual student hoard: candy bar, bus pass, crumpled dollar bills, iPOD, a long key chain, and a piece of folded binder paper. There was nothing else.

"He must have ditched the lighter somehow." The spittle reached Kendra across the desk. "No matter, we have a witness. We don't need the lighter." Zant pointed the behavior slip at Jon. "This is the 16th time I've seen you in my office this semester, but this is going to be the last time. Standard High is not the right place for you." Zant folded his hands in a "done deal" gesture.

The boy hesitated, then mumbled, "Do what you gotta do. Can I go to lunch?"

"You'd like that, wouldn't you? No, you are going to wait right outside until one of your guardians comes to get you. I'm giving you a five day suspension." He swept up the iPod. "I'll hold this for your guardian to pick up. You know the rules. If we see them, we keep them. Now get moving."

The VP waved the boy out and motioned for Kendra to stay put. Zant swiveled his chair, popped the lid off a plastic bin and placed the iPod on a mound of confiscated digital cameras, cell phones and like devices. Then, as if she wasn't there, he leaned to a small wall mirror, and carefully examined both sides of his face

3

before turning toward her again. His closely spaced, dark eyes studied Kendra as if he was deciding whether she was worthwhile prey or just a nuisance.

"Ms. Desola, that boy is a liability to the entire school. I'm not waiting for him to burn it down. I don't see anything 'special' about him. He's just a gangbanger hiding behind a disability label. It's too bad you've got misdiagnosed kids on your class list, but Downtown isn't responding to that problem, and our school can't fix these kids. Why spend more of our time on a new behavior modification plan when nothing will change? Or is Jon's problem just due to lack of supervision? I expect you to be monitoring your students."

Kendra cut off the tirade before she had to endure any more of the familiar browbeating. "I do monitor my students. And if you really want me to know what my students are up to, why don't you ever call me when one of them winds up in your office? But, to the point, Mr. Zant, I don't believe there ever was a cigarette lighter. Anita Hodges loves to get people in trouble, and is smart enough to know that no one will believe Jon."

"I'm not interested in her right now." Mr. Zant was clearly enjoying himself. With a flourish, he tilted back his head and popped a handful of breath mints into his mouth. Kendra wished, just once, they'd land in his thick hair, and that he didn't notice for at least two hours. His behavior was so strange, she wondered if he did share common eating habits with his pet spider, as her students often suggested.

Zant resumed, "You've got only 25 students on your class list, yet they all seem to wind up in my office. What do you do all day, then?"

Kendra stifled a scream. Zant was on a roll. It was pointless to state the obvious; she saw her students only during the periods that they were assigned to her classroom. Most of the day, they were dispersed all over the huge campus, either in the other classes for learning disabled kids, or mainstreamed in general classes. She had 25 different schedules to coordinate.

"Mr. Zant, this incident occurred at lunch. Are you asking me to give up my lunch to follow students around?" She glanced from her wristwatch to her sandwich bag. "Speaking of which, I'm out of time. I haven't eaten, I have a class to teach next period, and the bell is going to ring in about—" Kendra's bold declaration faltered with the untimely loosening of a hairclip. Strands of curly brown hair flared wildly around her ears.

Zant made use of the moment. "Call Jon's guardian and schedule a conference right away. Let's get moving on expulsion."

Kendra shook her head so fiercely that her glasses slid down her rather flat nose.

"That isn't for you to decide. You can't change a Special Ed. student's placement by yourself. It has to be decided by a team. Maretta Edwards should be there also. She's our parent outreach person."

Zant smiled sardonically. "You set up your meeting, then, but do not invite Maretta. I made it clear that you no longer have a Department Chair. That's just one reason why you Special Ed. teachers are the laughing stock of the faculty. You don't do anything all day but you want to have a Department Chair."

Zant had already turned back to his computer, as if these remarks didn't even merit eye contact. Perhaps the man wanted to bait her into another argument, but Kendra had neither the time nor the stomach for another round.

"I really must get back to my room," she said.

At the door, she had to step aside to make way for Allana Jarney, who stormed up to Zant. Kendra could just hear Allana ask, "What the hell do you think you're doing?"

***

Rain pelted Kendra's eyeglasses, blurring her view as she navigated a course through treacherous puddles and potholes. The walk from main building to the portable classrooms took several minutes.

When the original, two storey, brick building no longer held the increasing student population, a row of "temporary" prefabricated classrooms had been planted on what had been a softball field. A few years later, more of the wooden portables arrived, including the ones that now housed three Special Ed. classrooms. These additions, in their U-shaped configuration, made it almost impossible to supervise the students who chose to run from behind the buildings to the football field. The bleachers, that backed against a row of large oak trees, provided a spot for all sorts of undesirable activities both during and after school hours. From there, it was an easy sprint off campus, over or through the ragged chain link fence that marked the school boundary. Surveillance cameras seemed to have no effect on truancy, to say nothing about non-students who sneaked on campus for various destructive purposes.

Kendra crossed the deserted basketball courts. Today the students were sheltering near the portables. Kendra quickly leaped to one side, barely avoiding a collision with a boy careening down the handicapped ramp on a rolling desk chair. The lid popped off her drink, sloshing over her forearm.

"A perfect end to the perfect lunch," Kendra muttered, hugging the wall to dodge a stream of water cascading from the overhang. Several noisy students immediately burst upon her, nagging, complaining, offering up the latest tidbits of news. Kendra apologetically squeezed past them into her classroom and bumped the rickety door until it locked behind her.

She flopped into her desk chair and tore at her lunch bag. The condiments had soaked through the sandwich wrapper and were headed for her desktop. She ran to a supply corner to get paper towels and had barely grasped the roll when something moved at her feet.

Her scream brought the next-door teacher through the door that connected their classrooms. They both watched a small snake glide over the linoleum and slip through one of the many gaps in the plywood siding.

"Are you okay?" The man held a half-eaten cookie in his hand. "You're lucky it wasn't a rattler."

Kendra nodded, still out of breath from her dash across the floor. The teacher said, "Want me to check the rest of the room out for you?"

"No, I'm fine. See, I can even breathe now. That critter was harmless, go back to your lunch. These portables are like sieves, you know. This place is a zoo even without kids."

The teacher smiled and retreated to his room. Kendra cautiously approached the closet. The floor was still not bare. There was an envelope that should not have been there. The note inside read, "Check your email."

6

There was one new message in her email inbox. The subject line was "Your graduated students." The sender name was "A Friend."

Curiously, she opened the new message. It read, "You'll love this photo!" She saw that there was an attachment. She never opened unknown attachments on her home computer, but didn't the school network employ all kinds of elaborate security measures?

She clicked on the attachment. What opened was a vaguely familiar photograph of four of her male students seated in a convertible. But in this version, the centerpiece was Kendra. Her slim and scantily clothed body was entwined with two boys in the back seat. A caption read, "For your eyes only, for NOW."

She closed the attachment as quickly as her shaking fingers allowed.

"Who'd do this to me? Who the hell would do this to me?" she raged. "I do everything I can for the kids, work my butt off..." Then the tears came. She pulled off her flooded glasses and thoughtlessly wiped them on her shirt. Thudding shoes on the walkway outside acted as a curb to her self-pity. She still had to finish out the day. Would she come face to face with the person who'd done this before the day was out?

The photo was altered, but how could she prove that? The female body was almost identical to her own and, unfortunately, she didn't have any birthmarks to prove otherwise. None of the featured youths had a motive and they lacked the necessary expertise with Photoshop. Even to her eyes, it looked completely legitimate. What about other students, or even a coworker? It would be a fine mess if Zant had found out...but no, he wouldn't have found out anything yet. Damn it, who was after her?

Every teacher worried about accusations like this. At best, she'd be fired and never teach again, but criminal prosecution was more probable. Even if she wasn't prosecuted, her entire life was going to be scrutinized. She'd be ruined.

A bitter taste spiked her tongue. She cursed her stress-related habit of chewing on pens. Well, you couldn't get more poisonous than this email. Kendra looked more closely at the sender's email address but it told her nothing.

Something tweaked her memory and she went over to a bulletin board where she habitually pinned up photos. Most had been given to her by the kids themselves: shots of students dressed up for a dance, in their school sports uniforms, holding a baby brother, posed in gowns for their graduation picture. Although the board was still crowded with photos, she saw gaps where snapshots might have been dislodged. Or someone had removed them. She didn't see a photo of four boys in a convertible.

***

"Come in and shut the door." Mr. Zant waved Jack Sermon to the wooden bench that a now retired teacher had dubbed The Rack. "You're late, as usual. I have another evaluation at 1:15, so we have to rush." Zant's body language belied his words; the VP leaned way back in his chair, manipulating the limbs of a plastic action figure he'd confiscated from a student earlier that morning.

Jack shrugged. "Sorry. You know how things go. Soon as I start to leave the classroom, the kids all want something." He furtively pushed a pack of cigarettes farther down into his pocket. "And then someone asked me about a union matter." He sat back and released his grip on a small thermos jug and some rolled up documents.

"So decent of you to come." Zant replied. He set the plastic toy on his desk blotter and drew a sheaf of papers from an envelope. "Now that you've honored me with your esteemed presence, let's get going on this. Did you bring the teacher section of your evaluation?"

"I want to talk to you about that. Don't you know you used the wrong form? I'm a Special Ed. teacher and you used the evaluation form for a Program Specialist. That form is only good for someone in a managerial position. Perhaps you were confused, since some of my duties are actually administrative."

A choking sound came from Zant's direction as the VP took a sip from a cold drink cup.

Jack realized that at some point he'd picked up his thermos and was picking at its charging bull decal. He longed to aim the horns of the School Mascot at the Vice Principal. Jack continued, "To be sure, as a union rep., I take on tasks that most teachers aren't asked to do, but according to the evaluation procedures agreed to in our contract, you are obligated to use the credentialed teacher form to evaluate me."

"Thank you for that detailed explanation, Mr. Sermon, but let's not get bogged down in that petty stuff. A form is just a form."

"But Mr. Zant, this form doesn't address actual teaching activities or the special services that I provide to my disabled students."

"Mr. Sermon, all I want to know is did you or did you not fill out the section of the evaluation where you rate yourself?"

"No, I did not. I was waiting for you to give me the appropriate form. In a nutshell, I will not put my pen to your attempt to misrepresent my performance."

The VP remained motionless except for a delicate fingering of his toy. Each caress of the plastic was an abrasion to Jack's tenuously held temper. But Jack was determined to win this battle. He knew he was in the right.

Jack continued, "In case you don't know, I helped negotiate the section of our union contract that spells out how teachers are to be evaluated. The only area on this Specialist form that applies to me refers to conducting student assessments. By the way, you can't get me on that the way you're going after the rest of my department."

"It's true your paperwork is complete, Mr. Sermon, but that is only one part of your job. After all, we at Standard High are dedicated to having the highest degree of student achievement." Zant was clearly mocking the theatrical tone in Jack's manner.

"I'm glad you bring that up, because there is another big problem with your evaluating me. You never showed up in my classroom to do the scheduled observation, so how are you able to rate my classroom performance?" Jack felt his heart rate zoom. He toyed with the notion he might not live long enough to take the early retirement for which he longed. He rubbed sweaty palms along his thighs.

"That's right. I did miss the observation. I did get out to your classroom later on that day, but you, unfortunately, weren't there," snarled Zant. "Taking one of your little breaks, were you?"

Jack quickly deflected this line of discussion by going on the offensive. "You think you can write up an evaluation of my teaching for a period when you, in fact, observed nothing? I will be taking this to the Union."

"Before or after I document for the Principal that you were out of your classroom during a time you should have been there? And while I'm doing that, I'll tell her you've been seen smoking and lounging in your car—during class time, no less." Zant made a tent with his fingers. "Speaking of Mrs. Prescott, I don't appreciate that you went behind my back to get her to approve your so called 'Inclusion and Tolerance' seminar. I have the authority to make decisions about any activities we host at school, including your 'faggot forum'." Sorry if I tried to ruin your chance for a hot date," smirked the VP.

Not at all surprised at the jibe, Jack narrowed his eyes and mentally counted his blessings; he had only two years left 'til he could collect a full pension. Unless Zant managed to fire him. Yeah, Zant would definitely lie about what had been said in this room, so Jack curbed his reply.

"Mr. Zant, if you don't want to facilitate acceptance of the diversity in our community, that's up to you, but don't think that you can force your bigotry on others." Jack mentally added, *and speaking of hot dates, your ex-wife told me you couldn't heat up a teaspoon of water.*

Zant shook his head. "You don't judge me. I do the judging around here and if you don't like that, fine. You have any other remarks for me to put on the evaluation you won't sign?"

"Not at the moment." Jack's broad back hid the rude gesture he made with his rolled up packet as he lumbered away.

***

Nicole nudged the door ajar with her hip. "Mr. Zant, have you got a minute?"

"What is it, Nicole? Aren't you assigned to VP Favor this period?" Zant gave her a quick head to toe appraisal. Nicole was squirming in front of him, working her fingers into the back pocket of her exceedingly tight jeans. She surely was a "babe," as the students said. Zant wasn't that far removed from those years that he couldn't easily remember how it felt to be in class with girls like her. Next thing you know, she'd be calling him a dirty old

10

man, but what should he do with his eyes? These kids thought a dress code was a cipher to be broken, not a clothing guide. He forced himself to look at her face, at that lovely wide mouth.

"I already told you that I won't have you reinstated as a candidate, Nicole. Once you get a suspension, you can't run for office."

"This'll make you change your mind." Nicole held out an envelope decorated with her signature cartoon and moved forward to edge around the side of his desk. In a lower voice she continued, "Yesterday, after school, I was on my way to interview a teacher for the school paper and I saw the Special Ed. teachers having a little get-together in the room next door. I didn't mean to eavesdrop, but when I heard what they were talking about I thought, like, maybe I'd help you out a bit, you know?" She upended the envelope and slid out two cassette tapes.

When Zant didn't rise to the bait, Nicole made a gesture to put the tapes back. "Or, maybe you already know what they're planning to do?"

He could see his tarantula in its tank, crawling mere inches from the girl's arm. He was struck by the irony that the girl was a predator in her own way as well. However, her proposal was not without interest. The gleam in his eyes contradicted his careful words. "I don't make deals with students, Nicole. Save your business skills for your senior vocational task." He picked up his Army insignia paperweight and fondled it.

"Well, Mr. Zant, I think that you'll find it very worth your while to listen to this. Tell you what, you can have 'part one' now. After you hear how their meeting was going, I just know you'll want 'part two'." Nicole leaned forward, revealing several inches of cleavage. She dangled the tape before him. "I'm totally sure you'll want to show your appreciation by putting my name back on the ballot and then I'll give you the second tape. You know I should be senior class President."

The VP gave her his most professional smile. "I'll give it only my best, Nicole. Hand it over and go."

"I knew you'd see the light, Mr. Zant." She dropped the cassette into his hand and bounded out of the room, leaving a cloud of perfume behind.

Cripes, he thought, *that café latte girl was much more than her*

11

six feet of trouble. The tape seemed to jeer at him from his hand. Clearing his head, he locked it into a drawer. He'd listen to the tape later. That had been a real interesting little scene. The tape must have been made on the sly. It was probably illegal to even have it. Even if it actually did contain useful information, he had no intention of reinstating her as a candidate. He'd find a way to get the second part of the tape.

Zant wasn't surprised to find out that the Special Education department was plotting against him. He knew they wanted to get him fired and any one of them might be the ringleader—except Allana—she was too lazy. That busybody Kendra Desola was right in the thick of it, he was certain, to say nothing of that shrew, Maretta Edwards. Of course, Jack Sermon had more reason than anyone to want him gone.

And wouldn't Mr. Favor also relish that—less com-petition for the Principal's job that was coming open next year. He shook his head. He intended to be Principal, no matter what. He wondered if all the rumors about Nicole being "Favor's Favorite Flavor" had any substance to them. That would be useful information; he just needed proof of what the other VP was doing. He laughed as a plan came to mind.

He wished he had time to hear that tape now. But it was looking like another long afternoon. Even if he scrounged up a tape player, he feared being caught listening to the tape when Tamra Helens, the Special Ed. liaison arrived.

Hah, for all he knew, he'd hear Tamra on that tape! She would play both sides; he certainly knew what that woman was all about, every inch of her. He smirked at the memory. On the political front, however, he didn't count her in his camp even though she was an administrator by title.

He'd really had it with all these so-called "Specialists" like her, who knew nothing. All they had were a bunch of theories and an endless list of acronyms—useless labels the kids used to avoid taking responsibility for their actions. That was a lesson only learned here, long after completing the boring coursework required for teachers who wished to upgrade to an administrative position. Well, he'd pull this department into shape with or without Tamra Helens' help. He hadn't put in eight years as a sergeant in the US Army without learning the real way to administrate.

12

He ripped open a packet of mints and downed a handful with the dregs of his lunchtime soda. He didn't mind being in charge of attendance, student activities, and the after-school programs, but having the Special Ed. department on his back was a curse. Maybe he didn't have the expertise to deal with that arena, but it wasn't fair to load it on him in the first place. But no one wanted to oversee Special Ed. so it always fell to the lowest on the totem pole.

His VP job had turned out to be a far cry from the position of power and influence that he'd fantasized about. Instead, he caught all the flack from parents and staff while the Principal remained unscathed. During moments of introspection, he knew that he'd only been appointed VP because he had a relative up in the district office and this hole of an inner city school couldn't fill the vacant position. He'd been desperate to get out of the classroom, so he'd jumped at the opportunity.

Zant supposed that his frustration sometimes drove him to what looked like pettiness and retaliation, but he knew what needed to be done here, especially with those damn Special Education people. He was sick of their expectation of "special" treatment. One minute they wanted extra con-sideration because their students had different needs, yet the next minute they demanded the same kids should be treated like everyone else. He saw no logic to that. And the com-plexity of the laws and constant risk of legal action gave him a huge headache.

Yeah, this bunch of incompetent teachers needed to get their records in order or a few staff would be leaving, but he wouldn't be one of them. He wasn't going to allow the school to be sanctioned by the state review team. Yes, he was nominally the site manager of the Special Education staff, but he had justifiably assumed that their paperwork had been completed—under the watchful eye of Tamra Helens. How was he to know those damn teachers never finished their behavior plans and were doubly out of compliance by not holding the state-mandated, student education plan meetings?

At times, he regretted leaving the Army. In the military a rule was a rule. Well, not to worry. Since Maretta Edwards wanted to be the Special Education Department Chair, he'd make sure that she was the one who took the heat when the state review team arrived!

13

Mickey Hoffman

2.

Drip. Drip. The previous day's rain had continued through the night, and Kendra was in her classroom dealing with the results. The ancient chalkboards were so wet they bowed away from the wall. A saturated ceiling tile had fallen, and a shallow lake pooled in the center of the room in spite of the many buckets she'd placed in strategic locations. Unfortunately, there'd be no custodial help before school. If she hadn't anticipated the situation and come in early, the room wouldn't be in shape to hold classes.

She knew to expect a flood when heavy rain was forecast, so she positioned buckets before going home. Still, the water always seemed to drip somewhere new. Hopefully, today's roof leaks would not result in a repeat of the memorable occasion when a rain-soaked ceiling tile made a bull's-eye landing on a surprised student's desk.

Kendra had a second reason for coming in early. The bulletin board of student photos had to come down, especially considering what had already happened. Although teacher-training courses emphasized the need to maintain a careful, professional distance from students, she hadn't given the issue much thought as she went about her daily work. Some of the male teachers were so cautious that they'd only talk to students out in a hallway or other busy spot.

She dumped the last pail of reclaimed water and began to take down the pictures. The students would complain, but she had to protect herself. These poor kids needed a place where they could express themselves and get positive feedback, but it would be wise to review all the strategies she used to bond with them. A gust of wind blew the photos off the table where she'd been piling them. The classroom door had blown open again. There was something wrong with the latching mechanism, and all of her attempts to

15

have the lock replaced had failed. Today, the door was a priority. Her maintenance request form number S3402C was undoubtedly buried at the bottom of a drawer downtown. Time to wage yet another battle, this time with the main-tenance department.

Considering the never ending problems, she was some-what at a loss to explain why she still wanted to be in front of a classroom, especially this one. Six years to attain this level of certification, and the reward was Standard High? Yeah, she was a real winner, with her ratty classroom, and swamped with work. She smiled at the unintentional pun.

Back at her desk, she rummaged for her lesson planner, taking a moment to enjoy a large, framed photo of her cat. That dose of stress relief lasted only until she opened the planning book, which was jammed with notes about testing deadlines and the dreaded state standardized review. The overcrowded calendar reminded her of the first big argument with her boyfriend Brian.

The dispute arose after she'd cancelled a date so she could attend a weekend teacher workshop. Brian had just returned to town after being away on a job, and that Saturday was the only full day they had before he left again. She'd been unwilling to skip the workshop, and he'd been very upset about that decision.

When they first met, Kendra was supporting herself with a boring office job that didn't conflict with her college schedule, or their dating. Brian's sister was a teacher who'd influenced him with horror stories about the long hours of unpaid work. He kept trying to convince Kendra to switch majors and get an MBA. Kendra originally thought she could just ignore his conservative worldview; Brian was an entrepreneur, after all, who designed and installed computerized displays for trade shows and conferences. What did he honestly know about education? Still, maybe it was time for the two of them to sit down and discuss how their careers affected their relationship.

Kendra never tried to hide the negatives about her job. All she could do was keep telling him she valued and liked what she was doing. Yet he persisted in claiming teaching was not right for her. And since her transfer last year to notorious, gang infested Standard High, he worried she was trapped in an environment far more dangerous than she cared to admit.

To be honest, neither she nor Brian had correctly estimated just how demanding and time consuming teaching could be. And now, apparently, hazardous could be added to the job description. How would she ever tell him about the email?

***

"I didn't think it was relevant..." Julia sobbed into the receiver. "Or I would have told you, honest... What—what do you mean things don't look good? We can't give up! But can't you...what do we do now?" When her attorney finished delivering his lecture, she dropped the phone into the cradle and bolted from her seat, her careening chair unnoticed as it demonstrated Newton's third law of motion.

Julia had to use both of her shaking hands to unlock the restroom door. The tiny room held only sink, toilet and a small table, which creaked under her as she sat. She wadded some toilet paper in her fists and pressed it to her mouth to cover her sobs. Slowly, her self-pity turned to anger.

None of her relatives would have said anything bad about her to the adoption agency. Besides her husband, who knew that she had attempted suicide after that last miscarriage? She had given the doctors and later, her boss a convincing story. As far as medical records were concerned, her trip to the emergency room looked innocent enough. She'd just spent one night in the hospital after her "accidental overdose." Sure, there might have been speculation among the hospital staff, but with their overload of patients why would they give a second thought to her case? But somehow the information had gotten out, and the adoption agency wanted to call off the adoption, killing her chance to finally have a baby to call her own. The problem had to trace back to this place—Standard High, where everyone knew she was trying to adopt a baby.

How much had Zant learned about her personal life? He hadn't seemed suspicious when she requested a week of sick leave. When the adoption agency asked to review her family finances and employment, she and her husband had feared what could happen if her boss got interviewed. She asked her attorney about that part of the process and he said what the agency mainly wanted from her workplace was proof of sufficient income to support a child, and they'd probably just send a financial disclosure request to the Human Resources Department downtown.

Did Zant go out of his way to involve himself in the process, use his status as her superior to volunteer "input" about her character? All so well-meaning, of course, for the good of the baby. She could hear him putting on an oily, professional tone to attack her integrity. That son of a bitch.

There was rattling at the door; an aggravated staff member was asking how long she was going to be. Julia quickly wiped at her face, forsaking a glance at the mirror that would only throw back how disheveled she looked. She ran her hands through her short, straight hair, adjusted her rumpled tunic and exited quickly, before the impatient clerk got a close look at her face.

***

The offices were off limits to students during the lunch periods, but the hall monitor always let Nicole pass because she was the Vice Principal's TA. The one who was more likely to give her grief was Favor's nasty old secretary. Fortunately, Ginny didn't eat lunch at her desk too often.

Today Nicole sought a quiet place to think. She dragged a chair to a spot where she couldn't be seen from the hallway, and unzipped a pocket in her backpack. There it was: her insurance, her Ace. She was glad she'd decided to make two separate tapes. Her grades didn't quite cut it for the private college she had set her heart on, but when she became Class President, that should put her over the line. This tape would get her name back on the ballot.

She had done well yesterday, she thought, but what was that little smile she thought she saw on Zant's face as she was leaving? Nicole shrugged it off. He was probably thinking about her boobs.

Zant was a double-crosser, and she wasn't going to take his word for anything. But not to worry, he'd soon be so grateful he'd be in her back pocket, and she would also be able to play him off Favor to her advantage.

She heard footsteps. By the time Ginny came into view, Nicole was opening a drink carton, her lunch spread on the adjacent table.

***

18

Kendra stood at the windows. Classes were out, but she still had a lot to do before she went home. Students were milling around the portables, sharing after-school snacks, exchanging gossip. A yellow bus pulled up with a rival sports team and the players strolled past her classroom on their way to the nearby field. After all the rain, they'd have a muddy time out there.

A flock of crows had taken over the area, oblivious to the upcoming game. They picked through discarded paper and other trash that built up around the bleachers.

Okay, lots of schools were as dilapidated as Standard High, Kendra thought, and teaching was about the kids, not about the setting. Still, it was too easy to get buried in all negatives; having better surroundings might help give some perspective, bring home the truth that there was beauty and harmony in the world.

A booming car radio could be faintly heard from the side street, and Kendra saw four boys climb over the ten foot high, chain link fence to hitch a ride. Perhaps that was one good point about having a room here in the "outback." Things were relatively quiet. She rolled her shoulders around, trying to remove some of the knots. Clinking noises drew her attention to her TA, who was drying the last of the glass beakers they'd used for a science lab. She saw Jessica wave out the window to a girl who was obviously waiting around for her.

"I'll finish, Jessica. You can go home. Thanks for helping."

"You're welcome, Ms. D. Today's lab was amazing! Before I was your TA, I thought that Special Ed. kids just sit in class and color pictures all day. I, uh, thought they couldn't do nothing else, but you got them doing real work."

"I've had TAs in the past who would have liked coloring books better," Kendra said.

"You mean Monique? Oh, none of my business, sorry. Well, your class is fun, to me." Jessica stuffed her hair into a woven cap. Her friend now approached the classroom doorway.

"Hi, Nicole, how's it going?" said Kendra to the mature-looking girl who nodded vaguely at her.

"See ya tomorrow, Ms. D." Jessica hefted her heavy backpack and still managed to fly out of the room.

Admiring that youthful energy, Kendra suddenly and deeply

felt twice her 27 years. She leaned on the counter, closed her eyes and attempted to conjure a peaceful image of blue sky. The clear expanse was immediately overtaken with dark wisps. Nimbus cloud: maybe teaching Special Ed. was a mistake. Twister cloud: maybe teaching in a public school was the problem. Mushroom cloud: she should have considered more carefully before accepting this job at Standard High.

A beeping sound intruded, her cell phone's missed call alert. She dug the phone from the pocket of her sweater. Cell reception was spotty around campus, but this time, at least, the missed call had registered. Took Brian long enough to call back, she fumed. She knew he had a hectic schedule, but still! Maretta had returned her panicked call in five minutes, and with a class load of students coming in at that.

Kendra walked outside and headed toward the field, hoping for some additional signal strength. The mobile gods were smiling upon her; the display showed three bars. She pressed buttons and waited.

"Hey, sorry it took me so long to get back to you, sweetie," said Brian. "We had a big installation to finish, and there were pieces missing. By the time I checked for messages last night it was too late, and you didn't pick up this morning. What's up?"

"Nothing special, just wanted to hear your voice. Can't wait to see you this weekend. Oh, I do have a computer related question maybe you can help me with. About email." Kendra hoped that her voice didn't convey her anxiety.

"Email? Okay, shoot."

"Well, when you get an email, if you don't recognize the sender's name or address, is there another way to figure out where the email came from?" she asked, trying to sound matter-of-fact.

He said, "You can find out the service provider sometimes, or are you talking about mail from inside school?" Brian's tone revealed he thought the question was a bit unexpected, but she knew he was used to her insatiable, wide ranging curiosity.

"Oh, either way," she dissembled.

"Let's say, then, it was sent within a network like you have at your school. Each computer should have what's called an IP address assigned. Someone should have a list. The IP address wouldn't tell you who sent the email, of course, but you'd be able to tell which computer was used. Now, if it came from an outside account with one of the big internet providers, tracing is much more difficult. I'm not sure but maybe you could only get as far as knowing the provider. Does that help? Sorry, to be so vague, but this really isn't my field of expertise. Why do you want to know, anyway?"

"A student of mine is doing a report." She didn't like lying, but she wasn't ready to tell Brian about recent events. To change the subject she asked, "We still on for this weekend?"

"What's that? What report? You're kind of breaking up."

"Yeah, sorry, can you hear me better now? I was just asking if we are still going hiking this weekend," she asked, walking zig-zags to find a better signal. She cynically reflected that a bad connection was an advantage at times. Maybe her cell phone company was missing an opportunity with their advertising; they really weren't fooling anyone with their area coverage maps.

"Yep, hiking, absolutely. I want to spend the whole weekend with you," said Brian.

"Me too, but, um, I hate to ask, sweetie, but I need you to help me with something at school for a few minutes, if that's okay. But I promise, we'll still have a whole day of hiking."

"Heh? You're kidding, right? You have to go over to school on a Saturday?" There was an interval of silence that stretched so long she thought they'd been disconnected. "Kendra, I'm willing to help you, but we were supposed to have the whole weekend together. What's more important, your room or—"

A background noise came through from Brian's end of the phone. "Oh, hell! Sorry, I have to go. I'll try to call you later, okay?" He cut off.

Kendra regretted her decision to cut into their Saturday plans. The chalkboard upgrade could have waited, damn it. Like always, once she decided to do something, she just had to jump in and do it right away. One of these days, that little personality trait was going to lead to her undoing. She wondered if it already had.

***

"Any pizza left?'' A string of cheese flapped from the boy's overfull mouth.

Maretta pulled a box over and lifted the greasy lid. "Sorry, all gone," she reported from the far end of the room.

"Everyone was supposed to get two pieces," said Kendra, looking around to see how that had gone. The two teachers were holding a little reward party after school for students with improved attendance.

"I guess next time we'll put little name tags on the slices and hand them out," said Maretta, suppressing a laugh.

"Aw, Mrs. Edwards, that's cold," said a student, wiping his chin clean with a disreputable looking bandana. He quickly stuffed the red square back into his pants pocket.

"I don't want to see that again," warned Maretta.

Kendra offered, "I have a nice collection of headgear in my desk, want to see?"

"Okay, I know, no head rags at school," griped the boy. "But it's in my pocket!"

This was one argument Kendra was in no mood to have. She waved him outside.

Maretta waited until the kids were well away, and said, "I can't believe that email. Someone's either trying to mess with your mind or get you fired."

Kendra dabbed at her fingers with a paper towel, staring at the wrinkled square as if divining an answer. "Who'd go to such an extreme? Someone put a lot of work into doctoring that photo, and the way it was delivered... I didn't sleep last night."

Maretta gave Kendra a hug and then dragged two chairs over to a side table. "Here, let's sit, try to relax. I have to say this business scares me too. I'm so sorry I was hung up with relatives last night or you know I would have come over to stay with you. But I don't think you need to be afraid of anything physical, the snake was probably a coincidence; remember the squirrel you found in here a few months ago? Well, okay, I don't know about the snake, but we can't let it freak us out; we have to logically think things through. Who's got a reason to hurt you?"

"That's the problem, no one comes to mind. Maybe this is just some warped soul playing 'fun with Photoshop,' like when the students post nasty rumors on websites? Or, it might be a tactic to make me quit. Zant would love that and snakes are right up his alley. Heh, if he knew about our plan to get him reassigned, he'd probably throw in an alligator as well." Maretta smiled grimly as Kendra continued her analysis. "But if Zant wants me gone, he's got easier ways…unless he wants to humiliate me, too. I've heard rumors he's behind several staff resignations. Another possibility is that the email doesn't come from campus. What if it's from a parent, or even some mentally unstable person who hardly knows me?"

"Well, we need to find the sender fast, before he or she can go public. Let's assume the person works here. For starters, you didn't make any points with Allana or Jack at the last department meeting."

"All I did was state the obvious. If we're going to take a stand against Zant as a department, then we have to make sure we're not breaking any contractual rules ourselves. All four of us need to show up for work on time and then actually put in a full day's work."

"That's what I mean. You were too blunt. Our two colleagues knew you were referring to them and they didn't take it kindly. Maybe they think you're gonna rat on them. They don't want anyone interfering with their laid back attitudes."

That's what you call them, laid back?"

"No that's what they probably would say, if they even gave it any thought."

"Well this speculation doesn't help. I'm going to trace which computer was used to send me the email and when, if possible. I already popped into one of the computer labs and the library today. I don't think the photo could have been Photoshopped in either one of those places. The library computers don't have the right software loaded, and I think the computer teacher notices when someone is working on something out of bounds."

"Ah, well, at least you eliminated the library," said Maretta wryly.

"Not really. I didn't think of this in the beginning, but the emailer could have put together the picture at home, brought it to school on a CD, and then sent it from any computer new enough to have a CDROM drive. I haven't really learned anything that useful."

"Well, if there's something I can do, let me know. And now, I hate to unload more bad news on you, but I've got trouble of my own and I need to talk to you." Maretta's normally calm demeanor was breaking.

"What's wrong?"

Index cards fluttered to the floor as Maretta thunked her loaded carryall bag down on the tabletop. The fact Maretta didn't stop to pick them up showed how uncharacteristically distracted she was. She unsnapped a side compartment and pulled out a form.

"We have to call the meeting with the Principal immediately! Our department has got to let Mrs. Prescott know that we're not going to put up with Zant any longer." She handed the paper to Kendra.

"He called me into his office to tell me that I'm close to being fired because, according to him, I'm out of my classroom more than I'm in it. He demanded I keep a written log of every instance when I leave the classroom to account for my time, even for lunch or to go to the bathroom."

"That's bullshit! He's accused everyone in the department of abandoning their classes, but a time sheet? I can't believe this. It's not fair that because Allana and Jack are slackers, we all get punished. Honestly though, I wouldn't worry too much; you know how these things are. In another week, he'll forget all about it and latch on to something else to browbeat us with."

"Oh, I'm not finished. There's more. He wants to write me up for unacceptable classroom performance. He said, for one thing, I write too many referrals." Maretta's narrow face looked indignant.

"You're kidding!"

"Gee, maybe I should make our lovely Mrs. Jarney my role model. Allana doesn't write referrals. She just lets the kids cut class, then kicks back in an empty classroom." Maretta mimed her coworker's manner of lazing behind her desk. "And, she isn't caught walking the hallways because she's already sneaked off campus."

"What Allana does or does not do is not going to help you," pointed out Kendra. "Back to your problem, what did you tell Zant when he said you have to keep a time chart?"

Maretta's voice was tight with frustration. "At first I tried to reason with him. I reminded him that I have 25 students on my

24

caseload, and sometimes I have to leave the kids with an aide so I can go do observations or conference. I reminded him we're required by law to do those things, but he still ordered me not to leave my room during class time unless an administrator has specifically called for me." Maretta jumped up and paced along the wall cabinets.

"So the way it stands, Zant intends to give me a poor review, including dereliction of duty and unacceptable classroom performance. He said if I don't turn in the daily time sheet, he'll take things to the next level. You know what that means."

"Wow! He's really going after you. What did you say?"

"I told him that he had a better chance of winning the lottery than to see me hand in a time sheet. Then I walked out."

Kendra gasped. "And that was it?"

"Not quite. He shouted after me that if he doesn't get the time sheets I'll be needing that lottery win." Maretta paused in front of a display of student work and fell silent.

"How did we ever get stuck with such a jerk for a VP? No, never mind. I know. Jack told me; he sat in on the selection panel. Zant came on as energetic, full of ideas—a great act he put on. He knew all the correct answers, in fact, the rumor is he was fed the questions beforehand by someone. And unfortunate for us, he's been good at ingratiating himself with the higher ups. Yeah, we have an uphill battle ahead to get rid of him," said Kendra.

"Well, at our last department meeting we came up with ways we can prove our grievances are valid, especially if we do what you suggested and get Mr. Favor to help. Special Ed. surely isn't alone in wanting to see the end of Zant."

Kendra sighed. "Tamra Helens is in a position to legitimize what we're saying, but does she, or anyone in administration care a thing about the students besides their test scores? Tamra only wants to manage paperwork and hold meetings. Even if she did try to intervene on our behalf, I don't think she has enough credibility with Mrs. Prescott. No, we should rally the counselors and parents. Parents always have a lot of influence."

Maretta nodded. "It doesn't hurt to gather as much support as we can, but if push comes to shove, I'm not sure who'll be willing to stick their neck out. I would like Tamra to stand with us. She can't be afraid of Zant; after all, she works directly under District

Special Ed, not him. Surely she's seen enough to realize that he's not only making it impossible for us to do our jobs, he's on track to railroad half our students right out the door." Maretta's angry gesture almost dislodged a model of the calcium atom from its hook beneath a light fixture.

"Don't remind me. He's already expelled two of my students this year," affirmed Kendra. "At this rate, in a few months I won't have any students left, and I'll be transferred out to a middle school. Zant's happiest dream! God, getting booted from here would be so unfair, after I've worked so hard to create a good program."

Maretta raised her chin. "Well, *I'm* not going anywhere and I won't submit to Zant's bullying. I have been here for seven years. If he wants to play, we shall see which one of us lasts longer at Standard High!"

3.

Wednesday Morning

The inside line buzzed. The VP swept a hand toward the phone, starting an avalanche of papers toward the floor.

"Zant speaking."

"Tamra Helens just called." Julia took a breath. "She said she's been held up at another school and has to cancel your meeting."

"She did! So, did she reschedule?"

"No. Do you want me to call her back?"

"Call her right now and make sure you get through to her. And Julia, you got here late again this morning." Zant turned to see his secretary through the glass, but a fake houseplant screened most of her face. My god, there should be a rule to prevent that woman from decorating her workspace. He especially hated the shrine like arrangement of baby photos.

Zant was grappling up papers from the floor when a shabbily dressed man rapped on the open door. His visitor's badge identified him as Mr. Robinson. Zant took care not to show his amazement. For months, this man had avoided every meeting he'd been asked to attend.

"Mr. Robinson, come in, have a seat."

The VP yelled out the door, "Julia, bring in Ronnie Robinson's file."

Mr. Robinson said, "Uh, you wanted to see me?"

"Yes, Mr. Robinson, I want to see you. We've called and sent you letters. If I didn't know better, I'd think you were deliberately avoiding us. Your son's been truant for weeks. Here at Standard High we have a high commitment to school/parent relations, but as a parent, you have to cooperate with our efforts. Do you know that you can be arrested because your son doesn't attend school? You should be grateful I haven't notified the authorities—yet."

This challenge was dramatized by Julia's arrival. She carried a voluminous student file. Numerous pink truancy forms poked out between the manila covers. Zant dismissed her as the folder thunked heavily on to his desk.

The man shifted on the edge of his chair. "Uh, well, see, I thought Ronnie was here at school. He's up every morning, asks for bus money. How do I know he ain't getting here?"

"Mr. Robinson, it's hard to believe you don't know that your son cuts school. Our attendance office calls you every single time he's absent. Surely you're not going to tell me that you didn't get any of the messages?"

"Well, see, I changed cell phones a while back . . . and I didn't get no messages at home neither. Ronnie must have wiped them."

Zant flipped through the boy's file. "What about all these letters we sent? Or all the calls we made to your workplace? Or the note that the home-school officer personally dropped off at the office of your apartment complex?"

"That's why I'm here, cause of the note at the complex." Mr. Robinson's gaze slanted away. "I just ain't had time to come over here before. I, uh, lost my job, been busy trying to find a new one. . .and I'm losing my apartment, too, cause they tell me that I'm too far behind with rent. . . " His voice trailed off.

"Sorry to hear, but we need to focus on—"

"You got to help me! Ronnie went to, he was put in Juvenile Hall yesterday. The officers said that he was selling drugs up at the mall." Mr. Robinson's unshaven face showed a mixture of denial and defeat.

Zant frowned. The man's plea was a sad commentary on a society where schools were expected to take on parenting duties. "Unfortunately, sir, our school can't reverse your son's bad choices."

"I talked to Ronnie. He knows he needs to go to school now, turn his life around. So, if you'd just give me his work he can make up?"

"They have classes, teachers in Juvenile Hall, who'll give him work." Zant held back saying he didn't think Ronnie would be cutting *those* classes.

"My boy says he wants to make good on all his work for here so he can graduate. If you could ask his teachers, get it for me?"

Zant pictured the moving van that Mr. Robinson would need to hold all the assignments his son had to make up. "You'll have to contact his teachers. The counseling office can help you. But, since the boy's in custody, we can't force our staff to provide him with work. And I must tell you, since you've missed all the attendance hearings it's almost certain that Ronnie won't be coming back here when he gets out of Juvenile Hall. I've already applied for his transfer to continuation school."

Mr. Robinson rose. "But he won't go there! Ronnie says that place is for losers. And I'm gonna lose my custody over him if you expel him. Give my boy another chance, please."

"He'll have his chance at the continuation school."

"Ronnie was right about you! You just want to kick out all the poor kids. I heard about all the other ones you expelled. You shouldn't be at a school; you should get a job in the prisons, you SOB!"

Mr. Zant calmly walked to the door and summoned Julia. "Mrs. Chatin, please show Mr. Robinson to the counseling office. And did you make that call for me?"

"Mrs. Helens is holding on line one, Mr. Zant." The office door shut firmly as Julia gestured for Mr. Robinson to follow her down the hallway.

The parent stared at Zant's closed door and shouted, "You'll hear from me again, asshole."

***

"Mrs. Helens, I hear that you cancelled today's meeting." Zant idly doodled lightning bolts on his desk blotter.

"I know it was last minute, but something important came up," said Tamra without further explanation.

"What's more important than cleaning up the mess that Special Ed.'s created at Standard High?"

"Let's not waste time going over that again, Mr. Zant. If you still think your school's Special Education department is *my* responsibility, please talk to the Superintendent; he'll set you straight. He's in his office; do you want me to transfer the call?"

Zant penned a heart and shot it through with another bolt of lightning. "Ah, so now you've become pals with the Super? Have you invited him home to meet your husband?"

"If you have a point, make it. Otherwise this conversation is over."

The VP laughed. "No harm meant. But since you're chums now, I have an idea. You put in a good word with the Super about me—as it pertains to my becoming Principal next year—and I don't tell your dear husband about *our* past, shall we say, close friendship?"

***

Julia adjusted the monitor to compensate for glare coming from the light fixture above Mr. Zant's new terrarium. She groaned in disgust. A second tank! What was with that man, anyway? If he wanted to show a nurturing side, why choose such creepy animals? Did he want to appear macho to impress the kids? Whatever. But if he had to have this new arrival, Mr. Lizard, why must he set it up on the counter in back of her desk? This had to be another one of Zant's silent acts of spite.

Hopefully, when the Principal discovered the VP's creepy zoo was expanding, she'd finally take action. There must be a legal or safety issue involved with keeping these animals in a school. Although Zant was housing the spider in a back corner of his office, anyone with any sense at all could predict that before long, the tarantula would end up sliding down someone's collar. Hah! She didn't care if that spider ended up chewing on—

"Hey, Mrs. Chatin."

Julia's wishful scenario was cut short by Nicole's greeting. The girl's perfume wafted over the counter that divided the secretarial space from the VP's waiting room. Nicole jiggled up to the counter, readjusting her low-riding jeans. She was waving a long roster of names, showing off her bright blue nail enamel.

Julia glanced at the student dress code, posted on the wall near the waiting area. What an exercise in futility, to mandate "proper" attire to a bunch of adolescents who were in the full throes of their experimental years. She pitied the male teachers. They hardly knew where to direct their eyes for fear of being accused of something.

Nicole must be on an errand; this was the period that she was Mr. Favor's TA. Only, since she wasn't assisting a teacher, she shouldn't still be called a Teaching Assistant; but then, what would you call her? Julia stifled a snort. Oh god, she really needed to stop listening to the office gossip. Surely, there was nothing going on there. Nicole was a bit flirty and manipulative, but other than earning an in-house suspension for verbal defiance, the girl seemed to play by the rules. Still, she seemed to have the full run of Mr. Favor's office, and the adjoining administrative area as well. So, the jury was still out on their relationship. Julia deliberately returned her own gaze to her computer, pretending to read something on the monitor while she unenthusiastically addressed the student.

"You need something, Nicole?"

"Mr. Favor asked me if you'd, like, pull the attendance for these students."

Julia silently fumed. Did Ray Favor think that she was an idiot? He knew how to pull attendance; he was just too lazy. Favor treated her with as much disregard as Mr. Zant. Those two VPs were alike in many ways but the grapevine said they hated each other. Unfortunately, their rivalry didn't help her out.

Julia's tired response was more a statement than a question. "Can't Ginny do the job? She's Mr. Favor's secretary."

"Ginny has the day off because her daughter's getting married. I went and asked the Principal's secretary, but she said, like, she's too busy. So, you're the only one left that can help. Mr. Favor'd never ask you if this job wasn't an emergency, but he's already going crazy doing the master schedule. You're so nice, Mrs. Chatin. I know you'll help."

Julia swiveled to give Nicole her back. Let her wait. She couldn't even keep up with all the work Zant gave her, and the bastard always found a way to keep her from getting paid overtime. If she didn't need this job, she'd walk away—and to heck with the fallout. Another restraining force was that her brother-in-law, who was head custodian, had helped her land this position. In looking at the big picture, she knew that if she got another chance to adopt a baby, she'd have to show job stability. Yes, she'd stick it out, keep focused on her future.

Julia stood up with resignation and motioned toward the in box, which shared the counter with the terrarium and a half empty candy dish. "Put the job in that tray, Nicole."

"Mr. Favor told me to wait here. He needs that information right now cause those kids applied to be in the new Computer Tech. Academy and the acceptance letters have to go out by tomorrow night. He said to tell you he'll make it up to you." Nicole delicately unwrapped a candy, as if worried she might chip her nails, then uninvited, slipped around the counter for a closer look at Zant's new pet.

Julia gave the girl a "who are you kidding" look. "I'll do it, Nicole, but don't wait around. Tell Mr. Favor to pick it up later."

"I'll come myself, then," announced Nicole. She spun around and jogged off, long hair swinging across her back.

Julia retrieved the roster from the tray. Her arm felt the warmth from the terrarium light. Hopefully, the lid was securely on. Unwillingly, she flicked a glance at the lid, grimaced and reluctantly approached the glass tank. The occupant, after all, was just a poor animal who deserved better than a life of dodging trash. She shooed the lizard away and picked out a candy wrapper.

**

"What was this young lady doing pawing around on my secretary's desk?" Carl Zant pointed an accusatory finger at Nicole, who had dutifully followed him to Favor's office. The outburst startled Favor, who had been in deep concentration over the master schedule and hadn't heard them enter.

"Sorry, Mr. Favor, he didn't—" began Nicole.

"You can go now, Nicole, thanks for your help." There was no doubt this was a firm dismissal. Nicole sized up the situation and immediately left Ray's office. Zant watched Nicole walk away with amusement and a sigh.

"If you're done fantasizing, maybe you want to tell me why you came charging in here," said Ray.

"No harm in dreaming," said Zant, with an emphasis on the verb. "I hear you've actually done a little more than that."

Ray kept his expression blank. He wasn't willing to take the bait. A voice blared from his holstered walkie-talkie. He lowered the volume.

"Sounds like there's a fight; we should go out there," said Ray, rolling down his shirtsleeves.

"It's your day for yard duty, not mine," said Zant.

Although Ray didn't like dealing with campus violence, school safety was a shared VP duty and he'd happily take the opportunity to end this conversation. But his exit was stopped short at the doorway by Zant's burly arm, which, due to Ray's shorter stature, cut him off at the throat.

"You haven't answered my question," said Zant, dropping his arm.

Ray backed a step. "Which one was that?"

"What was your bit of fluff doing in my secretary's work area?"

Ray somehow held his temper, knowing that Zant might even welcome a physical response. "Nicole is my TA, only my TA, and I sent her to get attendance data."

"Well, get your own secretary to pull data for you. Julia is already behind on her legitimate work without you sneaking behind my back and using her," said Zant. "If you impinge on her time again, I'll have to tell Mrs. Prescott that you can't manage your own secretary—not that Prescott doesn't already know how you operate."

"Oh, now you're a human resources specialist, too? And here I thought you were just a specialist in Special Education and slimy animals."

Zant smirked. "At least my school pets have more than two legs. Don't think for a minute that you'll be selected for the principal's job with your reputation."

"I don't think going into reputations or relationships is a wise move for you. In fact I can vouch for that." Favor savored the effect this bombshell had on Zant, though the triumph proved short-lived.

Zant shot back, "In addition to your, shall we say, indiscretions, I'm aware of the favoritism you show with your scheduling. Someone might even construe that you're—"

The hurried arrival of a police officer cut off Ray's reply. "One of you coming or not? It's getting ugly out there."

"Tell you what, I'll go," said Zant, who loved playing cop.

Ray watched the two rush down the hall, the policeman describing the events taking place outside. When the voices faded, Ray closed the door, sat on the edge of his desk and thumbed his

BlackBerry for a phone number. The call was picked up quickly.

"Tamra Helens's office, can I help you?"

"Good afternoon. This is Ray Favor at Standard High. Is Tamra Helens there?"

"This is Tamra, Mr. Favor. What can I do for you? I hope you aren't calling to ask me for even more leeway with the master schedule." The way her voice kept fading in and out showed she had the call on speaker and wasn't giving the conversation her undivided attention.

"No, no, the schedule's under control. I'm sure you'll hear all about the assignments." Ray laughed.

Tamra's voice acquired a sharpness. "I hope not. Then, unless there's urgent business to take care of . . . this is a very busy time for me with the state review coming up."

"Actually, we do need to talk. I've thought of some changes that could be made here to finally get the Special Ed. department in compliance with District regulations. Make you look a lot better with the higher-ups. With your help, of course."

The background noises abruptly stopped. "Oh? And what's in it for you?"

"Are you still of the opinion that I'd be the best choice for the Principal's job next year?" asked Ray.

"I don't recall saying exactly that," hedged Tamra.

"Why don't we get together and talk. I'm sure you'll find that you and Special Ed. have an interest in *me* taking over the job from Mrs. Prescott. How about going for a drink at Max's? Strictly business, of course."

"Of course," replied Tamra.

4.

Wednesday afternoon

Allana Jarney peered closely at Julia's computer screen.

"It's the next field, I think," Allana suggested. Although all teachers were required to input attendance data, the software was so convoluted most of the faculty couldn't retrieve the stored information.

Julia bit back a retort; she knew more about this database than anyone. She quickly selected the names Allana had given her. "Do you also want attendance records for these kids, or just their schedules?"

"Both, please, and can I have duplicate copies? You're a dear."

From the corner of her eye, Julia caught the gleam of Allana's satisfied smile, the one Allana must have copied from a TV commercial for teeth whiteners.

"Hey, girlfriends!"

A heavily made up, 40ish woman with loose, highlighted curls approached. From the height gained by her sling-backed pumps, she had to look down to greet Allana.

Julia raised a hand to acknowledge Tamra, then returned her eyes, if not her thoughts to the computer. This was not good; chats near her work area might attract Zant's attention and then he'd fault her for socializing. Of course, the man would love to come out and flirt with those two, although his usual technique, a mix of arrogance and sexual innuendo, wasn't at all effective. In fact, Julia suspected that Zant had issues with Tamra Helens, but the tension seemed to spike his interest. Gee, maybe the VP could introduce the women to his new pet; the lizard would really excite them.

Actually, if Zant did come out, it could be interesting. Allana was supposed to be in her classroom, teaching, this period. Perhaps Tamra would ask Allana who was watching her class? Without a doubt, Allana's request for student schedules proved the point that the teacher didn't have a clue where her students were mainstreamed during the day. Julia supposed the upcoming state review had something to do with the teacher's sudden urgency to locate her students.

Julia went to a file cabinet, away from the whining of the ancient laser printer so she could better take in the women's conversation. Allana had moved to join Tamra on the far side of the counter that separated Julia's desk from the waiting area and was reaching for Tamra's hand.

"Wow, is this a new ring? It's gorgeous. Must have put a huge dent into your husband's bank account."

Tamra wiggled her fingers to show off an arrangement of diamonds and red stones that shouted for someone to ask if they were real rubies.

"Oh, he rates this a petty expenditure, like my Porsche."

Julia marveled as Allana comically shrugged toward the ceiling and asked the gods why she wasn't lucky enough to be partnered with a CEO. You had to hand it to Allana, she knew how to work people. No, Tamra wasn't going to ask where Allan's students were this period. Good lord, Allana could probably show up at 11:00 in her bathing suit and not be questioned.

Tamra said, "Well, nice chatting, but I must take care of business. I'm here to distribute the new student assessment forms. They've been revised again, I'm afraid. Shall I put yours in your box? And, as long as I've run into you . . ."

To Julia's chagrin, Tamra's voice became almost inaudible as she continued, "I was hoping you could set me up with more—"

"Of course," replied Allana. You want to meet me out back at my car in five minutes?"

"Okay. See you in a bit," said Tamra, taking the shortest path toward the faculty workrooms.

Julia pulled the printouts from the printer tray and put them on the counter for Allana. "Here you go. Sorry to move you along, but I have a lot to do and I'm not supposed to have socializing here." She scowled in the direction of Zant's office.

Allana lowered her voice to a whisper. "Are you going to come with us when we see the Principal about Zant?"

"I can't," murmured Julia. "It's different for clerical staff like me. We're too easy to replace and, in my case, I'm already close to being fired."

"That's a big reason to go. We've got to get Zant out of here!" Allana's hissing caused Julia to wonder if the woman qualified for a terrarium of her own.

"Ask the counselors to go with you, that would be best."

"Okay, I understand. Thanks for pulling the reports. But, Julia, I think it would do you good to show a little more backbone."

***

"Is Favor around?" asked Kendra.

Ginny looked up from a ledger and sniped, "Well, I don't hear any yelling, so he's probably gone off somewhere again. He doesn't have to report to me, you know."

"I'll just wait around, then," said Kendra, eager to end contact with this griffin.

No wonder Ray Favor preferred working with his student TA's. Kendra knew that she, herself, often got more willing cooperation from student assistants than she got from her burned out colleagues. Of course, you never knew how a TA would work out. They could be trouble. But there was no point in dwelling on her past issues with Monique, who had used her time as a TA in Kendra's room to catch up on her sleep. Still, for an intractable issue with a TA, you just told the counseling office and the TA was recalled. If you didn't see eye to eye with a fellow staff member, you were in for the long haul.

Kendra eyed a pair of students who were quietly waiting for their parents to pick them up. Ginny's presence seemed to put a damper on adolescent behaviors. That woman could make a fortune if she could bottle and sell whatever worked that magic.

Kendra moved to the hall so she'd be able to head off Mr. Favor when he returned. Once he got into his office, she might be unable to get in to see him. She ambled over to inspect a pair of computer workstations that were marooned at the end of the hallway outside Ginny's lair. Those computers were on her to-do list. Out of eyeshot, almost anyone could have used them. They looked reasonably new but dusty.

A door banged. The VP was exiting a small bathroom near the empty nurse's room. The era when the school could afford to have a permanent site nurse was long gone. These days, an itinerant nurse made bimonthly visits, setting up in the counseling office where she only reviewed records. The nursing room was now a storage area, a dump for castoff items, but the adjacent bathroom was still in good repair and prized by the few staff who had access. There was even a rumor that warm water flowed out of the sink in there.

Kendra called out, "Mr. Favor? Can I see you a minute?"

He glanced at her and kept walking. She trotted after him as he zipped into his office, clearly hoping to avoid her. Undeterred, she followed, ignoring a dirty look from Ginny

Without acknowledging her presence, Favor yanked a tissue from a box, used it to grab up a whiteboard marker, and violently flung the pen into a trashcan. "Damn cheapo pen, leaked all over me! And the stinking soap they keep here won't get the ink off." He wiped at his hands with another tissue, all the while swearing under his breath.

How typical. In one of his snits and he still hadn't made eye contact with her. This was but a normal workday interaction with Ray Favor, but he was actually quite amiable when he was off campus in a social setting. Too bad he was already agitated because he'd know why she was there, and he hated to talk to teachers about the master schedule even at the best of times. That was understandable because everyone argued incessantly about their class assignments and which period they wished to have prep. Kendra sat and waited him out.

Realizing his ignoring wasn't going to get rid of her, he tried to deflect her line of inquiry. "So, what's up with Brian? He hasn't shown up for basketball lately."

"He's on a big job that took him out of town. He'll be back for your next game. Anyway, this isn't the reason I'm here, but I was wondering if the two computers outside in the hall are on the school network."

Ray smiled. "Brian says you're flaky, and I can't see a reason to disagree with him. You'll have to ask someone else about the computers; I can't be bothered with runaway equipment. What *is* the reason you came to see me, then?"

"Have you got my classes on the master schedule yet? I'm supposed to put in a textbook order and if I don't know what I'm going to be teaching, how can I order books?"

Ray groaned, but brought out a whiteboard from behind a bank of file cabinets, propping it up for her to see. He must have been hiding the partially completed schedule from contentious eyes. Kendra found her name slotted next to the other teachers in her department. She scanned the columns. He had assigned her to teach *five* different subjects.

"Mr. Favor, you've got me teaching algebra? I'm not qualified to teach that, and most of my students aren't at that level." Kendra's voice wavered.

"The District wants us to challenge our students. That means they all have to take algebra next semester. End of story. We can't have our test scores staying down at the current level. As for having to teach so many different subjects, there is no other way to fit Special Ed. kids into the master schedule anymore, especially for algebra. There are just too many students who need it. Sorry, Kendra, I don't have the classroom space to fix your problem."

Ray's inflexible attitude was a product of his predicament. He had his orders. The school was overenrolled and he did what he had to in order to level out the classes. Special Education students were not high on the school's list of concerns. He'd put them wherever he could fit them and he'd assign their teachers to teach whatever subjects would insure each body had a chair each period.

"I see that I have to find out more about this math policy," said Kendra hotly. "I need to talk to Tamra Helens."

"I already had that conversation with her, but do as you wish. Don't blame her too much for folding on the issue. By the way, I believe she told me Mr. Zant was pushing for you to be the one to teach the Algebra.

Ray picked up his walkie-talkie and snapped it to his belt. Then, with a nod, he walked away, grabbing a folder from Ginny's outstretched hand without breaking his stride.

Kendra borrowed pen and paper from Ray's desk and copied her class assignments from the whiteboard. She wondered if Tamra had really given Ray the green light.

***

The computer technician was working in one of the computer labs, which was closed for maintenance. He was lying beneath a table, half buried under cables.

"Hey, Paul, you free to talk?" Kendra crouched to get a better view of the man, who was shadowed by a curtain of dangling wires.

"I am. I'm just doing some reconnections. The job will take me a while, though. I regret I may have to miss a lunch meeting," said Paul facetiously.

"Well, glad I found you. I've only got a few minutes before my prep is over. What I wanted to ask you is, well, I got a really over-the-top joke for an email and I'd really like to return the favor, but the sender used a silly fake name and I don't recognize the address. I'm pretty sure it was sent in house, so if I give you the IP address, could you tell me where it came from?"

"Ah, well there are more stupid jokes going through the network than anything work related, that's for sure. So much for improving work efficiency through technology." Paul laughed. "I can look for you. I've been thinking I have to update the list of IP locations anyway. If you can wait a few days, I can probably have the location of the computer for you—if the computer is one of ours. I can't tell you who sent the email, you know, just which computer it was sent from. That good enough?"

Kendra wanted to stifle any further questions. "You know, I do have an idea who sent the email, but I want to be totally sure before I send a reply, or it could be embarrassing. I'd tell you more, but it's girl stuff, you know?"

"In that case, I won't ask. I get enough of that with my wife and three daughters. Just give me a few days, like I said." He came up from the floor and started to coil a long piece of cabling.

Kendra masked her disappointment at having to wait. "Okay, no rush. The IP number is on this paper." She set it on a chair. "Thanks, Paul, I appreciate you doing this. I'll get back to you."

***

"Mrs. Prescott will see you now," said the secretary, bestowing a denigrating smile upon the last person left in the waiting area.

Jack folded his newspaper and shoved it into his ancient briefcase. He paused as he entered the Principal's frigid office. My god, he thought, the woman must be a throwback to an earlier evolutionary era. No warm-blooded entity could work in this room.

"Mr. Sermon, have a seat." Mrs. Prescott directed.

"That won't be necessary," said Jack, who knew that the offer of a seat was to give the woman the psychological advantage of height. Her office furniture had been carefully chosen; the visitor's chairs stood a good six inches lower than the principal's executive chair. Mrs. Prescott didn't go through the palsy-walsy charade of coming around her desk and sitting beside the staff. Give her a point for that, at least, granted Jack.

The Principal arranged a binder so that Jack could see her red notations on the grievance papers that the union had filed against her. She folded her hands. "All right, let's get straight to business then. You don't think this grievance is going anywhere, do you?"

"It already has," said Jack, slouching over her desk. "As the site Union Rep. I've been asked to tell you that the Super's office has the grievance under consideration."

"The only thing the Superintendent is considering is why our student test scores are so low. The District has directed me to provide teacher training, but your union doesn't want to do anything about the sub-par performance of its members. Just because certain teachers are unwilling to put in the required time and effort, I'm supposed to allow the school to deteriorate?"

"We're not taking action because we're lazy. We are objecting because you are making us waste our precious time—time that we'd like to spend doing things that actually could have a positive impact around here, like planning lessons and calling parents." The disparity between Jack's rhetoric and his own lax behavior was lost on him. "The after school in-services you mandated were more than useless, they were demeaning. Do you think that we don't know when speakers are talking gibberish? That awful woman who lectured to us for 90 minutes about some parenting study they did in Iceland? You've got to be kidding—we would have gotten more out of an actual trip to a glacier. At least that would have been science related."

Mrs. Prescott's chin jutted, but Jack was just warming up. He pointed at one of the highlighted paragraphs. "It says right here that you exhausted the amount of time that you can compel your teaching staff to stay after school without extra pay. You need to reimburse us for 2.5 hours from the last workshop alone. Also, while you're looking at figures, you might want to double check how much it really cost to bring in those worthless speakers. The union is calling for an independent audit."

She gave not an eye blink in response to the innuendo. "You, personally, won't be waiting for a check, will you, Mr. Sermon? I don't recall seeing your name on the last in-service sign-in sheet," said the Principal. "In fact, I double-checked and you didn't attend any of them. Not that I really expected you to, because you would have a difficult time driving your car into the library."

"What's that supposed to mean?"

"Do you think I don't know you spend half the day out in the parking lot having a smoke in your car?"

"Who told you that—Mr. Zant? That's one of your major problems, Mrs. Prescott. If you had real knowledge of what goes on around here, we would all be better off. You talk about all you're doing to improve things around here, but you—"

"Mr. Sermon, perhaps a change of venue would do you good. I hear there's a teacher vacancy at Center City Primary School. Shall I call the Human Resources Department?"

He shook his head. "You really don't know how Special Ed. works, do you? You can't reassign me! Special Ed. has control of where I work, not you."

She carefully closed the binder and snapped it into an expensive leather case. "Don't lecture me about what I know and don't know. Why don't you discuss your placement with Mr. Zant? He's explored the matter quite thoroughly. I'm afraid I have another appointment now." She crossed the space in front of him, grabbed her coat from the hook at the door and without looking back said, "Have a nice evening."

5.

Wednesday evening

Zant slammed the file drawer in disgust. Those papers had to be here somewhere. Julia had gone home again without finishing the work he'd given her. He reckoned she'd gotten just far enough to pull and misplace the file. He'd have to search through her whole workstation.

The secretary's desk phone began to ring. Zant ignored the trilling and relocated an ornately framed baby photo and a wreath of dried flowers to allow himself counter space so he could sort through a huge pile of documents.

The sought after form finally turned up, jammed into the wrong folder. It must have been deliberately hidden. Of all the nerve! If he saw fit to expel a student, that was his prero-gative. These bleeding hearted teachers always wanted to give the kids another chance. No doubt, Julia was helping someone, trying to obstruct this expulsion. This was just the last straw. He was definitely going to fire that good for nothing secretary. Too bad, she was fun to have around to play with.

Zant realized that the phone was again demanding attention. He grimaced at the wall clock. How annoying! It was almost 5 p.m. He doubted a parent was calling, but one never knew. Some parents seemed to think that the school staff was there to serve them 24/7. He gave an exasperated sigh. If he didn't pick up the call, a complaint might be lodged with the Principal. Standard High was supposed to be open to the "community" as a resource. He had yet to figure out how the school benefited from that exchange.

He waited another few rings and reluctantly lifted the receiver. He didn't intend to let the caller know his identity, so he answered in a neutral way.

"Standard High."

After listening for only a few seconds, Zant dropped the

receiver, whirled around and crouched in front of his newest terrarium. He took in a loud breath, exhaled a curse and charged down the hallway.

***

Jack slammed the door of the fridge and juggled his briefcase, thermos, a slice of pie, and a quart bottle of juice to a safe landing on the break room table. He hadn't eaten enough lunch and was now both hungry and feeling the effects of low blood sugar. Maybe he should have waited till he got home, but he still had something to take care of at school, after which he had to stop off at the union office, so he wouldn't get anything to eat for hours. He hated these long days. Thankfully, he could retire soon. In his next life— were there such a thing—he'd get a job where the lunch times were long enough to actually eat and you could go to the bathroom when you had to. Thinking along those lines, maybe he was already dead and this was hell.

He upturned a canister. "Oh great, not one lousy fork." He made his way toward a cluster of clerical cubbyholes located just outside the break room. Those women usually had a wealth of drinking straws, ketchup packets and plastic utensils in their desks. He was returning with a fork when he heard someone come up behind him.

"Hi, Jack," said Allana. "What are you doing here so late?" Although she made reference to the time, she showed no evidence of having worked a full day herself. Her makeup looked fresh and not one of her shoulder length hairs was misplaced.

"I could ask you the same thing. The last bell rang and you're still here? Your car break down or something?" Jack headed back to his chair with Allana close behind. She seemed uncharacteristically eager for his company. He waited for the reason.

"No, Jack, my car did not break down. I'm still here cause I turned in the forms for my evaluation and now I've realized that I goofed up on the goals, so I need to get the forms back and fix things before Zant sees what I put down. He's looking for any excuse he can find to give us poor evaluations."

"Tell me something I don't know," said Jack, cracking open his pie box. "I refused to even fill mine out. The ass-hole used the wrong form and that's just for starters."

"Do you think his office is open? I bet my mine is still sitting in his in-box."

"Who knows, but he stays late sometimes; you might be able to ask him personally to give it back to you," said Jack between mouthfuls of pie.

"Come with me, then, ok? I want you to stand outside and listen, in case he gets unprofessional again with me."

Jack almost choked on his pie. He knew that Allana's show of vulnerability was pure manipulation, designed to get his help by appealing to his pride at being a union rep. She'd even added her trademark smile for extra incentive.

She elaborated, "He's got a real sick routine with me; first he threatens to have me fired and then, 30 seconds later, he's making sexual innuendoes. I sure would love to stop him with my best Aikido move."

Jack savored a mental image of Allana twisting the VP's arm and wrenching him to the ground. "Okay, just let me finish eating first. I have to raise my blood sugar."

He abruptly aborted the move to his mouth, fork arcing in midair. This unseemly greeting was less than graciously received by Tamra, who just managed to dodge a piece of flying lemon pie filling. Allana, who had her back to the entrance, jerked around, obviously worried about who might have been within earshot.

Tamra put on an exaggerated show of surprise. "My goodness, am I seeing something momentous? Allana here after school?" Tamra gave Allana's arm a squeeze and turned to feed money into the drink machine.

"Nah, nothing at all momentous," said Allana. "I was just conferring with Jack about some books he wants to use." She gave Jack a look to shut down any other line of conversation.

Jack filled his thermos from the juice bottle and screwed on the cap. "My little 'pick-me-up'," he said. Jack noticed how the women looked dubiously at the battered thermos and exchanged glances, but he only nodded at Allana and said, "You ready?"

Tamra quickly said, "I won't hold you guys up, I'm on my way out." She popped the tab on her diet soda and took a few swallows. "Ah, that hits the spot. Those counselors can really yak, you know? I think the parent was sorry she ever asked for a conference. Have a good evening, see you." Tamra waggled the can in a goodbye gesture.

Jack heaved himself up, and replaced the juice bottle in the fridge. He accompanied Allana through the deserted clerical area. They paused near the attendance counter. Across from this stood Carl Zant's office. The blinds were tightly closed.

"Take a peek and see if he's there," whispered Allana.

"Give me a break," retorted Jack.

"I was just kidding." Allana walked over and softly knocked. When there was only silence, she tried the door, which opened to an empty office.

"All clear," she said. "Thanks, Jack. Sure you don't want to stick around and forage? Never know what you might find."

"I'd better not. If I saw what the bastard was writing about me, I'd have to do something to him." Jack's eyes speared the VP's desk chair. "Just kidding, just kidding. Okay, have fun. I'm going to use the facilities and head out, not to make a double entendre." He snorted a laugh, turned and left Allana to her business.

***

Allana wondered if Jack believed her reason for this surreptitious visit, not that she cared. He was a fool.

She took in the room. This place was messier than ever, but the lack of organization made it safer to rummage without leaving a trace. Zant would probably never realize that anything had been moved. Or removed.

She passed over a tier of desk trays. Damn it, they were jammed so full she couldn't remove any papers without tearing them. Too risky. But perhaps what she wanted would be more hidden. She turned her attention to the desk drawers.

Two drawers later, a walkie-talkie broadcasted from its resting place on a shelf. The chief hall monitor was signing off for the day. Allana realized that she'd been in the office far too long. And the very fact that the walkie-talkie hadn't been turned off could mean that Zant was still somewhere on the premises. Definitely not good. Such a pity, she could have used more time, but she wasn't going away completely disappointed.

***

Ray changed gears with more force than necessary. What a waste of time—a dinner break. Just a lame excuse for the higher ups to eat off the district budget. After the hour was up, Ray would have to go back downtown for more, point-less discussion. He'd better call his wife before she started to look for him. She still wouldn't believe he was really at a meeting at this hour.

Ray could have gone to eat with the rest of the group, but he wasn't in a table-talk mood. Might as well get some use out of the dinner break. He'd given the excuse that he had left a pertinent file in his office. And he wanted to avoid his superior's inevitable questions about how things were going at Standard High. For all they cared! The Superintendent and his cronies seldom visited the school because they knew it was easier to sweep those problems under the rug from their offices downtown. Ray was familiar with the touch of that broom.

He jerked his car to a gravelly halt. The driveway gate was still unlocked, probably because custodial staff was still on campus. In the dusk, a spotlight illuminated one of the security cameras. Ray gave it the finger and laughed. The only CCTV camera that actually worked was mounted on a façade near the basketball courts, but had been knocked off target—deliberately, he assumed—so that it gave only a view of the northern sky. The requisition order for maintenance on the cameras had been sent off the previous summer. Perhaps the requisition was lying in the sun on a tropical island somewhere, having a cold drink.

He'd just leave the car in the driveway and cut in through the west door. The alarm system wouldn't have been activated yet, either. Not that Ray believed the alarm system was even operational. The campus security equipment was the responsibility of the Principal, although you'd never know it. Ray wasn't about to step in to take up the slack for Mrs. Prescott. The worse she performed, the better he would look after he took over her job.

He passed empty cubicles and entered the mailroom. With a final check to make sure he was alone, he reached into Mrs. Prescott's box and fished out the contents. He concentrated on the large, brown district mail envelopes. Finding one that looked promising, he undid the string ties, spreading the contents on a tabletop for closer inspection. This was an even better find than expected! He powered up the copier.

***

What a heck of a mess! Nate Bowen flopped the mop over a wide swatch and began to clear a pathway toward the sinks on the back wall of the boys' room. Well, it could be worse. At least the sinks weren't overflowing. A regular student trick was to block drains and let the water run until it overflowed. There were constant complaints about the custodians' failure to fill the paper towel dispensers, but who had to unplug the drains and dry up the flooded bathrooms? Not the students, not the staff, nor the adults who professed outrage over the school's inadequate bathroom facilities.

Nate had been a custodian for ten years and hardly noticed the overall condition of the bathrooms anymore. He just cleaned up and got out as fast as he could. A less inured viewer would be quite disheartened. The students quickly damaged whatever repairs or improvements were made, although those remediations were few, and far between. The stalls that still had doors hadn't been fitted with latches in years because the students would latch them from inside, then slither under the door, leaving the next person locked out. The towel and soap dispensers had been pulled from the walls innumerable times leaving a scabrous pattern of naked bolts and broken plaster. Toilet paper was often used to make spit balls. The ceiling was liberally coated with paper missiles.

Today, however, the bathroom was messed up in an unexpected way. Nate sighed. He hadn't seen this in a long time. In addition being troublesome to clean, a soapy floor was dangerous to walk on. He'd have to put in a lot of extra time before this bathroom was useable. Almost every day there was some vandalism that took extra time to clean.

Take the graffiti—in spite of daily wiping, graffiti still covered every wall. He'd long passed the point of reading any of it himself. Some of his colleagues were avid readers and told him about the more outrageous postings. Of course, nowadays the students had cell phones to text message their endless comments. He also knew about emails and websites that students used to slander their enemies. That could have a good side; maybe bathroom graffiti would soon be a thing of the past.

Meanwhile, he would rather not read or hear the gossip. His job went a lot easier if he just concentrated on his custodial tasks. Nate liked working the late shift. By the time he arrived, most of the students and staff were either leaving, or long gone. From time to time his shift was less solitary, as when he was asked to set up the library for use by a com-munity group. Man, that room was heaven, compared to this.

Nate wrung out the mop and dried his hands on a towel he kept on the janitorial cart. He adjusted the earphones from his mp3 player. He liked to stay in his own little world while he worked, to make the time go faster. Nate wheeled the cart down the dimly lit hallway toward his next destination.

It wasn't his job to mop the hall, but he noticed something on the floor and walked over to get a closer look. There appeared to be traces of soap going down the corridor. With a sigh, Nate wielded the mop and began to clean up the sticky tracks. This was a safety hazard so he couldn't let it go, although the added work meant he wouldn't finish his regular duties before quitting time.

The smears continued to a stairwell that led down to the North parking lot. He hoped he didn't have to clean the steps. Glancing down the length of the staircase, he pulled up short and let go of his mop mid-pass. It clanged down a flight before coming to a stop. Below the mop, a man was lying twisted in an awkward pose.

6.

Wednesday night

Kendra fumed at the can of coffee, which seemed to taunt her from the topmost shelf. Brian must have stashed it there without thinking. She couldn't reach that height without a stepladder. She recalled, with frustration, she'd last used the ladder to change the patio light. A glance out the window confirmed that the ladder was still out in the yard. In the rain. Of course it was.

Why was it that when her nerves were already shot, everything conspired against her? At the moment, she felt so stretched that even the misplaced ladder brought tears to her eyes. Yes, it was an overreaction, but the last five hours she'd been filling out the forms for her teacher evaluation, but the goals and lesson plans still didn't conform to what Zant would grade "acceptable."

Wearily, she slipped on a pair of scuffs, and went out to retrieve the step stool. She was carrying it back to the house when her neighbor's powerful porch light came on, and a stout woman appeared at the railing.

"How nice to run into you, Kendra. Haven't seen you in a while." Mrs. Ireland's piercing voice carried across the low fence that divided their tiny yards. Kendra could have commented that this meeting seemed hardly coincidental, but she only nodded at the fence, and headed for her back door.

Undiscouraged, the woman called out, "Glad I finally caught you. Would you ask that boyfriend of yours to shut the drapes if he wants to parade around your house half naked? Bad enough the way he was lying around your yard all summer, wearing next to nothing."

"That's called a bathing suit, Mrs. Ireland," shouted Kendra without looking back. "If you don't like what you see, then I suggest you change the channel." The back door absorbed the woman's indignant protestations as Kendra closed it with a little extra force.

On another occasion, Kendra would have laughed at the

situation. Her windows had mini shutters instead of drapes and she habitually kept the lower tier closed. Petite Mrs. Ireland would need to stand on a chair to be able to see anything below Brian's chest. Sometimes Kendra wished she lived in a place where people ignored their neighbors.

Well, she was wide awake now; didn't even need the coffee to stay up until she finished the damn evaluation. As if she had a choice. The deadline was tomorrow. Damn Zant! Four weeks ago, she'd sent him her original submission. But only this morning, the day before the deadline, she found it in her school mailbox, rejected. As if that wasn't bad enough, a different template was attached with "USE THIS ONE INSTEAD" scrawled on a sticky note. Requiring a complete rewrite. Zant probably knew about the new format all along, and was now having a good laugh at her expense.

For some reason, the district felt the need to change lesson plan requirements frequently in an attempt to conform to popular theories and politically correct trends. Teachers were forced to write learning goals using the latest buzzwords, whether they made any sense or not. One year the word "facilitate" was very popular. She got so sick of hearing that one she started to chart the times the word was used during conferences. After that, the favorite term became "metacognition," soon followed by "standards based curriculum." The current term was "differentiated learning." Kendra knew it was useless to let this bullshit bother her, but she knew all the rhetorical juggling wouldn't do a thing to improve student learning, to say nothing of it being a waste of her time.

The lamp in her tiny office was casting a yolk-like pool of light on the hallway floor. Under other circumstances, she might have grabbed her camera and taken some artsy shots, but at the moment, she wasn't feeling inspired. At this time of day, she never was. Maybe she should have gotten up at 4 a.m. to do the rewrite.

Bobbins lay on the kitchen table, curled peacefully around the salt and peppershakers. The cat purred in response to her touch but made no other sign he was aware of his surroundings. She could hardly believe just minutes ago he'd been sprinting from one end of the house to the other, chasing after some imaginary prey.

Kendra was envying the sleeping cat when the ring of the phone startled them both. No one who knew Kendra would call her this late, after 10:30. Maybe she shouldn't answer. After two more rings, she surrendered to curiosity.

"Hello?"

"Hope I didn't wake you? Want to go catch a movie tomorrow afternoon?" asked Maretta, all too cheerfully.

"You're calling at this hour to ask me that? And, I believe tomorrow is Thursday?"

"That's right." Maretta's words came out in a rush. "Bet you five bucks school will be closed."

"Okay, you have my attention. I don't mean to be grouchy, but can you get to the point?" Kendra hoped Maretta wouldn't delay the punch line much longer. Her friend loved drama and was known to be a fountain of gossip even on occasions when the pipeline was nearly dry.

"You haven't heard then. There's trouble at school!"

Kendra rubbed her face. "What are you talking about? When? Was there a gang fight?" Kendra unwittingly threw out a series of questions without stopping for an answer.

"They haven't given details yet—" Maretta paused for dramatic effect. "But something happened to Zant. He was taken away from school in an ambulance!"

"No way!"

"Could be a heart attack or something, but the school is roped off and there are police cars, like a crime scene. Makes me wonder—there are a lot of people who'd be happy to get rid of the bastard; do you think someone jumped him?" Clearly, Maretta was enamored of the possibility.

Kendra struggled to make a coherent story out of Maretta's sketchy summary. Something had happened to Mr. Zant.

"What? How do you know?"

"For heaven's sake, Kendra, turn on the TV, channel 7. I bet half the city knows by now. The Principal will be furious."

Kendra dashed into the living room and found the station. They were interrupting their regular programming for "breaking news." The crawl at the bottom of the screen listed the many previous instances of violence at Standard High. The news camera was panning the school's main entrance and the street that fronted the school. Local residents lined the streets, gaping at the burst of unexpected activity.

"Ok, Maretta, I have the station on. Look, now they're showing footage of the ambulance. Wow, I don't believe this."

Kendra was distressed by the sight of the paramedics sliding a gurney into the ambulance, but that feeling was suddenly accompanied by a most inappropriate upwelling of relief as she realized that she wouldn't have to stay up to finish the lesson plans. Zant wouldn't be doing her eval-uation tomorrow.

Maretta took the opportunity of a commercial break to continue their conversation. "Do you think someone finally got fed up and gave Zant some payback?"

"Whoa, you're off on a tangent. You shouldn't even be thinking stuff like that." But the topic was too juicy to discard. Kendra settled into her TV chair for a longer conversation, folding her legs Indian style.

"I'm not just talking about angry students either. Did you know he even had a big fight with our golden girl, Allana, the other day? And here, we thought her charms made her immune. One of the counselors, Mrs. W., told me that Zant and Allana were going at it head to head, or fang and designer nail—sorry, couldn't help that. Anyway, Mrs. W. told me that she happened to be walking by and saw the two of them arguing. Then, all of a sudden, Zant burst out laughing. Even Julia stood up and stared at Zant's office. And you know Julia, she usually pretends not to notice what goes on in there. So she must have heard something out of the ordinary."

"Now that you mention it, I might have heard the start of that argument the other day, but I only caught a few words. That doesn't mean it's relevant to what happened tonight."

"We don't know what is or isn't, do we?" said Maretta.

Kendra considered the possibility of a faculty member attacking Zant. No, Maretta was just transferring her own antipathy toward the VP on to other people. Although, to be fair, Maretta wasn't the only person in the Zant Haters Club. Kendra, herself, had a membership card. Maybe Maretta's theory of foul play was on target.

"I have someone on call waiting, talk to you later," said Maretta. "I'm sure I'll be up for hours; call me back if you want."

***

The reporter was now conducting an interview in front of the school marquee. A neighborhood kid jumped in front of the camera and was pulled away by unseen hands.

"Thank you, Sergeant Halstead, for that update. And now back to our studios."

Kendra had missed the entire interview. Now the station was returning to the regularly broadcasted sitcom rerun. How long had she been staring into space, lost in memories of her antagonistic relationship with Mr. Zant. God, it was really late now and the thought of a warm bed was very inviting. She turned off lights on her way back to the kitchen. A moment after she placed her phone in the charger, it began to ring.

"No movies tomorrow," said Kendra as she answered. Her voice was hoarse with sleepiness.

"Movies? What do—"

"Oh! Sorry, Jack, I thought you were Maretta," she explained. "Have you seen the news?" Kendra sat at the table and buried a hand in her cat's warm fur.

"Ah, you've heard, then. Yep, the late shift custodian found our esteemed VP lying below the North staircase, out cold." Jack's smug tone showed how much he loved having inside information. "The paramedics acted like Zant's condition was real serious." Jack did not sound unhappy at that prospect.

"The north stairs? He fell down the stairs, then? How could that happen? Or was there a fight? What do you think Zant was doing over there, anyway? That's kind of out of his way, back by the auditorium."

Jack laughed. "Whoa, one question at a time. Who the hell knows what he was doing out there. Maybe he was rehearsing for a new reality show, *Administrators with Issues*. Seriously, though, the exit to the north lot is at the bottom there. Maybe he was going outside for some reason, although he doesn't park with us peons, so he wouldn't be going to his car that way. He could have been making a security check. Who knows? All the media cares about is that something bad happened at Standard High. This is going to be a huge story that feeds right into the recent gang problems on campus."

The clink of ice cubes against glass punctuated Jack's next words. "But what affects us right now is that the big shots downtown are having a cow over the bad publicity, and want this portrayed as a simple accident. But the district's insurance company—they've got the opposite view. If it's a crime, the insurer won't have to pay out for an accident. Anyhow, the situation's in limbo right now, but to satisfy both sides, school's closed tomorrow. That gives time for things to settle down and a potential crime scene won't be messed up."

"How did you find out all this stuff?" Kendra couldn't help asking, even though she hated to fuel Jack's ego. He endlessly tried to impress people with references to his past teaching awards and his knowledge of legal codes, but it had been years since he'd shown any interest in actual teaching. In fact, he was quite careless about his classroom responsibilities. Jack's laziness was bad for the students, and created more work for his colleagues who ended up having to pick up the slack. Kendra was only able to tolerate Jack because he was a good-hearted man. She thought it was sad that he'd given up even trying to teach, but realized Standard High could do that to a person.

Jack hesitated briefly. "Look, I don't mind telling you what I know; just don't let this go any further, okay? We don't know where the situation is going."

"I won't say anything, I promise."

"Okay. What I heard is that Nate was doing his cleaning rounds in the north hallway and found Zant lying there, out cold. So, Nate walkie-talkied the shift super, who called 911. Then he called the head custodian. Mr. Ken found out and notified the Custodians Union. You can guess why he got the union involved; Zant was found lying there at the end of the second shift. Usually at that hour, only custodians are on campus. Of course, it's not fair to suspect one of them, cause who knows how long Zant was lying there before Nate found him? Anyhow, their union called our union, who called me to ask if the school had any activities going on with teachers maybe around. Everyone's already worrying about damage control but the only thing that's certain at this point is that Zant's in the hospital."

"Wait. The TV news reporter was talking like they know that a crime was committed. That's really irresponsible."

"Yes, but a heart attack or an accident doesn't quite get the ratings. The media loves stories about high school violence. And, until Zant regains consciousness, or the cops find an eyewitness to what happened, how does anyone know the truth? Of course"—he paused for dramatic effect—"if someone confesses . . ."

"There are surveillance cameras on campus. Won't that clear it up?" asked Kendra.

"Might, but for the time being, it's a mystery, and the TV audience will eat it up. So, don't expect the story to die quickly. This puts a lot of pressure on the school board, you know? So, Mrs. Prescott and all the honchos are meeting as we speak. How I'd love hear that discussion."

"Yeah, for real, they must be hysterical with all the negative publicity."

"And it could be worse for them in this case, because a VP got hurt, not some gangbanger, or a peon employee like us. A crime looks bad enough, but they can't forget about the bottom line either. Who knows what Zant's family is going to want in compensation, even for an accident? I bet his 'ex' is hoping he never wakes up." Jack huffed enjoyment of his own joke. "I don't know about the rest of his family, or even if he has any."

"I never thought about that," said Kendra. She visualized a hoard of Star Trek aliens wearing the letter Z on armored chest guards.

"Well, get some sleep, and try not to shed too many tears. Consider this your official notification that school's closed tomorrow. The union told me to help spread the word."

"Okay, thanks, Jack. Keep me posted, will you?" Kendra's desire to know the latest overcame her normal reluctance to talk to Jack.

"Will do. Have a nice night, Kendra." He hung up.

Those details were interesting, thought Kendra. Tonight wasn't the first time paramedics had been called to the school—not by a long shot, but usually the cause was a student brawl. Maybe Jack was right and the only difference was that, this time, an administrator was the one on the gurney. Jack was certainly flippant about the whole thing, but she really wasn't in a position to throw stones.

Without thinking, she dialed Brian's number, but heard his voice mail kick in. He must be on the plane, on his way home. She didn't leave a message because she realized she wasn't in a rush to have the conversation. Brian was going to react to the news with a fresh diatribe against her job and, at this point, she would have a hard time arguing why she shouldn't quit.

She was too wired now to sleep. She needed something to take her mind somewhere else, away from real life. Her favorite on-line computer game would be perfect. Maybe there was a raiding party she could join with her sorceress. While the game loaded, Kendra tucked the dreaded eval-uation papers out of sight.

***

"Okay, calm down, Nicole. Yes, I know about it. I'm sure it's not serious. Look, I can't stay on the line right now. Don't worry. Go take care of your grandmother."

In the background, Ray heard Nicole's disabled grand-mother asking for something. The burden of taking care of the old woman was forcing her to grow up in a big rush. She'd been trying to cope by herself since her mother had deserted them, while social service bureaucrats argued about which agency should step in. Now 18, she showed the world a false maturity. In truth, her childhood had been cut short, leaving her in an uncertain stage of development. Like many kids at the school, she was "at risk". It wouldn't take much more adversity for her to choose the "easy" road to riches, a life of drug dealing. Ray was only trying to keep her on the right path, but it occurred to him again that he should never have given Nicole his cell number. He could wind up "at risk" too, but for a different reason. Ray tried to keep their relationship impersonal but it was hard to push away such a needy woman-child and damn, she was gorgeous.

"But, Mr. Favor—"

"I'll talk to you tomorrow, all right?"

Ray slipped the cell phone into a pocket. Why hadn't Mrs. Prescott called him with an update? She was probably still huddled with the big bosses. She was in tight with them, in line for a job downtown because of her political finesse.

This incident meant more bad publicity for Standard High. When he took over, he'd clean up the school. Mrs. Prescott was a skilled politician, but she was clueless about how to take the school back from thugs in the student population. Carl Zant was clueless too, yet he really believed he'd be the next principal. A serious injury or illness might hurt the man's chance to achieve that even more than his lack of competence.

But Zant's hospitalization wasn't all roses for Ray. He was going to have to take extra work at a time when he was already working overtime on the master schedule. Well, he'd use Zant's lazy secretary, have her do a day's work for a change instead of spending the day making googly eyes at baby pictures. If he tried to give any extra work to Ginny, she'd hang him by his necktie.

Ray thought back several hours earlier, to an encounter with Zant at the break room vending machines.

"I got a nice little present from your favorite TA," Zant offered with a mean smile.

Ray slotted coins into the vending machine and waited for the punch line. There had to be one. There was only silence. Zant wasn't going to make this easy.

"Make your point. I'm busy." Ray grabbed his soda from the niche.

"No point, just wanted you to know she's full of surprises, that girl, and she's willing to share," said Zant. He walked away laughing.

Recalling that vignette made Ray very, very angry. Zant should have considered whom he was playing with this time. Ray could deal with whatever Zant had cooking, if there actually was anything to deal with, which he truly doubted. If Nicole really was involved with Zant in some way, Ray would find out. Was that why she'd been so hysterical tonight? He realized that his wife was calling him; Mrs. Prescott was on the line.

***

As he reached the intersection, Brian questioned what he was doing even as he impulsively swerved across two lanes and turned into a cul de sac. Moments later, he pulled his car to a stop where the narrow street ended at the rear boundary of Standard High. Before him, on the other side of a long span of tattered, chain link fencing lay the football field, a drab green expanse lit only by widely spaced perimeter lights. Far beyond lay the main campus, shrouded in rain and fog.

He scanned the field and the bleachers. What did he expect to see, a gang war, or a witches' coven at the 50-yard line? Realistically, even a wino could find a better spot on a chilly evening.

Brian glanced at the residential buildings nearby. Most of the ground floor windows were barred, drapes tightly closed. Weedy lawns sported "Keep off the Grass" and "No Trespassing" signs. Again, he asked himself what he was doing there. For all he knew some neighbor was calling the cops to report a strange car. The joke would be on him, then. He'd never be able to explain this to the police.

Well, since he was already here, he might as well get out of the car and try to get a better look. Brian leaped over an overflowing gutter to the fence. This was the closest that he could get without trespassing. The view from here was less than satisfactory, but Kendra's portable was visible. The line of sight was poor, but as far as he could tell, the door did look tightly closed. Brian felt somehow reassured, then ashamed that, somehow, he was spying on Kendra. He was here only out of concern for her safety.

She insisted she was safe at her classroom, but he took a more realistic view. The motion detector didn't work and the door didn't latch properly. Who knew what Kendra might encounter in her room at 7 a.m.? At that hour, way back in her portable, she was on her own. Kendra wasn't willing to change her early morning habits and he was almost afraid to bring the subject up again. For sure, she would have a fit if she knew he was over here. This was a fool's errand if there ever was one. In fact, she might even break up with him if she thought he was being over protective. No, she wouldn't call it that; she would say controlling. Brian pushed away from the fence, rubbed a residue of grit from his hands, and ran for his car.

It had been a long day. He looked at the dashboard clock and groaned. Then he remembered he'd left it on Daylight Savings Time. Even so, the evening had gotten away from him. If he went over to Kendra's house at this hour he'd wake her up. That was never a good idea. He'd rushed to catch a flight, hoping to get home in time to have a late dinner with her, but the plane had been held on the runway for unexplained reasons. To make matters worse, the airline wasn't able to locate his checked baggage. All the travel was starting to wear him down.

His job wasn't stress free, as Kendra assumed. She thought he was so free and easy because he was an independent contractor. In fact, he often worked for people he loathed, and was stuck writing bids for jobs he didn't want, just to ensure he would have enough work. He'd been lucky thus far, but he knew that eventually he would have to take out a loan and try to compete with the big guys. Still, even if his income wasn't predictable and steady like Kendra's, at least his working conditions were safe.

He drove to the four lane street and made a left, away from the school. It barely registered with him that a news van was heading in the opposite direction. The neighborhood quickly became more upscale only blocks from the campus. Traffic was blessedly light. He relaxed into the seat and gave his home refrigerator a mental scan. He'd stop and get a sandwich.

***

Mr. Helens poked his head into his wife's cozy library. Tamra looked up at him with surprise. He'd been working in his home office and usually didn't leave there till midnight.

"Sorry to bug you; there's a call for you. A man. Says he's from school and that it's important."

"Thanks dear," said Tamra. She was stretched out on her lavishly upholstered loveseat, right next to the phone, but she'd turned off the ringer, as was her habit in the evening. Especially tonight when she needed time to think. She supposed it was the Super's office so she could hardly avoid the call. She waved her husband back to his study.

"This is Tamra."

Jack's enthusiastic voice caught her by surprise. "Heard the news?"

"You doing a Neilson survey?"

"Funny, hah hah. Matter of fact, maybe I am doing a survey. A survey of the people who were on campus after school today," said Jack.

"What are you babbling about?" Tamra's voice brimmed with irritation.

"I just wanted to tell you how impressed I am."

"If you don't start talking sense, I'm hanging up.

"Aren't you worried about an alibi?"

"What?"

Jack clicked his tongue. "Hey, I'm offering you the hand of friendship, trying to give you an alibi in case someone asks where you were this afternoon. After all, you really helped me out, if you get my meaning."

"No, I guess I don't," said Tamra.

"I wouldn't have expected you to take credit, but I wanted to voice my gratitude. I'm sure you had your rea-sons. Zant wanted to put all the blame on you, didn't he?"

Tamra held the receiver away from her ear as if the sound waves might somehow transmit a plague. "Are you implying that I had something to do with the accident at school?" In spite of herself, Tamra's voice went up an octave. With alarm she got up and walked to the door, opening it a crack to see if her husband may have heard the outburst. His door remained firmly closed.

"Don't be paranoid. I'm not taping this, if you're worried."

Tamra felt the soothing touch of the plush carpeting beneath her bare feet as she walked to a window to gaze out at the dramatically lit garden below. Her life at work was a separate universe. She felt secure in this setting, in command.

"You've lost your grip on reality, Jack. I have nothing to be concerned about. I don't know why you even want to go down that road, since you were there after school as well, and if you want to talk about motive—"

Jack's chuckles turned into a thick smoker's cough. "Sorry. Let's not get into an argument. I just wanted to thank you and say that I wouldn't think of saying anything about your presence at school so late. All I ask in return is that you make sure my job is secure."

"Have you been smoking something other than tobacco? I don't appreciate your innuendos about Mr. Zant's accident. Pick someone else to slime, and don't ever call me at home again!" She clicked off and hurled the phone away in a fury. The Jack Sermon substitute bounced once on a sofa cushion and rolled soundlessly to the carpeted floor.

7.

Thursday

Teachers and clerks clustered in groups around the cafeteria tables, discussing what they'd seen on TV the night before. The custodians were huddled in a far corner, as if to avoid unwanted questions.

Calls had gone out the previous night to inform the staff that school would be closed, but this morning another call requested their presence at an afternoon meeting. Attendance was almost perfect. At Standard High, only a major incident could get the whole staff to attend a meeting.

"I was getting ready to visit the grandkids," complained a supply room clerk. "First they said no school, then we get called in anyhow. I guess I could have just kept going on with my day, but I want to hear what Mrs. Prescott has to say."

"Poor Julia," whispered a teacher's aide, "She looks really awful, doesn't she? I wonder if she knows something, being Zant's secretary and all."

"If I were her, I wouldn't be wasting too much time feeling sorry," said a nearby music teacher. "Mr. Zant treats her like dirt."

"All the same, she works with him every day," countered another tablemate, "and that brings things closer to home."

An untimely "Shwoosh" could be heard above the chatter. Allana Jarney was demonstrating her golf swing in front of two male colleagues. In spite of the wintry weather, she wore a short skirt and sleeveless top. Although her demeanor was carefree, her presence at a meeting revealed that she was as curious as everyone else.

"May I have your attention, please?" Mrs. Prescott stiffly gestured from left to right, her severely tailored suit perhaps impeding a more fluid motion. Even the habitual rabble-rousers at the back table went silent, another indication that conditions were out of the ordinary. She gazed briefly at Mr. Favor and then raised her eyes to an impersonal zone a few feet above the heads of the hushed audience.

"Thank you for coming on such short notice. I'm sure you all know that there was a serious incident here yesterday. Carl Zant was found unconscious and taken in critical condition to the intensive care unit at Memorial Hospital." The Principal's face betrayed no emotion, but she was speaking too slowly, choosing her words carefully.

Bodies shifted restlessly and hands popped up all around the room. The staff clearly wasn't going to sit and listen quietly to more of this non-information. Jack Sermon stood up.

"Mrs. Prescott, we're all upset about Mr. Zant, but we know he's in the hospital. Can't you give us more details? If not, why have we been called in here today?"

No one was shocked by Jack's rudeness; he was like that. Sometimes, his pugnacity was useful. Heads nodded in support and someone called out, "Yeah, why?"

Mrs. Prescott blinked and turned slightly away from Jack. "I'm afraid there's bad news. I am very sad to tell you that Carl has died. He—"

There was a heartbeat of silence and then everyone began to talk at once. This time, a coach helped to quiet the room. "Let her finish!" he yelled.

Mrs. Prescott continued, "I'm afraid I don't know all the details either. I do know the cause of death was from head wounds he received in a fall down the stairs. The doctors were not able to save him. Carl's family has arrived from out of state and they will hold a memorial service. You'll be informed as to when that will be. They're asking that no flowers be sent. They will let us know where to send a charitable contribution in Carl's name."

As the crowd reaction approached the decibel level of a student lunch period, Ray Favor stood up to take the lead.

"School will reopen tomorrow morning. We believe Carl Zant's death was an accident. His wounds were consistent with an accident, but due to the circumstances, the police will conduct a routine investigation. As you probably noticed, the area where the accident occurred is blocked off to allow forensic team access. Please do not cross any boundary tapes."

Favor held up a hand in a futile attempt to silence the room. "We know that it is unthinkable that anyone would have wanted to hurt Carl, but the police need to make certain that no crime has been committed."

"We've been asking for more security around here for years," shouted an irate teacher. His comments were roundly seconded.

Publicity about gang activity and poor academic performance had long marred the school's image, making it hard to recruit and retain good staff. A fresh exodus from Standard High would surely follow this incident.

"Rest assured, the district is committed to school safety. Teachers and staff, all of you, please reinforce this with the students. Although we're certain the incident was just an accident, we are immediately going to hire two additional hall monitors and we've been given funds to purchase more surveillance cameras. But let's not dwell on that. I assure you we have no indication that there was any criminal activity during the time period in question."

A teacher shouted, "What time period was that, anyway?"

Favor ignored the chorus that echoed that question and continued, "All right, all right. Quiet down! Listen up. Tomorrow, the library will be open before school, so that all employees can provide the police with a short, written statement. So, please schedule a few minutes to help the investigators. I know each of you will cooperate fully." Favor parried all demands for more details.

"Let's just get things back to normal as quickly as possible. I am sure none of us want this unfortunate incident to ruin Standard High's reputation." Immediately, derisive laughs came from the back of the cafeteria.

Mrs. Prescott took over again. "We know that some students may undergo emotional trauma. Some of them were quite close to Carl, especially Special Ed. students who were under his wing."

This remark created a great deal of eye rolling. Mrs. Prescott appeared not to notice. She went on, "The district is sending special counselors who will set up shop in the Community Outreach office tomorrow. If you have any students who are upset and want to talk, send them over there. Concerning school operations, I will be sending out a memo to announce who will temporarily take over Carl's duties until a new VP can be hired. I think that is about all I have for you at this time. Thank you for coming."

***

64

Kendra selected a good vantage point and watched for Maretta. For the millionth time, Kendra wished she had better eyesight. The parking lot was a confusion of more than one hundred people, all trying to leave at the same time. Finally, she caught sight of her friend coming down a line of parked cars, and trotted over to meet her.

Maretta launched right in. "Thanks for waiting, I wanted to get some papers from my room. Want to go for a coffee? I could sure use one." When Kendra nodded her head, Maretta continued. "Well that was a shocker. God. I can't believe it. Poor Zant…and poor Standard High."

"Yeah, it all happened so fast. I can't deal with it."

"Don't be so upset. I mean, it's natural to feel bad, but look at it this way; if Zant sent that email, you won't have to worry about getting any more of them."

"There's plenty to worry about. I've been thinking there was a good chance Zant sent it, for whatever reason— to get me to quit, or to make my life miserable. But now, I don't know if it's worse if he's the one who sent it or not. What if he was murdered? The email gives me a grade A motive for murder. And suppose Zant didn't send it. What if the email came from the real murderer as part of a plan to set me up as the prime suspect? If the cops find out about the email, it might not matter whether or not Zant sent it because they could say I killed him because I *believed* he did."

"You sure can make something complicated. Don't get so worked up! Nobody even said Zant was murdered."

"Oh, that makes me feel much better. If it was an accident, I only have to worry about being arrested for a simple sex crime I didn't commit."

"Come on, Kendra, relax! As far as we know, nobody but the two of us knows anything about the email."

"What if the cops get into the school mail system and turn up a copy? Even if they don't, you know I'm just not comfortable at all with police."

"Come on, that was years ago. You need to get over it."

"Someone planted the evidence that put my brother in jail. You think he got over it? Five years gone out of his life for nothing."

"All right, now's not the time to review your paranoia. Just hold it together if they ask you any questions. You haven't done anything for God's sake."

"That's what I'm saying. Does it ever matter? Oh God, my brain is going to explode. I need to go home."

"Yeah, let's go. Maretta led the way to where she was parked. A passing car tooted goodbye and they waved as she asked, "So, what time did you leave school yesterday?"

"See, see? Now you're asking me for an alibi. Okay, okay, I went to the materials lab around 4:00, so I wasn't here very late. But campus was almost empty by the time I left."

"Oh, I was just wondering if you stuck around late and saw anything odd. I assume that's what they want us to make statements for, in case someone did see something suspicious. But they ask us for information without telling us what time frame they're looking at. The administration seems to be keeping things back from us.

Kendra nodded. "Yeah, if they're so sure it was an accident, why the hush-hush?"

"Well, as for alibis, I left campus right after 6th period because I had a dental appointment."

Kendra said, "So, you were out of here too, that's good."

"Um, well, it's more complicated than that. I had a teeth cleaning and was done in less than an hour." Maretta paused. "Truth be told, I came back here cause I forgot something. I was so irritated at having to come back, I just sped in and out, and I didn't pay attention to the time. For all I know, I picked exactly the worst moment to be on campus. Should I say that I was here? I didn't see anything, anyway. You think one of the cameras could have picked me up—those things don't actually work, do they?"

"My advice is to tell the truth. Why worry when you haven't done anything wrong? I think you're more freaked out than I am. Maybe you shouldn't drive right now. Want me to drive?"

"I appreciate the offer, but it's okay, I'm just a little nervous. You know, we should think twice about staying on campus late from now on. Who knows what really happened to the man. And all this publicity! My relatives are pumping me for juicy details and they don't believe me when I tell them I haven't got any. What about you? You talk to Brian yet?" The two of them rounded Maretta's car.

Kendra sighed with resignation. "Yeah, I called him this morning, told him that Zant had an accident last night on campus. An accident doesn't sound all that bad does it? But you know Brian; that was enough for him. Even though he was barely awake, he went into a long harangue about how Zant must have been attacked by some gangbangers and how I should clear out my room and never come back."

"That thought pops into my head every morning," said Maretta, with a grim smile.

"Brian overlooks the satisfaction I get out of my job, maybe cause every time he's come here he's had a bad experience—like kids yelling obscene things at him, stuff like that. He refuses to have lunch here with me anymore, says the ambience brings him down."

"As it does to us all," said Maretta, slowly waving an arm to encompass the expanse of the campus.

"Yeah, true. But wait till Brian hears that Zant's dead. He doesn't know about the email yet either, and I'm really afraid to tell him about it now."

They drew up at Maretta's car and the two women hugged. Maretta said, "I'll take a rain check on the coffee. I'll back you up no matter what happens. Go home and try not to think too much. Call me later, ok?"

***

As Allana pulled into the lot, she saw that in spite of the eatery's popularity, Tamra had managed to snag a highly desirable table by the window. Allana decided to take it for a good omen.

"Over here," Tamra called out to her, waving.

Allana savored the comforting smell of spices and fresh bread while she threaded through the rows of glass-topped tables. Two lines of customers snaked back from the counter. At this hour of the day, most of the patrons were tourists from the nearby venues. The overall commotion made it unlikely that anyone could hear a private conversation.

"I left my office as soon as you called," said Tamra. "Sorry I didn't give you an update this morning after I found out Zant died, but I went straight in to a meeting." She pushed a glass and plate across the table. "I ordered for you."

Allana wasted no time. "Tell me everything. You must know more than what Mrs. Prescott told us. Why is she keeping the staff in the dark?"

"You seem worried. What were you really doing on campus so late last Wednesday?"

"Hey, you were there, too and if anyone should be worried it's you. After all, I wasn't the one who was screwing Zant." Allana's lips scrunched into a show of distaste. "How you could let that SOB near you, I'll never understand, but I see you're not looking exactly heart-broken."

Tamra stirred artificial sweetener into her ice tea. Allana knew Tamra was stalling, weighing the danger of further discussion. Allana could admit that her personal strong points were not loyalty or openness, so she couldn't blame Tamra for being cautious. One could have a professional relationship and the occasional get together with a coworker, but actual friendship and trust required more commitment.

"Come on, Tamra, I won't say anything, I promise. You must know what really happened. The administration won't tell the staff anything. Do they think Zant had an accident or not?"

Tamra seemed focused on a paper napkin, tearing it into bits in a methodical way but answered reluctantly, "I'm not included in meetings with the Superintendent, so I have to add up bits of information as they come my way. Early on, I saw some cops and lawyer types come out of the Super's wing. Shortly after, I went to deliver some paperwork and I chatted with his secretary. She was working on a press release. That's when I found out Zant was dead.

"A while later, I heard there are conflicting opinions and purposes. The on site evidence and Zant's injuries are consistent with a finding of accidental death, but the district's insurance company demanded a criminal investigation cause they don't want to have to pay out for a fatal accident. The last thing the Super wants is a homicide on school grounds, but they don't want to be seen to be covering up anything either. I didn't find out any more, but obviously the police did agree to investigate."

"So, you think the police suspect it *wasn't* an accident?" Allana bit her beautifully glossed lower lip. "Favor said we have to write a short statement for the cops. Will we be interrogated too?"

"Maybe." Tamra waved off a bouncy server who was making the rounds with a pitcher of water. "An investigation puts me in an awkward position. I pray the cops don't find out about Zant and me, not that there ever was a whole lot going on, just one or two 'encounters.' And we were very, very careful. I told Zant from the start that I won't risk my job or let anything wreck my marriage."

"If you're so worried about losing your husband, you shouldn't have cheated on him. He treats you so well, and never complains about your credit card bills. Not that I want to sound sanctimonious or anything—I know I'm not exactly a nun."

In truth, Allana was genuinely surprised that Tamra would have done something that could jeopardize her marriage. Tamra's main mission in life was to placate her wealthy husband. Perhaps this proved that Tamra wasn't as in control of herself as she led people to believe.

Tamra replied, "You're right. I don't know what I was thinking. I know my husband. You've heard, I guess, that most murders are domestic." Tamra mimed stabbing herself in the chest. No smile accompanied the gesture.

"Now that you mention it, maybe Zant's ex-wife got him, then," said Allana.

Tamra sniffed. "It wouldn't surprise me if the cops found a voodoo doll planted by his 'ex'."

"Joking aside, that would be best. That takes the whole thing off campus."

"They might be looking at his ex. She could have come on campus, who knows? But we might as well expect the cops will focus more on his work associations. Scene of the crime and all that."

"That's why I'm nervous. If the detectives really start prying, all sorts of things could surface, like the shortcuts we took with some of the student files, and there's—" Allana took a swig of her juice concoction. "I guess I have to warn you."

Tamra's shoulders hitched up. "Warn me? About what?"

"See, I was in Zant's office for my evaluation, and he was saying how he couldn't wait to take me down a few notches. He said he was reviewing my credentials, that he was sure I was faking something, but he'd be willing to overlook any

69

discrepancies if I'd 'treat him nice'." She made quotation marks in the air, and continued, "Then he started to look me up and down, said he'd like to find out what kind of a dancer I am. What an asshole! So, I changed the subject, got him talking about himself, instead. That wasn't hard to do, he's such a self-centered pig, I mean, he *was*. Anyway, he started talking about his macho workouts at the gym, how important it was to him." Allana shifted uneasily in her chair and looked at the distant pastry counter.

"You're warning me about his fitness program?"

Allana's eyes met Tamra's and quickly fled. She continued, "Um, no, he was talking about how he'd like to build more muscle mass, and my entrepreneurial side took over. I asked him if he'd ever thought of trying HGH. Zant seemed really interested in having some treatments, so we scheduled one for next week."

"I never thought you were that dumb, Allana. Or were you just too eager to stick a few needles into him? Anyway, what does all this have to do with me?"

Allana hesitated. "After he made the appointment, he turned around and demanded that I have sex with him, or he'd turn me in over the HGH, so I told him that if he reported me, I'd go public with your affair, and I pointed out the obvious—that if the affair came out, that would end his chance to become principal. I'm sorry, Tamra, I didn't have a choice."

Tamra clutched her ice tea glass so tightly that Allana was afraid it would shatter. "For god's sake, Allana, how could you bargain with my private life! After all I've done for you, helping you finish your damn paperwork and everything. I feel like making you do it all over again, the right way, and see how long you keep your job without my help."

Allana thought that was unlikely, since Tamra would look bad if the deadlines weren't met, but she needed to soothe her companion, and fast. "I'm sorry, really I am! If actually sleeping with the creep would have worked, I would have slept with him, but you know as well as I do, he would have gone public anyway. I had to protect myself."

Neither woman spoke for several minutes. The pieces of Tamra's napkin were now arranged on the table in the shape of a cross.

Allana broke the silence. "What I did doesn't matter now. Zant can't do anything to either of us. I didn't even have to tell you any of this, but you've been a client and friend of mine for a while now, and I wanted let you know what happened and to assure you that all my clients have complete confidentiality."

"You call making a deal with that swine 'client confidentiality'?"

"It wasn't a deal. I called his bluff, is all. I'm telling you, I would have slept with him if I thought he would have let me off the hook."

"Why am I not totally convinced of that?" Tamra pushed away her drink.

Allana squeezed Tamra's hand. "We'll be okay. If the cops ask, you won't talk about me and I won't mention you."

"You don't have to pressure me. I don't have any reason to rat on you. I think the investigation is just for show, anyway, to make the insurance company happy."

"Still, I'd feel better if I knew what was on his BlackBerry. I wonder if the cops have it."

Tamra shrugged. "I never put anything of a more personal nature in writing and if I'm on his calendar, that can be explained as administrative contact."

"Hell, I think I might have sent him an article about side effects. I guess that might look funny coming from a teacher. Well, even if they find something like that, I've gotten rid of everything related to that now."

"Does this mean you won't be taking the risk to stay in business any longer?" Tamra frowned with disappointment.

"I'll deal with your sagging flesh when everything gets back to normal. Which I hope is soon."

"I'm sure the bastard just slipped on something and fell down the stairs. The students love to sit on the stairs and eat lunch. Zant probably didn't see a slice of left over pizza and slipped on it."

"Well, that's the kind of detail I'd like to have," said Allana. "We're at a disadvantage if we get interviewed. You should hear the rumors that are flying around school."

"As long as we're not the subject of any of the rumors, why care?" Tamra adjusted her sweater around her shoulders, picked up her wallet, and gracefully rose from her chair.

"I will make sure the gossip focuses on someone else," said

Allana, handing Tamra the check.

***

When Kendra got home, she saw Brian's car in the driveway. She found him napping on a chair in the back yard. She sneaked up and yanked the cap off his head. He sat up and grinned at her.

"Glad to see you're fully clothed. A hat, even. My neighbor has added "peeping time" to her daily schedule. She's quite enamored of your manly charms."

"Ah, well, then she has good taste," replied Brian, without a hint of irritation.

"I have to warn you though—if you see her standing on a ladder in her dining room, make sure you've got your pants on. You don't want to have to call 911 if her heart stops." Kendra's voice broke up in giggles.

"Love thy neighbor," quoted Brian flippantly.

"Since I woke you up, I wasn't sure you'd remember I have the day off," said Kendra, pulling up a chair alongside him.

"Oh, you woke me up good with that call. I did get back to sleep though. I wasn't going to lose any because that asshole is in the hospital. I just got up again about an hour ago, and came over, but found you gone."

"Sorry, I had to go to an emergency meeting at school. Guess what? Carl Zant died!"

"No way!"

"Oh yeah." She bobbed her head emphatically, yanked her glasses off and fussed with the earpieces.

"When you weren't here, I figured you were out doing errands or something."

Kendra went back to her story. "The principal said Zant died from head injuries."

"Now, don't tell me you're going to cry over him," said Brian. "Not to be a monster, I don't rejoice when anyone dies, but from what I knew of him, he wasn't exactly a nice person, and on a personal level, he made your workday hell."

She blew fluff off her lenses. "I'm not sure yet how I feel. There's more to tell, though. The police are investigating the incident." She popped her glasses back in place.

Brian groaned. "I told you, didn't I, as soon as you said he was taken away from campus in an ambulance? Do the math: injury plus Standard High equals crime scene. Kendra, honey, fights, theft and property damage are bad enough, but homicide? Come on, time to wake up. That job isn't worth it."

She gave him an annoyed look and he changed tack. "So, was it a gang thing?"

"That's what's kind of freaky; they're not telling us anything. The cops are there, but they keep calling it an accident."

"You sound skeptical about it being an accident your-self."

Kendra didn't want to give a straight answer. There was no advantage in feeding Brian's hostility toward the school, or in letting him know how much animosity there was among her colleagues. "Let's just say that Zant didn't treat anyone else much better than he treated me."

"In that case, there must be a long list of suspects. As-suming the cops go that route."

"I'm included in that list, you know." She frowned and picked at the wicker fibers on her chair.

"Justifiable homicide, that would be my verdict," said Brian with a laugh. "Hey, I'm kidding." He noticed that Kendra wasn't laughing with him and leaned over to land a kiss on her forehead, as if to soothe a child.

She didn't notice his touch. Yes, she thought, perhaps someone had decided that murder was justifiable.

8.

Friday morning

Julia flicked on the light, and surveyed the chaos of Zant's office. The desk was covered with mounds of papers that crested at one end of the phone cord. Framed military memorabilia hung over a long table, the surface of which hadn't seen daylight since Zant moved in. The detectives had finished with this room, and had given permission for her to work in it.

Julia's current task was to pack up Zant's personal possessions and to organize the files to make things ready for the next VP. She didn't quite know where to begin, but she was sorry she wasn't wearing the outfit she wore to do yard work. Or maybe one of those moon suits designed for biological hazards. Too bad the whole room couldn't be shoved into a dumpster, but she'd been told to sort into four categories: Special Ed. Department, attendance, school activities, and Personnel files. Zant's personal items were to be taken to Mrs. Prescott's office. Maybe she would begin with those.

Regarding his personal effects, Julia realized no one was feeding his pets now. She shuddered just thinking about their dietary needs. Someone else would have to take charge. Maybe the biology teacher, or one of the Special Ed. teachers? Yes, the Special Ed. teachers were always looking for an opportunity to teach their students responsibility, weren't they?

The passing bell sounded. It was the end of first period. School had resumed without much fuss. Thus far. The students were eager to discuss Zant's passing but very few had sought the available counseling. Within the faculty, speculation continued over the cause of death. Rumor had it that detectives would be interviewing selected employees. Julia huffed. If the police were looking for people who might have been motivated to harm the former VP, they wouldn't have a difficult search. She could easily name four or five—herself included.

After the meeting broke up the previous morning, she'd rushed home to avoid curious colleagues who wanted to ask questions, to get inside her head. This morning, people who normally didn't even say hello to her were stopping by to convey their sympathy. She didn't know or care if they meant it. As a rule, she tried to treat everyone decently but she didn't go out of her way to socialize at work. She wasn't interested in making friends.

Julia's TA shouted his arrival. She dispatched him to visit the teachers she believed were most likely to take in a tarantula and a small lizard. The boy left with a hall pass and quite a show of amusement. Hopefully, he'd stick to the mission at hand and forego a side trip to friends' classrooms.

Too bad the student couldn't help with Zant's office, but files were confidential. What's more, she believed there might be inappropriate items stashed in the office. Without enthusiasm, she began the packing. At least this task gave her valuable time to herself.

***

"Good morning, if you can say that at a time like this. There was a note in my box this morning; you wanted to see me?" Jack lumbered into Maretta's classroom, briefcase in hand. The air soured with a wash of stale tobacco. He'd probably smoked his way through his prep period.

Maretta frowned at both the odor and the inconvenient timing. "That note's been there for a week, Jack. I said to come after school, not during passing period. But never mind, since you're here, have a look at this."

She brought out a workbook and flipped a few pages as he watched with disinterest. The cover was marred by graffiti-like doodles and random pencil marks. There was little actual work to be seen.

"Heh, this is Sam Luong's. A few days ago he told me he'd lost it." Jack extracted a bag of corn chips from his case and gave full attention to the sealed end.

She pointed at the book. "I found it hidden on a shelf, wedged behind some dictionaries," said Maretta.

"Sam has a habit of misplacing his books so he doesn't have to do any work."

75

Jack was looking at her like she was an imbecile. Maretta almost gagged as he crammed a handful of chips into his mouth and wiped his plump fingers on the collar of his grimy shirt.

"Let me rephrase my question, Jack. Why did you put Sam in the same workbook that he completed last year? He passed your freshman English class, so, presumably, he doesn't need to do the same work all over again?"

"Um, well, I've got a number of students in 2nd period that haven't covered this stuff yet—"

Maretta cut in before Jack finished his self-serving explanation. "So it's much easier for you to give them all the same book. What do you think he's in Special Ed. for? You do know that we're here to individualize their coursework."

"I hardly think that you are in a position to lecture me about learning strategies. I am an awarded reading teacher, you know." Jack puffed his already rounded chest. "If you'd take the time to look at Sam's assessment testing, you'd see that he's only in the 74th percentile of— "

"Hold up, will you?" Maretta was thinking more about projectiles than percentiles. I'm not in the mood to listen to any of your long-winded justifications. I believe you've assessed him correctly. Can you just use a different workbook? You don't have to make him do the same exact things all over again. How do you expect him to feel? That's why he's been refusing to work."

"You have a better idea? I wasn't aware you're a reading specialist," retorted Jack.

"Better than an idea. You can use this." She pulled a textbook from a shelf.

Jack looked at the book dismissively. "What if, in my judgment, this isn't appropriate? I believe it's up to me what work I assign in my classroom. Who do you think you are?"

"Just one of your respected colleagues. I'm being perfectly reasonable. Sam is on my list. I wrote his learning goals, and intend to make sure he progresses. You don't want him to give up and fail, do you?"

"No, of course not," said Jack, relenting to a degree. "But, I really don't see the harm in having him repeat skills. You know the recent studies about long term memory—"

"Spare me. Will you start Sam on this book or not?"

"All right, since you seem to be so hysterical, I can't, in good conscience, be the source of your nervous breakdown. I'll do what you want."

Maretta noticed for the first time that Jack looked unusually strained. She thought she could even detect some sadness in his face. It had been a very bad week. Just when she was rethinking her long held belief about the man's lack of empathy, he grinned and asked, "So where were you when our fearless leader took a dive? Not behind him, I hope. If you were, you must have been at the head of a long line."

"The man's dead, Jack, how tasteless can you get? If you can't take Zant's death seriously, at least keep your fantastic conjectures to yourself." She pointed at him. "And don't you dare say anything like that about me to anyone else. What have I ever done to you?"

Jack swallowed a mouthful of chips. "Well now that you mention it, you faked my signature on an education plan. We're all behind on getting them finished, but it wouldn't take you that long to just have me sign—"

"What the hell are you talking about?"

The snack bag crinkled as Jack set it aside. He removed a clipped sheaf of papers from his briefcase, turned to the last page and held it under her nose. "I didn't attend this meeting for one of your students, but here's my signature. Explain that, Mrs. Edwards."

"I would love to, but she's not my student this year. I offered to take this girl off your hands last year, but now she's on Allana's roll. Anyway, I think you're just confused. I wasn't at the girl's meeting either, but we all have to sign as long as we see the student for at least one period. Kendra and I signed this—see? Tamra's been circulating stacks of these in a panic lately because of the state review. I bet you just signed this one on autopilot."

"Not for this kid, no way. Look again—at the kid's name. Remember? I was having so many problems with her and her family last semester, we made a deal and swapped students. Since then, as you know, I won't have her in any of my classes. So why would my signature be on her goal sheet? If it was my signature, which it isn't."

Maretta reasoned, "Tamra must be working off an old roster list. What else is new? So, when the packet was completed and ready to go back to the teacher of record, it came to you. That proves Tamra thinks the kid is still on your roll."

"Okay, but you haven't explained why my signature is on something that I didn't sign."

"No, I can't, unless you signed it by mistake."

"Not a chance. Well, then, we seem to have a bit of a mystery, but I owe you an apology." Jack gave a small bow.

"Accepted. If you don't mind leaving, I have to let the kids in before the bell rings."

"Speaking of leaving, I saw your car leaving the lot pretty late yesterday afternoon, way after school was out. If you need an alibi, I'd be glad to help." Jack popped the last chip into his mouth.

"You must be mistaken, Jack. I wasn't here. But you've just told me where you were. Should I be interested?"

The question achieved the desired response. Jack licked his lower lip, tossed the empty snack bag into a wastepaper basket, snatched his case and hurried out the door.

***

"Hey, Julia, how's it going? I hear you need a new home for the menagerie?" Kendra smiled inwardly when Julia looked from her to the wall clock, as if to check if Kendra should be away from her classroom.

The secretary shook her head. "Wow, 3rd period already? I never even heard the bells. I wanted to ask, can you take those animals? Someone has to at least feed them until they find new homes." Julia's tone made it clear that the "someone" in question wasn't going to be Julia.

"If nobody else wants them." Kendra went over to get a closer look at the spider tank that sat in the corner behind Zant's desk. "Ick. To be honest, Julia, I'm not exactly sure how you take care of something like this."

"Zant kept pet care books around here somewhere. Maybe they're buried under all the candy wrappers on his desk," said Julia with a poker face.

Kendra moved to the desk, but was stopped short by something poking at her leg. With the image of the "creepy-crawly" still fresh in her brain, she swatted at her leg in alarm. But the attacker was only a shard of splintered wood. The desk had a center drawer and two on the side. The damage was at the bottom drawer, the only one fitted with a lock.

"Uh, Julia? This desk is busted up, you should probably call the Plant Manager about it."

"Busted?"

"Yeah, the wood is cracked, someone's going to get gouged by this."

Julia came over to get a better look, and said, "I never noticed this before, but I hardly ever came around to this side of the desk."

Kendra wondered if Zant had lost his key, and his temper on the drawer. Or, perhaps the damage dated back to a previous tenant, though that was unlikely. No one could work near this desk for very long without getting jabbed.

The secretary sighed. "I should empty this drawer and tape over the splinters before someone gets hurt." She tried the drawer, which easily opened to its full extension. The two women gasped at the display of bullets and other contraband undoubtedly confiscated from students during their disciplinary sessions with the VP.

Kendra was happy for a chance to see inside the VP's desk. Somewhere in this office she hoped to see the snapshot that had disappeared from her bulletin board. She'd love to find it here, especially now that Zant was dead. When she got the original back, she could more easily prove she'd been set up, if the need arose.

Julia muttered under her breath and said, "I guess he turned the blades and guns over to the police, but what am I supposed to do with this stuff?"

"Yeah, you should maybe call someone. . . I'll just have a look for the pet books."

"I'm going to talk to the detectives, make sure they saw this." Julia looked at Kendra speculatively. "They searched the office. I wonder why they didn't say anything about this drawer full of lovely collectibles from Standard High."

"If they believed it had something to do with Zant's accident, I'm sure they would have asked about it," said Kendra.

"That makes sense. Hey, Kendra, don't you be moving around too fast. You're kicking up a lot of dust."

"I noticed. Didn't they ever clean in here?"

"Heh, how could they? The custodians wouldn't do anything except empty the trash and mop the parts of the floor they could see."

Kendra took a risk and said, "Since you're going through everything, could let me know if you come across any student snapshots? I'd like to take a look and see if they're the ones that were taken from my room. I wouldn't be surprised if Mr. Zant wound up with them. He always made the kids turn out their pockets."

Julia grunted with disinterest. Kendra hoped that meant yes, and quickly changed her line of questioning. "Have you heard anything about who might fill in until a new VP is hired?"

"The talk is that it won't be anyone from here," said Julia.

"I was wondering about that. In some schools they choose someone already on the faculty."

"From what went on at last month's faculty meeting, I think someone would have to hold a gun to Mrs. Prescott's head before she promotes one of you teachers."

"Yeah, well, maybe relations will improve now. Zant was a major source of friction."

"If you don't mind, let's not talk about Zant." Julia pulled a rapidly filling trash bin closer to her side.

"Sorry, I know he treated you badly, but you weren't the only one—I guess that wasn't much comfort."

Kendra heard the secretary clear her throat. "I try to not pay attention to other people's business."

Kendra took the point and backed off. "I'll be out of your hair as soon as I find those pet books. I better round up a custodian to help me take the two terrariums back to my room. Can I use your phone?"

After making the call, Kendra resumed her foraging. As she lifted a three ring binder, a business card fluttered out from some hidden resting place. She picked the card up from the floor and was surprised to see it was from a law firm specializing in adoptions. A recent date was scribbled on the back. She put the card back on the desk.

Zant as a prospective parent? That was unthinkable. Maybe he was trying to help a pregnant teenager. No, that was also out of character. Come to think of it, she did know one person who was trying to adopt a baby. But Julia had already told her to mind her own business, in almost those words.

Kendra pulled at a file drawer, but it went off its track, and the drawn out, metallic screech drew Julia's attention. With a grunt, Kendra used a shoulder to keep the entire cabinet from toppling on her. She regained her balance, shook the dust from her sweater and sneezed.

Julia put her hands on her hips. "What are you doing in that file cabinet?"

"I, um, thought the books might be in there."

"Those files are confidential! Maybe you should just go! I'll let you know if I find the pet books."

Kendra was on her way out when a man came to the door. There were sweat marks visible on his tan uniform and there were new worry lines on his plump face. "You need help with something, Ms. Desola?"

"Yes, thanks for coming, Nate. Are you working the day shift now?"

"Yeah, well, after what happened, I sort of wanted to be here during the daytime, at least for a while, so I switched with someone else. Kind of sorry I did, cause a detective's been questioning us custodians all morning, especially me. Over and over again."

"Not to worry, Nate. They can't believe you did anything wrong. They're just doing their job," said Kendra in what she hoped was a reassuring tone.

"I hope so. They keep saying the questions are routine. So what's this about tanks?"

"When you have time, could you please take Zant's spider and lizard tanks over to my classroom? I get to be the new zookeeper."

Nate gave the tarantula a look that clearly showed he'd prefer to use a can of insect spray on the creature, but he nodded and replied, "I'll have to go get a cart. If you'll be in your room next period, I'll come by with them." Receiving the okay, he glanced again at the spider tank, made a face, and sauntered out.

The reference to the time made Kendra realize she'd have to run to make it back to her room before the passing bell triggered the student stampede. She glanced at Zant's desk on her way out.

The business card from the law firm had disappeared.

***

Ray Favor leaned over the distraught teenager. He could smell her perfume and something else, a hair product or soap. He gave himself a mental slap, and backed away, perching on the edge of his desk.

"Nicole, get a grip, okay? I don't have time for drama." In hopes of cheering her up, he added, "Your hair looks nice today; I love those braids."

Nicole showed no sign of hearing the compliment. Ray glanced at the closed door and continued in a low voice, "Are you going to tell me why you're crying, or not?"

The girl snuffled into a tissue and wiped at her smeary mascara. Without meeting Ray's eyes, she began, "They're saying . . . saying Zant was murdered. What's going on around this place?"

"Don't believe that crap. There was no murder. You should know better than to believe what you hear around here. But if you're that upset and you think you need it, I can give you a pass to the counseling—"

Nicole cut him off. "Whatever you say, the cops are still here, asking questions. What if they hear the stupid rumors going around about us, and . . . and they think. . . and my grandmother finds out. It will kill her, I know it will."

"Where are you getting these ideas? Look, first of all, you're over 18, so you're not going to be taken away and put in foster care, or anything. I'm the one who should be concerned about talk like that, not you, because I'd lose my job. But why are you bringing this up unless you've been telling tall tales?"

"No, of course not. I'm not that immature," protested Nicole.

"All right. Good. Now fix your face and get back to class, I've got work to do."

Nicole nodded. She got out her makeup case and began to line her eyes.

***

Allana stretched in her chair and propped her bare, pedicured feet on a low cabinet. Her class was quiet: nine students were sprawled and dozing, the other was occupied with something on a classroom computer. The only sound she could hear was the faint, repetitive slapping of a semi-detached poster caught in the breeze of a ventilation duct. She gave a contented sigh. It was marvelous what a bit of creative classroom management could accomplish.

She considered whether or not the students would even wake up if she slipped out for a few minutes. She didn't want to get caught doing anything that might attract notice, but, somehow, she needed another look around Zant's office. If there was anything in there that could hurt her, she wanted to find it first.

God, she'd been stupid to take Zant as a client. She'd known from the start that giving HGH treatments was a big risk, but after her Spa business went under, she decided that if you didn't take risks, you'd fail. This damn teaching was nothing more than a way to pay her mortgage while she built up a new business.

She'd lied just the tiny bit, telling Tamra she'd gone only as far as to schedule one appointment. Zant took several treatments from her before he made his move. She'd thrown his affair with a married colleague back at him and though it shut him up at the time, she wasn't sure if that gambit would have stopped him for good. She also feared Zant had figured out who her other clients were and had collected evidence that could land her in jail.

Suddenly, the door burst open to admit two jeering students and a hall monitor. The hall monitor's walkie-talkie was turned up to headache inducing levels, undoubtedly to demonstrate his policing power. The escorted students slid into empty desks. Heedless of their rain soaked clothes, the boy pulled out an iPod and his female companion began to file her nails.

"I found these two at the coffee house down the street when I was doing a neighborhood sweep," said the monitor. "They said you told them they could go there."

Allana met the man's challenge with calm. "I only told them to get out of my room. They were causing a disruption."

"Did you write referrals?"

Allana waved the question aside with a wave of her hand. "What's the use of writing referrals? The kids always end up waiting for hours until a VP sees them, and most of the time, they don't get seen at all. Then they go home, and the next day the waiting starts all over. By that time, whatever they did to get a referral is old history and they've missed a day's worth of class, which is usually what they wanted in the first place. Then they might get suspended, so they get to go home again. What kind of punishment is that?"

Mrs. Jarney's rational—though self-serving—defense fell unheeded, like the powdered sugar from the doughnut the truant male student was now eating. The hall monitor was staring intently at the computer user, who was making assault weapon noises.

Allana wanted this man out of her room. She adopted a more cooperative tone. "Leave the kids here, I'll deal with them."

The hall monitor hesitated, gave the two truant students a final, malevolent look and left.

"You the bomb, Mrs. Jarney," exclaimed the boy who'd just been reprieved. "Want a donut?" In total knowledge and disregard of the school rule to not eat in class, the boy began to hand them out to his peers.

"No, I don't want one, and how stupid can you be to get caught off campus? No wonder you guys are in Special Education." Allana thought it was stupid to worry about damaging adolescent self-esteem when they spent all their time being nasty to adults.

"So are you, Mrs. Jarney, hah hah, you're in Special Education too," the boy's female companion sneered. "We know about you, how you lost your beauty shop and wound up teaching at this sorry place. So don't you be telling us *we're* lame! Anyhow, I was just put in this class because my mother thinks I'm going to kill myself." The girl sniffed with the indignity of it all and continued with her manicuring activities.

Another student piped up, "Hey, Mrs. J., now that you mention going off campus, we heard you got caught sitting in your car with that new football coach during class time." Laughter erupted around the room.

"Talk about stupid," said a girl with black lips and nostril studs, "Me and my sister, we leave all the time way before lunch and *we* don't get caught. Next time you want to leave early, maybe you should follow *us*."

"Aw, I hope you don't get fired, Mrs. Jarney, I like you," said a half prone boy.

"For sure, if you get fired they'll put us in Ms. Desola's or maybe even Mrs. Edwards's room. They'll make us do work," mumbled another kid through a mouthful of doughnut.

Mrs. Jarney looked at the clock. She didn't need to listen to this. Nine minutes left to the period. They weren't going to get anything done this late. Might as well send them out. It would give her extra time.

"Okay kids, class dismissed."

Before she finished the sentence, the room was empty.

***

"I heard you were tackling the mess in here," said Allana, "and I wondered if you could use any help. I know how upset you must be feeling, so I came over the minute I could get away. Anything I can help you with?"

"There might be," said Julia, wondering again at the teacher's amount of free time. She wasn't really buying the 'Mother Theresa' act.

Allana went on, "This is a huge job. Are you the only one doing this? That's not fair. Anyone else come around to help?"

"Have you come to ask me questions? I just gave Ms. Desola all the answers I have." The secretary made a show of going back to her labors.

"Of course not, I came to help."

"All right then, since you've come all the way up here, I will accept your offer to help. But I don't need you doing what Ms. Desola did. She made the mess in here even worse, from what I can tell, going through every-thing."

"So Kendra was here?"

"Came to see about Zant's pets. She's taking them. Hey, don't you get started again with the questions. I'm sick of them."

Allana stepped forward. "Okay, no problem, I'll just get started."

Julia spread her hands to ward Allana away. "It really would be better not to have you around any of these files. No offense, but I've realized if something gets misplaced, I'll be the one who gets in trouble. How about if you take these two boxes over to Mrs. Prescott's office."

It was obvious from Allana's disappointed look that

delivering boxes wasn't the job she wanted, but she hefted a box and walked toward the Principal's domain.

While Allana was on her errand, a family showed up at the attendance counter, and Julia went out to deal with the irate woman, who was accompanied by three, shrieking little brats. Out of the corner of her eye, Julia helplessly watched as Allana returned and shut herself in the VP's office.

Fifteen minutes later, when she was free to resume her packing, Julia found the second box still in place on the floor of Zant's office. Allana Jarney was nowhere to be seen.

***

Maretta scrawled an account of her whereabouts for the police department staffer, who stood patiently waiting. This was an inconvenient class interruption, but she could only be angry with herself. She bet she wasn't the only one to miss the 7:30 a.m. appointment in the library, either by chance or by design but who expected that the police would so doggedly follow up on strag-glers, even to the point of interrupting classes?

Since she didn't know the exact time of Zant's accident, she refused to admit she'd come back to campus. She didn't think the police would check her statement. The whole investigation was just a formality and this would be the end of her involvement.

The students were enjoying the break, becoming more rowdy by the minute. This particular class was quite a trial even on the best of days. Maretta handed her statement to the waiting woman and stood up to take charge of her classroom.

Two of the girls were engaged in a tug of war over one of the little do-dads that they used these days to adorn their backpacks and purses. The item currently in contention slipped between their grabbing hands and ricocheted to the floor. Laughter broke out. Maretta sighed inwardly.

"Clarice, bring that up here."

"That's not fair, Mrs. Edwards, she pulled it off my backpack!" Clarice made no move to comply.

"It ain't yours—you stole that in the first place, girl!"

86

accused her adversary from the desk behind.

"Shut up! I didn't steal anything. I found it in the girl's room this morning before school." Clarice was adamant in her innocence. Maretta knew from experience it was hard to tell when Clarice was lying.

"I will leave that issue for you two to work out after class. In the meantime, may I have that please?" Maretta's voice took on a darker tone.

The girl sullenly handed over her precious trinket. Maretta placed it in a basket on her desk.

"Thank you, Clarice. Now let's get back to work."

"What page are we on?" asked three students at once. Maretta repressed a sigh and motioned to the whiteboard, where the page in question was clearly posted.

"William, would you read question 31, please?"

"The bell's gonna ring, Mrs. Edwards."

And the bell did ring. The students jumped up and clamored out the door. Clarice was among them, having completely forgotten about her precious backpack ornament. Maretta shook her head and hoped that next period would be less chaotic.

***

Jack wriggled deeper into the driver's seat. He watched a dirty rivulet run down the windshield to its delta, a midden of pine needles, bird feathers and bits of soggy paper jammed beneath the windshield wiper mechanism. Maybe he should break down and get the car washed.

He yanked at his bunched up jeans. Some coins slid from his pocket, clinking their way to a totally inaccessible crevice between the center console and the driver's seat. He groaned. Ah, what the heck, leave 'em. What was the loss of a few cents compared to the job that he was about to lose? That damn Zant lived just long enough to carry out his threats.

All the time he'd put in at Standard High was worthless to him now. It was one thing to spend the best years of his life in this hellhole, never getting any appreciation for it, but he'd kept himself going with the certainty of a nice retirement. Now that proved to be a pipe dream. He was ninety-nine percent sure he was going to be fired.

Oh, he'd try to fight it, but Zant had carefully prepared "evidence" against him that the union wasn't going to be able to counteract. He was going to end up jobless, with only a monthly Social Security check to live on. Hell, not even that, because he was still too young to get even that pittance. His only relative couldn't afford to help him out—in fact, his sister depended on him, on the income he was going to lose, on the pension that he wouldn't get. He searched the pocket of a cast off jacket and extracted a half crushed candy bar, which he unwrapped and ate in 3 bites. He hardly noticed the taste.

Jack knew that without his job, he'd lose his house, and, of course, his health benefits would go, too. With his health issues, he wouldn't live long after that. So what? Better than living with the other homeless under the expressway, right across from the lot where his ex-students reportedly dealt drugs from a top line Mercedes.

Well, maybe that scenario was a bit over the top, but what would he do now? Maybe get a job at the big discount store down the street because no one else would hire an old wreck like him. He could work there with all the high school dropouts. But, heck, why scoff at them? They showed some real cleverness, the way they sneaked on campus every day to stand in line for a free lunch. He even could come with them; that would take care of one meal a day.

Jack started to sweat. He wanted a beer. Well, he could do the next best thing. Out of habit, he glanced around, and seeing no one else in the faculty lot, lit a cigarette. It would feel really good to burn a few holes in the notification letter that lay near his feet. Yeah, that might make him feel a tad better, but wouldn't stop the disciplinary hearing from happening. Being a union rep, he knew all about the ugly procedures coming up. He saw his job going up in smoke along with the stream from his cigarette.

Zant was a real bastard to single him out when there were plenty other staff members who got up to stuff that someone should write a book about! Jack cracked the window open a bit more and thought about what he'd seen while sitting out in his car. All the times he'd seen Allana driving off campus when she was supposed to be teaching a class. Custodians loading school property into their cars. Campus monitors who drank on the job. That was only the tip of the iceberg. Time to use this knowledge to pay back the people who'd gotten him fired. If he was going down, he could at least have some fun drawing the cops' attention to the activities of his back stabbing coworkers.

Yeah, he knew which of his colleagues helped put him in his current predicament. Jack mulled over his revenge list. Allana was on it, of course. Tamra surely was in league with Allana, who would never catch up before the state review without cutting corners. Tamra would want to "expedite" Special Ed. procedures; it was her job to certify compliance with the Special Education mandates. A few faked meetings and forged signatures would solve both women's problems of accountability. Tamra was making sure the state auditors would find completed paperwork, even if done illegally. Who knows what else those women were into? Staging a fall down the stairs maybe? But he hardly felt bad about that. If anyone deserved it, Zant did.

Back to the important issue, Tamra's role in getting him fired. Her role as a liaison made her seem less like an administrator, but he really should have treated her with more circumspection, shouldn't have mentioned Zant's new necktie matched the one poking out of a gift bag in her carryall the week before. Hell, it was just a joke, but Tamra had become openly antagonistic after that. She must have used Allana to spy on him because the things Zant cited as cause for termination could have only come from close observation.

Although he had to admit some personal respon-sibility—slacking off with his daily teaching duties—how was it fair that the biggest rule violator on campus was the one to report him, while she got away unscathed? Allana's turn would come soon. But he needed first to decide on what to do about Tamra. Instead of staying under the radar, she'd called and asked to meet him, being vague about the reason. Maybe she was sorry and would help him? As unlikely as that was, he couldn't miss the chance. The important thing was to come up with a plan before they met next Thursday morning.

The rank smell of the burning cigarette filter roused him from further thought. He stuck the butt into the ashtray and after a look outside, slipped out of his car and headed back to his classroom.

9.

Friday afternoon

Kendra left the main building by the west exit, taking the long way back to her portable to enjoy a few quiet moments outside. During the two lunch periods, this area was off-limits to students and usually deserted, so she was surprised to see someone sitting on a brick ledge at the far end of the building. As she got closer, she saw it was Zant's secretary.

Once again, Kendra couldn't help but observe how "un-put together" Julia was. Some of her wardrobe conformed to what was often described as "office attire," but Julia liked to finish out an outfit with shoes or sweaters that would be more appropriate for a camping trip.

The secretary was leaning forward, elbows on her knees. At close range, Kendra could see that Julia had been crying. This encounter might be awkward because they weren't on familiar terms. Even so, Kendra wanted to help, if she could.

She tentatively asked, "Julia, are you okay?"

For several seconds there was no response, then the woman shrugged. Kendra took it as permission to continue.

"Is something wrong?"

Another shrug, followed by tears. Kendra wondered if Julia was upset over Zant's passing. Yet, if she read the woman's face correctly, grief battled rage. Along with a desire to help, Kendra now felt the pull of curiosity.

"Julia, are you crying about Zant? This must be a bad time for you." She patted Julia's arm.

"Zant. It's about Zant, all right," Julia muttered, "but not that. . . ." For a moment she looked angry, then caught herself and looked away.

"In a few days things will look better," suggested Kendra, not knowing what to say.

"How can I feel better? You don't know—my baby, no, now there's no baby. The baby is off. . . ." Julia's voice tailed off.

"Are you saying something has happened to your baby?" To her embarrassment, Kendra remembered that Julia didn't have kids and was trying to adopt.

Julia didn't appear to notice the slip. She blew her nose and said, "I put all my hopes on getting this baby, but we got turned down."

"The adoption didn't go through?"

Julia took a few ragged breaths. "Things were messed up, but I thought we still might have a chance. Then, last night, the attorney called, said it was definitely off. Now I have nothing to live for." She shrank down farther, her head in her hands.

"Of course you do." At this point, Kendra wished she could think of something else to say or do, but perhaps the best thing was to sit with the sobbing woman and give silent support. The fact that Julia was opening up like this must mean she wanted someone there.

A car drove by and the driver, a counselor, slowed and greeted them. It looked like she intended to stop, but took the hint when Kendra shook her head. This reminder they were in a public place seemed to motivate Julia to pull herself together. She sighed. "Sorry, I'm acting like an idiot. My husband's the smart one, the strong one. He told me that being childless is not the end of the world. I wish I was more like him."

Kendra gave Julia a one-armed hug and said, "We all have ways of coping. You'll find your own way, in time. Want to go to the ladies' room, wash up a little? It will make you feel better."

Julia led the way to a women's bathroom that was usually reserved for front office staff. Kendra wondered if Julia's job with Zant afforded her access to this relatively luxurious bathroom, or if Mr. Ken had given her a key on the sly. There was a small rest area with a two-seater couch and an upholstered armchair. Nearby were a magazine rack, a reading lamp, and a bronze pedestal ashtray, which was being used as a plant stand. These accoutrements surely remained from an era when females were ostensibly delicate enough to require a secluded place to rest, and found time to do so.

Julia went to the sink and splashed water on her face. Kendra brushed at her skirt, which was smudged from the dirty brick ledge.

Between splashes, Julia said, "I'm sorry, I don't know what got into me. Maybe, I'm just too worn out. I was up all night. My poor husband. But today, I thought I was okay. I don't know what happened to me just now, something just set me off."

"Hey, you don't have to apologize. What you really need is time. Maybe you should take a few days off?"

"I've used all my sick days, or else I wouldn't be here. In fact if I could quit, I would. After we finish paying the lawyer, I intend to find another job."

"We'd hate to see you go," said Kendra diplomatically. "Why don't you wait a while and then decide? I know I make lousy decisions if I'm upset."

Julia put her nose closer to the mirror. "Oh god, I have to fix this face." As she rummaged in her bag, it slipped from her shoulder, spilling the contents everywhere. Julia squatted and began to pick up her things. Kendra reached under the chair and came up with a vial of liquid eye makeup. To her chagrin, she found that the cap was loose. She wiggled her stained fingers.

"Whoops, this opened up!"

Julia looked at Kendra's hand and said, "No problem, just toss it. I'll pick up the rest of the stuff."

Kendra went to the sink and turned on the water. There was no hot water, of course, but there was soap, undoubtedly supplied by a staff member. The soap was good quality and pleasant to use, but scouring powder would have done better in this case.

Julia applied lipstick and hoisted her purse. She said, "Thanks, Kendra. I feel better now. I'm sorry I bothered you with my problems."

"Not at all. You've been under a lot of stress the last few days. The rest of us can stay in our rooms, but you've been in Zant's office, cleaning up his mess. That alone would be enough to upset anyone."

Julia warmed to the subject. "Yes, it's been awful! I thought that Mrs. Prescott would come by to help sort things out, but she's hardly looked in. To make it worse, the cops made another mess, moving things around, looking for God knows what. They asked me if Zant used a BlackBerry, where was it. Like I knew?"

"Did they ever find it?"

"Not that I know of. Afterward, I worried that it got thrown out by mistake, maybe caught up in one of those piles of newspaper, but it's not my responsibility to go through every single item in that room."

"No one could blame you."

"I hope not. God, you wouldn't believe what crap that man had in his office." Her eyes narrowed as she visualized the room. "It was bad enough he had a dumpster's worth of old newspapers all mixed up with important files. Then, he kept everything he took away from the kids—not just that stuff you saw—and tons of his own little knick-knacks, and that's only the tip of the iceberg." Julia smirked. "He hid clean underwear in a file cabinet! Can you believe that?

"Be glad it was clean underwear."

Julia smiled grimly. "Well, I should get to work."

"Yeah, I have to run, too." Kendra frowned at the stains on her fingers. Lunch was almost over. She hoped her "dirty hands" didn't create a classroom disruption.

***

"I hope everyone's given you their full cooperation," said Mrs. Prescott, who looked across her desk at the two detectives. Ray Favor, who'd escorted them in, stood to one side, and observed that Mrs. Prescott hadn't gotten up to greet the detectives the way she would have if she'd con-sidered them important to her career.

Detective Howard said, "All your staff reported their whereabouts and we haven't found anything suspicious. Her stiff pose did nothing to back up her casual speech. Her male partner added, "Forensics didn't come up with anything either."

"So, that's that," said Ray.

"I told you everything would go smoothly. I'll be sure to tell the Super how professional your investigation was," said Mrs. Prescott.

"We'd like to check the feed from your security cameras," said Detective Tapia. He smiled but his brown eyes were all business.

"But—surely we know now that the whole thing was an accident," said Mrs. Prescott.

"Let's leave the conclusions until we're actually done, ma'am," said Detective Howard.

"Yes, of course. I'm sure you know what's best. Mr. Favor, please show the detectives whatever they want to see. I'm afraid I have to leave for a very important meeting, or I'd be happy to accompany you." She made a show of gath-ering up her things.

Ray gestured to the door and followed the detectives out. He guessed that the male was in his 50s, maybe fifteen years older than his female partner, but he looked energetic and sharp witted. Detective Howard on the other hand gave Ray the impression she was an android that could use a few days in a repair shop for some retooling.

Evidently, Mrs. Prescott was still clueless about the awful condition of the school security cameras. Ray was careful not to let his superior awareness come through. The closed circuit data center was housed in a tiny room near the computer technician's office. Ray made a show of being less than familiar with the appropriate key, saying, "This is really under the purview of Mrs. Prescott, so I don't have much reason to come in here. She's in charge of the campus security equipment."

Ray clicked the light switch but the bulb was burned out. "Oh well, there's enough light from the hall I guess. Let's see now…" He reached down and checked a unit, but came up empty handed.

"These machines sure are old. Is the tape jammed?" asked the female detective, leaning in to lend a hand.

"Um, no, there doesn't seem to be any tape," said Ray, moving aside.

Detective Tapia flicked a pocket flashlight over the faceplates on all the recording units. All were empty. Tapia looked interested in this turn of events. "So, where would the tapes be? You are using tapes, right? Anyone else besides you and the Principal have a key to this room?"

"Not that I know of. You can ask Mrs. Prescott."

"Howard, go back and ask the Principal before she splits." Tapia ran a finger along a small, curved scar on his chin.

Ray felt the room closing in on him even with only two of them inside, perhaps because he now felt more vulnerable to interrogation. He quickly moved out to the hallway and asked, "If we don't have anything on tape, is that a problem?" He genuinely didn't know the answer, as far as it concerned the cops, but if Prescott was running the system without tapes, that definitely would be a professional problem for her.

"Tapes could be very useful to our investigation. These machines look like they're in bad shape. We should test this equipment, see if it's even working. If it's not, then we can at least look for tampering." He gave Ray a long look. "You got any fresh tapes around?"

"Probably right next door, you want some?" At a nod from the detective, Ray scurried over to the media storage area and retrieved several blank tapes.

"Stick those in and let's see what we get, if you don't mind," instructed Tapia. "I see the recording light's on; that should mean something's happening. While we wait, any chance we can get a light bulb?"

"Sure, be back in a minute." His trip was cut short when he nearly fell on the female detective who was back from the Principal's office.

Howard announced, "There are only three keys to the CCTV room. The head custodian, Mr. Ken, has the other one, and Mrs. Prescott said she didn't know why no tapes were loaded."

While Tapia checked the number displays on the tape decks, Ray entertained himself visualizing Mrs. Prescott making excuses for her ineptitude at a School Board meeting.

"Mr. Favor, can you find us a VCR? From the looks of things around here, I assume your school isn't into DVDs yet? Should be enough time gone by now to see if we got anything."

"There's one in my office we can use." Ray gestured down the hall.

The three soon settled in Ray's office. A review of the tapes revealed one stationary view of the sky and four scenes of absolutely nothing. Ray leaned back and cautiously said, "Uh, I guess the cameras don't work."

"I guess they don't," said Howard. "This wouldn't be the first school with broken equipment—" The female detective was silenced by her partner's cutting look.

Tapia asked, "Mr. Favor, can we take a look outside at the cameras?" His tone came across heavier than a request.

"Of course, but I'm afraid I won't be able to go with you. I have lunch supervision today. I'll get a custodian to help you. He can hook you up with a ladder, whatever you need."

Ray waited until a custodian came and sent the three of them off. He knew they'd find no external damage, except for the camera that had been knocked out of line. The problem was that the lines were faulty, but the repair work was on hold because the original installation had been done improperly, and the district was waiting for the seller to make repairs free of charge. With money so tight, there was no way that the district would pay for repairs unnecessarily.

Ray didn't know for sure why Mrs. Prescott didn't push to get the security system into working order, but he suspected that she'd delegated that task, as was her practice, and hadn't followed it up. Ray could have shared his knowledge with the detectives, but he wanted to reinforce his lack of involvement with the security system. Anyhow, the detectives would learn about the situation from Mr. Ken, who handled all the maintenance requests. Prescott was so good at avoiding blame, Ray hoped Mr. Ken wouldn't end up taking the heat on this one.

Ray put the useless tapes on a shelf. When he became principal, this school was going to write a grant and get some updated technology. As much as he hoped the latest turn of events might diminish Mrs. Prescott's reputation, Ray hoped this equipment issue didn't make the investigation drag on longer. He didn't need the police poking around.

***

Kendra needed to speak to Nate. She'd been teaching her 6th period class when he delivered the two terrariums to her classroom. Fortunately, the cart was covered with a tarp. As far as the students knew, he was just bringing her a load of copy paper and they lost interest when he pushed the cart to a corner and left. As soon as class was over and the students gone, she removed the tarp. The spider was there, but she didn't see the lizard.

She assumed the creature was hiding behind a branch or rock, but a quick search told her that it was no longer inside the terrarium. She realized, in fact, she hadn't actually seen the lizard that day. Kendra called Julia, but the secretary hadn't noticed Mr. Lizard's truancy. The only person left to ask was Nate.

Kendra went to her "treat" cupboard, put cookies into a little bag and headed out. On her way to the main building, she wove through a group of rowdy adolescents, the same ones who, when presented with class work, instantly sank into a stupor virtually impossible to dispel.

The wide doors to the custodial area stood ajar, framed with safety warning notices. To one side, the old bookroom stood silent and locked, the caretaker long since retired and not replaced. She went upstairs to the custodian's all-purpose room. She was surprised to see that the center of the room was taken up with a large table, spread with a golden yellow cloth on which dozens of miniature, fantasy figurines were arranged. Kendra approached for a close look. The size of chess pieces, the little statues were grouped according to their role within the genre: warriors, wizards, nobility and so forth. "Wow, this is quite a set up." exclaimed Kendra to no one in particular.

A female custodian looked up from a load of cartons she was stacking against a wall. She laughed and came to join Kendra. "Not what you expected to see in here, I bet."

Totally lost, Kendra asked, "What's this for?

"For our Mr. Ken, for his birthday. He's really into these little things. I swear, he acts like a kid sometimes, but then, he's a guy so what I can I say? Anyway, he collects these, I forget what you call 'em, but some of them are nice, don't you think? Julia Chatin—you know she's his sister-in-law—thought he'd get a kick out of this, and she ordered a birthday cake made to look like a witch's spell book. We all got silly costumes too. I have to cover the table soon, before he gets back from downtown. It's gonna be a surprise. She let out a loud laugh, then, abruptly became serious. "Because of what happened we ended up having to postpone the party 'til today. Better late than never, I guess." The woman finally paused to catch her breath.

Kendra turned one of the figurines in her hand. They were fashioned with a high degree of detail and originality. Kendra was familiar with this kind of collectible. Some of her online gaming friends even made them to sell at SciFi conventions and the like. They just seemed very out of place at Standard High.

She set the piece down. "This is fantastic; I'm sure Mr. Ken will love it. When's the party?"

"Later on this afternoon and, boy, can we all use a little Friday fun. Those detectives have been driving us crazy with their questions. Mrs. Prescott told us we have to cooperate with them. Like we know anything? And, if one of us custodians did see something, who would care? Nobody ever listens to us—we're just janitors. Like I told them way back last year—this school ain't safe. Gangbangers are sneaking on campus all day long. But they just told me to carry my walkie-talkie, stay alert and make sure to lock up. Like I don't? Every time I clean a classroom, I lock up afterward. It's the teachers who don't remember, no offense. I found the computer lab unlocked more than once. It's a miracle the place hasn't been cleaned out."

"Maybe the computers are too old to be desirable? Like those two computers near Mr. Favor's office—they could be stolen easy. What's the story with those? Does anyone use them?"

"Not that I know of. It must be a spillover from the junk in the nurse's room. If they do get taken, I'm sure I'll get blamed, cause I clean over that way. Like it's my job to patrol the halls. Those detectives, they acted like it was our fault we didn't notice anything on Wednesday."

"What about the security cameras? Whatever happened back there, it should be on tape, no?"

The woman shrugged. "I guess so. But I don't have anything to do with that. Gosh, I'm sorry, I guess you didn't come out here for a chat. Can I help you with something?"

"I was looking for Nate, do you know where he is?" Kendra fervently hoped she did, thus providing an exit opportunity.

"Right behind you, Ms. Desola," put in Nate. He laughed when Kendra jumped at his voice. "Didn't want to interrupt your conversation."

"Hi, Nate. I brought the cart back. Thanks for moving the zoo for me." She held out a bag of cookies, which Nate gratefully accepted. Before he could express his thanks, she asked, "I have a question for you. When you were handling the terrariums, did you see the lizard?"

Nate expression changed to paranoia. He was clearly worried he might be linked to another mishap of some sort. "Can't say that I did, Ms. Desola, but I really didn't spend any time looking. Something wrong?"

"Don't you go blaming Nate for nothing, he took enough crap

already!" piped in the female custodian.

"I'm not blaming anyone. The lizard is not in its tank and I'm trying figure out where it is," explained Kendra.

The woman clicked her tongue and went back to her earlier task by the cartons. Nate frowned. "Jeez, that's not cool. But you know the way things disappear around this place. Not your fault, I'm sure, Ms. Desola. I wouldn't take it too hard."

"I'll feel terrible if I find out something bad happened to that animal, even though I'm not really into reptiles."

Kendra looked at the time. "Nate if you have a minute, could you have a look at my classroom door lock?"

"Sure, I can take a look, at least. If you're going back, I'll walk out there with you now."

Kendra walked with Nate toward her room. "I know you probably don't want to talk about Zant's accident, Nate, but no one's really told us much about what happened. The situation doesn't make sense to me. First, they tell us it was an accident, then they open an investigation. Do the cops really think someone killed him? I mean, how could someone push a big, ex-Marine like Carl Zant down a staircase?

"I got nothing much to tell you. The detectives didn't tell me anything. They just asked a lot of questions, like did I run into the VP a lot after school. I told them that I never saw Zant over there before. They asked me what rooms I clean, and when I told them we got this one person who does the halls with a machine, they got all suspicious, asking me what was I doing then, cleaning over by the stairs. But, for real, Ms. Desola, after I finished in the boy's john, I saw that there was some more goopy stuff tracked from the bathroom down the hall, and I was just starting to mop it up when I found Mr. Zant lying there." Nate jiggled his key ring, his eyes on the portables ahead of them.

"From what you say, it does sound like an accident. Zant must have been on his way to the stairs and just skidded on something."

"I think that is the stone truth," agreed Nate. "He was wearing those dressy leather shoes, easy to slip in them. Nobody expects a freaky accident like that, but like they say, stuff happens."

"Were you the one who called for help?" Kendra knew the answer but couldn't resist the chance to delve a bit deeper.

"Soon as I saw him I called my supervisor right away—and

100

now, I get questioned like I'm a bad guy. Why the cops want to make a simple accident into something else, I don't know." He shook his head in a "how could that be" gesture.

She came to a stop at her classroom door. "The media is partly to blame. And the local politicians are screaming, so there has to be some kind of investigation. I'm sure the cops don't believe what happened has anything to do with you."

"Hard not to worry when detectives ask you questions for an hour."

"I'm sorry you're having such a bad time but this won't last. By next week you'll be wanting to switch back to your regular shift." She gave Nate a smile.

"That's what I'm hoping, Ms. Desola."

"You never know, something good might come out of all this. When it's all over, the district might spend some money on school improvement to get some favorable publicity. In the meantime, I'm not holding my breath. Anything you can do with this damn door will be greatly appreciated.

10.

The Weekend

"Sorry to bother you at home, Ms. Desola. Can we come in?" The detective held up his ID for her to see. His partner stared at Kendra impatiently.

Kendra didn't want to let them in, but did she really have a choice? She motioned for them to wait while she closed the French doors to the living room so that Bobbins couldn't run out, then invited the unwelcome duo into the foyer. But no farther. That way they couldn't plant anything in her house.

"I'm Detective Tapia," said the man, cheerfully ignoring the lack of hospitality. He motioned to his side. "This is Detective Howard. We won't take too much of your time."

Kendra looked from one to the other. The male was wearing a suit, but looked like he spent a lot of time outdoors. She had the feeling he was sizing her up, like maybe estimating how fast he'd have to run to catch her if she bolted from the scene. His partner had her hair pulled back from her face, accentuating the dark circles under her eyes.

Kendra said, "If this is about what happened with Zant, I already wrote down where I was. I didn't see anything before I left for the materials center. After that, I came home."

"Right," said Tapia. "We wanted to ask you about something else. Carl Zant's office might have been burglarized. What can you tell us about that?"

"What do you mean?" Kendra's came out sounding like an indignant squeak.

"We heard you were very interested in Mr. Zant's desk. That true?"

"I never said that! I only pointed out that there were splinters around one of the drawers. His secretary, Mrs. Chatin, was there when I noticed it, ask her."

"We were wondering what you were doing behind his desk,"

said the female detective smugly.

"I was looking for pet books, that's all!" said Kendra angrily.

"Pet books?"

"Yeah, he kept two pets in his office and Mrs. Chatin asked me to take care of them." Kendra suddenly saw where the questions were going. "If anyone broke into the desk, it could have happened anytime. There's a lot of theft on campus."

Howard hooked a finger under her belt. "Interesting point you make, Ms. Desola."

"Well, I don't mean to say that's what happened. I didn't find—I only wanted to get the pet books."

"Take it easy, miss, said the apparent leader of the team, as he exchanged a look with his partner. "We aren't accusing you of anything. We didn't get on campus 'til Thursday, you know. It would help us to know if the desk was forced open before or after the incident."

When Kendra didn't respond, he continued, "The thing is, Mrs. Chatin said she never noticed anything wrong with the desk until you came in. She told us you were trying to persuade her that the damage was old. Now, why would you do that?"

"Huh? I never said anything like that, and if I broke into the desk, why would I call her over to see?" Kendra berated herself for attracting Julia's attention.

Tapia's sidekick took up the questioning, in Kendra's eyes playing "bad cop, bad cop."

"Mrs. Chatin said you were acting suspicious, asked a lot of questions."

Kendra's outrage broke through her anxiety. "For god's sake, this is ridiculous. Did I commit a crime? Is Inquiring about Broken Furniture a felony or a misdemeanor?"

Tapia ignored the outburst and said, "A broken drawer didn't faze us at first. We've spent enough time in public schools to know what the furniture's like, but the timing on this is interesting. Sure you didn't try to get a peek into the desk, then try to talk your way out of the damage?"

"For the last time, I did not break into that desk. If you're looking for suspects, you could start with people with easy access to his office, like Mrs. Chatin."

Tapia said, "Okay, let's assume you're telling the truth. Then, I still wonder why you thought Mr. Zant's desk was so interesting. When a detail like this stands out, I have to ask."

"Sorry, I already told you what happened, no matter what Mrs. Chatin says." Kendra stepped past her interrogators and went toward the door, hoping they'd follow, but they remained in place, twin pillars framing the entrance to her living room.

Detective Howard broke the silence first. "Perhaps we could get your impressions about Mr. Zant. You worked with him closely, didn't you? What kind of an administrator was he?"

This change in topic was unwelcome. Kendra wasn't going to give them a reason to single her out. "Mr. Zant did okay with some things, but he wasn't a very popular administrator."

"We heard you argued with him a lot."

"That's no big deal. We disagreed about the students, not for personal reasons. I felt that he was too heavy-handed with them. Excuse me for asking, but it doesn't sound to me like you think his death was an accident." To Kendra, this was starting to sound like a murder investigation and the prospect of that was making her even more anxious.

Detective Howard waved off the observation. "Just a few more questions, if you don't mind? Mr. Zant disciplined students. Do you know of any students with a grudge against him? Gang members, maybe?"

This had occurred to Kendra as a possibility, in spite of her reluctance to admit that any of her students would commit murder. Most students took in stride what Zant dished out. Once they wound up in his office, they didn't expect kind treatment, but more to the point, her students didn't care if they got suspended.

"I can't think of any kids like that. You can ask the other teachers, or have you already done that?" asked Kendra.

"Which one of your colleagues do you suggest? The female detective looked up from her notepad with a sharp look, expecting at least a few words of gossip. Detective Howard was about to be disappointed.

"Let them speak for themselves." She hoped one of them wouldn't be talking about emails.

"What about angry parents?"

Kendra shrugged. "I don't know any who are that angry."

"All right, Ms. Desola, I guess that's all for now. Thanks for your time," said Detective Tapia.

"Have a nice evening," said Howard. Kendra thought the woman looked pleased that she'd already spoiled any chance of that.

Tapia paused on the steps. "If anything else comes to mind, give me a ring," said Tapia, handing his card over. "Curious people like you can be helpful sometimes." He suddenly broke into a half-smile, and followed his partner out the door.

She watched them get into a car and drive away. She felt violated. Her hallway had become unsafe. She fled the interrogation spot, into her living room, and dived on to the couch. This was better, a nest. The pale green walls were decorated with some of her craft projects and other art that she'd purchased. She tried to lose herself in the Edward Hopper reproduction she'd hung over the bookcase, but at the moment the starkness of the shadows made her feel lonely. Kendra wondered if this was how it started for her brother before he was arrested, unjustly convicted and sent away.

Maybe she should call Brian, get advice about the situation. Or, should she call an attorney? Before she spoke to anyone, she'd better calm down and think.

The sun made patterns on the pale green rug where Bobbins lay fast asleep. Motes of dust floated hypnotically through the shafts of light. Kendra's eyelids drooped and she peered through her eyelashes at the gyrating specks. Suddenly she felt herself swooping into that tiny galaxy, careening haphazardly, but never colliding with the other, drifting particles. The projectiles gradually developed smooth curves, becoming egg shaped, then morphed into sculpted marble heads. She strained to identify the vaguely familiar stone faces as they sped by. Just as the nearest one began to speak to her, a snort and a bump from Bobbins brought her back to the living room.

The sun was now hidden behind the buildings across the street. She must have dozed off, then. What was the last thing she'd dreamed? She'd been right on the verge of learning something important—no, there was nothing left, just a sensation.

Kendra often remembered her dreams, much to Brian's amusement when she recounted them in detail. This one was really weird. Flying through faces made of dust? If only she could have gotten a better look at that last face. Perhaps she felt dirty after the cops' accusations? Or was she feeling ashamed that there was fur on the floor? Perhaps it was a play on the word face—she'd lost face?

Oh god, the detectives. They'd upset her so much she'd blown a chance to learn more about what had happened to Zant. Would the detectives have given her such a grilling if this wasn't a murder investigation? Did the police think she was involved? And what the hell was Julia up to? Kendra realized she couldn't trust the secretary, who definitely had some hidden agenda.

Perhaps the cops were visiting the rest of the staff this evening. She should call up Maretta, Jack, a few others and find out. Yeah, she'd do that . . . later.

She sank down to the cat's level and put an arm around him. Bobbins gave a throaty purr of approval and put a large paw on her chin. The touch was vastly comforting. Kendra closed her eyes.

***

"How did you know the driveway would be open?" asked Brian. "I thought they were beefing up security."

"See that? There's a soccer game later." Kendra waved at a coach who was sorting through a pile of equipment. "The field gate's open too. Drive down there. We can go over to my room that way."

"I keep telling you, this place is like a sieve. Well, you've got protection with you this morning," he beat his fists on his chest and laughed.

"Oh, right." She rolled her eyes up and pretended to think. "What was the name of that karate school you flunked out of? No matter, come on, we can have the whiteboard up in no time and be on our way."

"When they delivered the board, how come they didn't put it up for you?" groused Brian. He opened the back of the SUV, took out his electric drill, and hid their packs under a tarp. He checked to make sure the doors were locked.

Kendra was already several yards away from him and didn't hear his last comment. Brian increased his pace and caught up with her as she arrived at the portable.

"Look, the door's off the latch!" She gave it an angry shove and stomped in, Brian at her heels. The whiteboard that they'd come to install was leaning against the wall, but Kendra's eyes were on her desk. She walked over and started to curse.

"What?" asked Brian, looking around.

"Someone's been messing with my desk!"

"Are you sure? If someone broke in, the whole room would be a mess. You've been telling me the door refuses to lock and it was windy last night, so it probably blew open," observed Brian.

Kendra's arm sliced the air in frustration. "Okay, so they didn't have to force their way in, but I think someone has been in here, at my desk."

"You don't have anything valuable in the room, though, do you?" Brian went to the wall and set out his tools.

"No, of course not. I wouldn't be that stupid. But they don't necessarily have to be looking for valuables. There are plenty of kids who would trash a classroom just for fun."

"Maybe they were looking for your famous stash of cookies," said Brian, only half-joking.

She knew that he was downplaying his concern to soothe her. He'd been very supportive the night before when they'd discussed her session with the detectives, almost dispelling her paranoia with nonthreatening explanations for their behavior. Only Brian didn't know about the email. He simply couldn't realize just how jumpy she was these days.

She heard the sound of Brian's electric drill. Poor guy, here he was, helping her on a Saturday morning and she was carrying on, making a big deal out of nothing. He was probably right; some vagrant or other sort of opportunist had come around looking for anything they could steal and had seen that the door wasn't locked. They'd come in to look for something that could be easily carried away and must have quickly figured out that they were wasting their time. Nothing appeared to be missing. She decided to drop the issue. Brian was prejudiced enough against Standard High. And this was a day for fun and relaxation.

The whiteboard wobbled, fighting Brian's efforts to pull it to its designated spot. She walked over and grabbed one end. "You want me to hold up one end of the board?"

"Yeah, I have the holes drilled now. Let's get this up and be on our way before the traffic picks up."

***

"Hey, I like this spot, let's stop a while." Kendra flopped down on a conveniently situated rock. There was an unobstructed view of the narrow canyon below, and the river foaming over the rocks on its way down from the mountain. She adjusted her hat against the sun.

"Aw, come on, it's only a couple more miles to the end," complained Brian.

"What's the point of being up here if we don't take time to appreciate where we are," muttered Kendra, who lowered her daypack to the ground. "If you don't mind, go on ahead, and I'll just sit here and do some bird watching, ok? I think I need a few minutes to get my energy back."

Brian rolled a pebble under the toe of his boot. "Don't get me wrong, I didn't mind helping you put up the whiteboard today, but you'd be feeling a lot better right now if you didn't work so hard and left that job behind on weekends." He shifted his pack and squatted down to face her. "Sorry. I don't mean to blame you. I'll go up to the summit and wait for you, no rush." He gave her arm a reassuring squeeze.

Kendra watched him disappear around the switchback and dug out her binoculars. She could hear a woodpecker knocking on a nearby bough.

Five birds later, she shouldered her pack again and marched up the trail to the summit, where she found Brian lying in full sun. Another small group of hikers sat in the shade of a large boulder that marked the end of the trail.

Brian was using his jacket to make a pad on top of the scree beneath him. His sunglasses were pushed up above his forehead. He was, as usual, unconcerned about the possible effects of too much sun. She dropped her binoculars at his side and knelt to remove her pack.

"Feeling better now?" he asked.

"Yes." She tried on a limpid smile.

"I didn't expect you would be so upset by Zant's death. You should be relieved because you won't have to work with him

108

anymore. After all, you've been ranting and raving about him from the day he was hired."

"Yeah, I know. But there are other issues..." She'd almost decided to bring up the email, when he sat up to face her.

"Whoops, my fault. Now I'm the one that brought up your job. But, since I did, I'm going to say my piece." When she didn't object, he went on, "You've become obsessed with trying to help those kids, against your own welfare. Try to look at your behavior objectively. For instance, remember the day where you spent your own money for a padlock for a kid who didn't even thank you, then you had a run-in with some whack-job of his drugged-out parent, and you topped that all off with a night of insomnia, worrying over something Zant said to you? And do I need to remind you that same kid stole your wallet two weeks later?"

Kendra could feel her face turning red, not from sun, but because what he said was pretty much on target. She picked up a pinecone and fixed her gaze on it.

Brian sensed he'd made enough of an impact. "Just one more thing. You don't get paid nearly enough to compensate for the hours you put in, or what you put up with. Okay, I'm done. Sorry. I think if you can step back and just look at the facts, you'll know I'm right." Brian took hold of her hands, twining their fingers together.

Kendra silently acknowledged he'd made some valid points, but she wasn't sure he understood how teaching was more than just a way to make money; it was a calling. She knew he felt she gave less attention to him than she gave to her job. Perhaps he did have a reason to feel underappreciated because here she was, unable to let go and relax on a beautiful hiking trip. Still, she couldn't help but try to justify her behavior.

"Work is so different for you, Brian, you pick and choose the people you work with. Besides, school problems are complicated in their own way."

"Complicated doesn't have the right flavor. I've been around Standard High enough to see the picture—a picture only a museum of horror would hang, I might add." Brian sat up, took a drink from his water bottle and offered it to her.

"Listen, Kendra, take this business at school as a wakeup call, a signal to get out of there before something worse happens. Pick a different career, one that suits your personality better."

Now she was glad she'd held off telling him about the email. If Brian knew, he'd really go ballistic, demand she quit her job, and they'd have a big fight.

He went on, "From what I can tell, even Ray Favor doesn't take the job as seriously as you do and he's a VP. I don't mean this in a negative way, but you're too high-strung to be a teacher. The way you always have to follow up on every little detail—with a job like teaching, you're dealing with human beings, there's no way everything's gonna turn out neatly, the way you want it to go."

Brian's voice softened. "Why can't you be more laid back about your job, like that Jarney woman, for example? I bet she doesn't think about work all the time."

Kendra snapped, "I don't think snakes have the brain capacity to think about anything." She vigorously twisted off a circlet of pinecone scales.

"Why don't you go back to your old career? Working in a business environment wasn't so bad. Or pick any job you can leave behind at five o'clock. That will leave you the time and energy to put into the creative activities you love. You've become a different person since you started teaching. I want the old Kendra back."

This more intimate twist brought her close to tears. "Am I that bad?" she said flatly. The words lay more as a statement than a question.

Brian hugged her to his side. "I didn't say that, not at all. You're miles from bad. Speaking of miles, look at this gorgeous place. We both need to forget about everything else that's going on and enjoy our day, okay?"

Brian pulled her down to lie against him and closed his eyes. The touch of his body relaxed her. The sunlight felt rejuvenating. After a while, she rolled on one side to look at him. She tickled his ear with a pine needle until he grabbed her hand. They lay quietly together.

***

"What else do you want to get?" asked Brian, guiding the

shopping cart toward the produce section. I hate coming here on weekends; I hope we don't have to wait in line too long. I still say we should have just gone home and ordered some take out. I'm so hungry I feel like gobbling stuff up right off the shelves."

"One of my students said one time he stood right in the aisle and opened a box of cookies. He stuffed the box up his pants leg when a store employee went by. Those baggy pants, you know, you could put half a bakery in them." When Brian gave her a look, she quickly added, "Of course I say something to them when they brag about doing stuff like that."

"Okay, not another word about school for the rest of the weekend, honey. We agreed on that."

"Yes, Mr. Rosinski, sir." She gave him her best interpretation of a salute. Brian was right. She'd been able to keep to the agreement all the way down the mountain and throughout the ride back to the city. Until now. Bad habits were called that for a reason.

They rounded the end of the aisle and came upon the Pharmacy area. To Kendra's surprise, Jack Sermon was standing at the "pick up" window. Before she could duck around the bend, Brian and the cart came forward, blocking her escape route. Jack noticed her at the same moment, but when he saw Brian, looked uncertain whether he should acknowledge her. Kendra felt trapped in a purgatory of social correctness.

The pharmacy clerk got Jack's attention by reading out the medicines to confirm that he was giving the right ones. Kendra recognized the drugs: insulin and a treatment for high blood pressure. No shocker there, with Jack's weight and reddish complexion.

Brian tugged her arm. "Let's go."

"I can't just disappear now that he's seen me, I have to at least say hello," she whispered. Brian grumbled under his breath and surged away, side swiping a shelf of cheese crackers. Kendra was pushing the boxes back into position when Jack appeared at her side.

"Haven't seen you here in ages, Jack," she said, in a lame attempt to make small talk. She felt the eyes of other shoppers on them. Jack's attire was attracting attention. His burgundy sweatshirt was several sizes too small and the accompanying sweatpants rode under his protruding stomach, which, thankfully, was almost covered by a t-shirt. He made an ineffectual effort to tug the band of his sweatshirt downward. Kendra cringed and whipped her eyes away.

"Hi, Kendra. Yeah, I think half the school shops here, but these days I only come here when I have prescriptions to pick up. I found a cheaper store, but maybe I should come back for the pleasure of your company."

"Picking up snacks?" asked Kendra, desperate for a new topic of conversation.

"Snacks? This is my normal diet," said Jack with a degree of self-deprecation. He gestured at his cart, which held a variety of desserts, bottled juice, and a huge box of microwave popcorn. "Have to make sure there's a reason for taking my medicine. I hate paying for drugs I don't need," he said with a smile.

"Oh, you must take better care of yourself than that?"

"Care, eh? The way things are going lately, I'm beyond caring about anything except replacing the batteries in my remote control." Jack's joke lacked a smile.

"I have to admit, I haven't been in a very good mood either lately," said Kendra, assuming Jack was referring to the uproar over Zant's death. "But it will all blow over soon."

"Blow over. We'll see, won't we?" Abruptly, Jack nodded a goodbye and wheeled his cart quickly past her without another glance.

11.

Monday

The classroom reeked from rain soaked clothing, cheap cologne, and a more endemic odor known as "corroding classroom." Kendra was pleased that the quirky door lock was working today, and it was extra blessing during her prep period, but there was a bad side to being closed in.

After a weekend away from work, she felt more positive. She was still humming songs from a concert of world music she and Brian had seen on Sunday. To prolong a good weekend, she'd arrived at school uncharacteristically late, just before the first bell.

After using the first part of her prep to go beg at the custodian's office for a professional locksmith to fix her door, she was back to grading papers when the phone rang. It was a counselor.

"Kendra, I need some test scores from you. I emailed you a list."

"Sorry, Mrs. W, I'll get to it today." Kendra hung up. So much for having a good day. It would suit her just fine if she never opened a school email again, but now she could hardly avoid it. The inbox listed the email from Mrs. W. and below this was an anonymous email with the subject line, "You're famous!"

Oh no, not again! God, maybe she shouldn't have touched the keyboard or the mouse because of possible finger-prints—no, that was really stupid. This was electronic mail, not a paper document. But the threat felt immediate, so much so that she spun around and checked the room to see if she was alone.

She opened the message. A single line of text appeared above a web link. The message read, "This goes to the Prin-cipal next."

Her fingers locked on the mouse. Wherever the link took her, however vile a site it was, it might give her a new way to trace the sender, but what if the site contained a virus or the message disappeared with some kind of self-destruction program and she was left with no evidence at all. Okay, maybe that idea was a bit far-fetched, but there must be some truth in those movies about computer hackers.

There was a way she could at least prove the email existed. A few clicks and two copies went to her home computer. Now, for the reveal. She didn't like what the URL said, but clicked on the link anyway. The web site loaded quickly, a Megan's Law website, with Kendra's face, mug shot style. Below, there was ID information and the particulars of a purported conviction. The page looked legitimate, but she knew better. Somehow, she found the presence of mind to send the page to the printer.

She used her web browser to access the real Megan's Law website, and input the name of a sexual predator who'd been in the news recently. She compared this with the phony page she'd printed out. There were differences, but the mirror site was good enough to pass casual scrutiny, good enough to mount a very successful smear campaign. The bright side was that she now knew at least two things; her antagonist was alive and had excellent computer skills.

The bell rang, announcing the end of her Prep. She couldn't deal with a room full of students right now. She panicked at the sound of the door opening, but it was her 4th period instructional aide. Kendra quickly folded the paper evidence and shoved it into a pocket, and punched reset on the computer. She showed her aide the chapter review questions and asked her to get the class started. Then she dodged around the first group of arriving students and sprinted for the nearest bathroom.

***

Jack watched three enterprising youths who were fiddling with a padlocked chain on the parking lot gate. The heavy rain evidently didn't damper the kids' desire to slip off campus, or at least away from the supervised areas. In the first place, students weren't allowed on this side of campus during lunch, and one of them was smoking—two violations of the rules, right there. Whether the smokes contained something more than tobacco was a question Jack didn't really want to ask. Heck no, he wasn't going to ask for trouble. His only defense was his fists, but who knew what those kids were carrying on them? Also, if he put hands on a student, he could be sued or charged with something. Now, wouldn't that put icing on the shit cake he'd been baked?

Jack elected to stay in his car, on the far side of that chain link fence. He silently rooted for the chains, which reduced the probability any faculty member would find slashed tires, graffiti or a key mark on their car at the end of the day. The school didn't offer compensation for auto damage; the policy was "Park at your own risk." Except for those three at the gate, the other kids who'd chosen to be outside were staying where they were supposed to be. For the time being, the faculty lot was secure and Jack would be unnoticed.

A red umbrella caught his eye, and he waited to see if his timing would prove to be correct. Yes, it was Allana, heading for her car, and doubtless, the wide world beyond. Jack got out of his car and hailed her.

"Hey, Allana, come here a minute."

The umbrella tipped to expose a none-too-pleased face. Jack beckoned her over. "What's up? I don't have time to talk."

"I think you will find it's a talk worth having. Come on; get in my car. You're getting drenched," said Jack.

"I'll give you one minute." Allana closed her umbrella and propped it against the dash. Water droplets soaked a clutter of fast food wrappers that lay on the floor mat. She made a face and stuck her nose out the passenger window to demonstrate that the atmosphere inside the car was less than pristine.

"I've been thinking," said Jack. He stared at the back of her head. "Seems to me that there was more to Zant's accident than people think. Do you agree?"

"Why should I?"

"You can't have forgotten our trip to Zant's office on Wednesday afternoon."

"This is your important conversation?" Allana made a move to leave.

Jack continued, "I'll be more specific. I'll break down the main idea for you, just like we do for the kids, so it's easy to understand. When I came out to my car about 20 minutes after we parted company, your car was still in the lot. Do you really think I fell for that ridiculous story you gave me to explain why you were sticking around school so late?"

Allana's back lost some of its slouch, but she didn't reply. Encouraged by her show of tension, he added, "I'm sure you've already reported your true whereabouts to the cops, so, if I relieve my conscience and call them to confirm your story, that won't make trouble for you, right?"

Allana twisted to face him. "You're an asshole, you know? You had way more reasons to get rid of Zant than I did. He was annoying to me, but that's all. You want murder suspects, how about the rest of our department? I hear that your little favorite, Kendra, was snooping around his office. She was the one who originally suggested we try to get him fired, you know. Who knows what she was willing to do?"

"Ms. Desola is idealistic and completely harmless. Let's chat instead about your special motive. Do you think no one's noticed the signatures you forged? I bet you never actually held those meetings, even if signatures mark everyone as present. You're lucky the parents we deal with never read anything that's sent from school. And I guess you were counting on us being so sick of all the last minute paperwork we wouldn't look through it. But I did, and I'm sure Zant did too."

She pointed a crimson fingernail at his chest. "I don't know what you're babbling about, but I do know that you were here late on Wednesday, too. So, be my guest; do whatever you like. The second you report that you saw me on campus, they'll know that you were here, too, and I'll be happy to vouch for it. I can even supply a few reasons why you might have been hanging around. And, let me tell you—you pathetic loser—I'm sorry I felt sad for you all this time, seeing how you sneak out here for all your secret, happy hours."

Jack growled, "Oh, the boxing gloves are off! I'm glad you admit where that little rumor came from. Get ready to hear some juicy stories about yourself."

Allana jumped out of the car, and pointed the tip of her umbrella at Jack's face.

"Don't try it," she shouted, and ran off through the cars.

Jack's angry reply was muffled by the rain. "I won't go down alone, Miz Jarney!"

***

The rapping became more insistent. Kendra wanted the kids to give up and go away. They always told her they hated going to class. Too bad that didn't extend to their free time, when they did an about face and clamored to come in.

This was her lunch break and she didn't need any interruptions. Cautiously, she lifted a corner of a window drape. No surprise, Robert and Haksim, two of the most hapless freshmen on her list, were outside. Reluctantly, she opened the door a few inches and grunted a greeting.

"Can we come in?" Haksim pleaded. "It's an emergency. I was goofing around with Angelina's stuff and . . ."

Robert added, "Please, Ms. D, he really stinks bad!"

By way of explanation, Haksim placed his hands at the opening, much closer to Kendra's nose than she would have liked. The smell of cheap perfume bored into her nostrils.

"Thanks for that, Haksim. I get the point, but why come to me? Are the bathrooms out of service again?"

"I been there, but the boy's room got no soap, but you got some good stuff." Haksim spoke with triumphant certainty that he'd just made a brilliant, logical deduction.

Kendra let out a long sigh of surrender. Having a sink was useful, but also a curse. Students were always asking to use it. Not that she could complain. It sure beat the school where she was forced to get water from a janitor's closet and lug the sloshing buckets back to her room. You couldn't teach science without water.

"Ok, I give up. Come in." She let the boys in quickly, before any other students could see. Wanting to come inside was definitely contagious, especially on a rainy day.

"Just don't make a mess at the sink. I still doubt you're going to be able to get rid of that smell. I'm glad you don't have any classes with me this afternoon because I have misplaced my gas mask. Just kidding, just kidding. But I pity Mrs. Edwards and Mrs. Jarney."

"I just saw Mrs. Jarney leaving," announced Rob helpfully.

Haksim put in, "Oh, Rob's not going to Mrs. Jarney's class the rest of the week. She kicked him out again."

"Huh? Did you get in-house suspension, Robert? What did you do this time—no let me guess. Picking on someone or refusing to work, right?" She grabbed a towel to sop up some of the water that was pooling around the faucets.

"Ms. Desola, you on the pipe? Mrs. Jarney didn't give him work. You think she ever gives us work in there?" Haksim laughed at the absurd idea as his friend nodded in agreement.

Haksim finished his tale as he dried his hands. "For real, Robert didn't do nothing wrong. He was bored, so he took out his CDs. Mrs. Jarney always lets us, you know. Then some of them fell on the floor and I don't know why, all of a sudden, Mrs. Jarney, she's real mad and she says she's tired of him messing around, disrupting the class and to get out, don't come back 'til next week. So then, Rob, he left. And then, you know, I was the only one in there, cause nobody but us showed up for the class yesterday. So, she tells me to go too, get out, and I seen her leave right after me."

Haksim came to the end with a tiny smile that showed he was aware how this reflected on Allana's teaching practices.

Kendra already had a clear picture of Allana Jarney's workday but she didn't want to get into that with a student. She only said, "Robert, you didn't answer my question. When she kicked you out, did you get a referral to in-house detention?"

"No, Mrs. D., I didn't get no referral, but I know she won't let me back. And I got nowhere to go. Can I be in your room this afternoon?"

***

The streaked cafeteria windows let in tepid afternoon light that failed to cheer. The cafeteria tables that were folded up and wheeled to one side after lunch were now being set up again for the meeting by a slow-moving custodian and two teachers who'd been conscripted to help. One of the pair insisted that one more table would be enough since staff meeting attendance was back to its normal 40%.

Mrs. Prescott and Mr. Favor sat in close conversation, flanked by the teachers who clung to any administrator they could get to accept their toadying. Kendra made her way toward the most distant table.

"Over here, Kendra!" Jack waved a pen to invite her to sit with him. She didn't want to, but felt obligated because he was being so emphatic. She slung her purse down and sat on the other side of the table. They were alone, which was to be expected, since most people tended to avoid Jack and thus, avoid hearing him talk about how much he knew.

"What's new, Jack?" Kendra caught her breath, realizing she was going to suffer for asking him such an open ques-tion. But instead of going off about some obscure learning paradigm, he leaned toward her in a conspiratorial manner, his voice uncharacteristically hushed. "Where were you on Wednesday after school? I didn't see your car. You were out of here, right?"

Kendra sighed, but decided to answer. "I don't know why you're asking, but I drove over to the Materials Lab after school."

"For how long?" pressed Jack."

"Since you're interested, I needed to get materials for my hands-on curriculum." She gave Jack an ironic look and added, "You know, the stuff you guys are always making fun of? Who knew it would come in handy for more than actually teaching the kids something? Anyway, I hung around the materials lab for a while, talking to the woman that works there."

"Glad to hear it." If Jack realized he'd received a jab for his teaching methods, or lack thereof, he didn't dwell on it. In fact, he seemed suddenly preoccupied, his eyes uneasily scanning the room. This behavior was making her nervous.

"Mind telling me why you're glad?" Kendra's voice ac-quired an edge.

He leaned toward her and mumbled, "You know, I do respect you; you do a lot for the kids. Instead of being ap-preciative, Zant kept hassling you. So, I'd hate for you to be singled out if the cops decide to take the investigation further."

"Why would I be—Do you know something?"

Jack looked uneasy. "Listen, I heard you've been snooping around. Take my advice and stop. You don't know what you might stir up," advised Jack with solemnity.

Before Kendra could ask Jack to explain, a teacher at the next table poked at her and gestured toward the front of the cafeteria. The meeting was already in progress. The Principal was speaking, and Mr. Favor was giving Kendra a squinty look of censure.

Mrs. Prescott finished reading the agenda. "And now, before we get to business, I have some news I know you'll want to hear," said Mrs. Prescott. Coming in the wake of Zant's death, even the hardened cynics in the audience sat up straighter.

"The autopsy results on Carl Zant—cause of death—have been made available. He died from excess fluid in his brain, a result of head trauma from the fall down the staircase. No evidence was found that points to the incident as being anything except an unfortunate accident, and therefore we expect the police will be discontinuing their investigation very soon."

"The sooner the better!" shouted a PE teacher. Cheers broke out and everyone began talking at once.

Mr. Favor rose and boomed out, "All right, all right. I'm sure we could discuss that forever, but some of us would like to finish this meeting, and go home. Unless, of course, any of you would care to stay over and work on curriculum mapping." Ray gave an evil grin.

Immediately, the room quieted and an English teacher called out, "What's the next item on the agenda?"

***

In spite of Ray Favor's stated intention of moving things along, the meeting dragged on well past the allotted hour. Kendra was envious of anyone who showed the guts to get up and leave at the time the meeting should have, by union rule, come to an end. But she was surprised that Jack didn't stay on because time at the end was always reserved to discuss union business. And he'd left before she could find out why he'd cautioned her.

After the meeting, she exchanged some small talk and then went to the mailroom. Kendra wasn't in a big rush to get home since the afternoon was already shot, and Brian was working late also.

Her mailbox was stuffed with the large, brown envelopes used for internal mail. Kendra went to the adjacent break room to sort through the contents. Most of it would undoubtedly end up in the trash. She was mindlessly pulling memos and meeting reports from their envelopes when she caught the name of a notorious boy who was under Allana's primary jurisdiction.

Kendra was irritated that she hadn't been invited to his meeting, even though the boy was in two of her classes. Kendra leafed through the pages to check the meeting date. The signatures of the attendees caught her eyes instead. First came the signature of the boy's guardian, followed by the scrawl of Mr. Zant. Below were the signatures of Allana and Tamra. At the bottom, she stared at a reasonable facsimile of her own.

Unless she was going senile, she hadn't signed this form and she certainly hadn't attended the meeting. Kendra decided to hold on to the file until she made up her mind what to do. At the very least she needed to read the goals that bore her signature of approval. These were legal documents, and someone was tampering with them.

She squared up the papers and stuck them into her bag. A glance at the clock explained both her need to find a bathroom and why she was unlikely to find one that was still unlocked. Earlier in the day, she could have asked another staff member to open the nearest one, but the area was now deserted. Her bathroom key didn't work on the bathrooms in this part of the main building. For some reason, the administration would only give teachers a key for the bathroom closest to their classrooms. She could find no logical reason for that.

Kendra would never forget her student teaching stint at a nearby school. The first time she stayed late she discovered she was locked out of the building which held the only staff bathroom she could unlock. She found the girl's rooms locked also. She'd run to her car, and sped home to the bathroom. The following day, she sought out a teacher who'd worked at the site for many years hoping to find out what to do next time. The elderly teacher gave her the look she reversed for real greenhorns and said, "It's too dangerous around here after school for them to leave anything open. I try not to stay after school, but if I'm here and I have to go, well, I pee into a cup and pour it down the sink in my room." That was the first time Kendra second-guessed her decision to become a teacher.

Kendra was so lost in thought she didn't notice that someone was walking beside her. When she felt a tap on her arm, she jumped in fright.

"Easy, Ms. Desola. Sorry, I didn't mean to scare you." Nate looked embarrassed.

"It's okay, I'm just tired. I see you're back on your regular shift now."

"Yeah, well, the guy I switched with wasn't happy and to be honest, I really prefer working the second shift. This place is a crazy house during the day, no offense or anything."

"No, I totally understand."

He tipped the box he was carrying. "Can you use this? I found it lying under a stack of chairs in the old nurse's room. Funny what turns up in that place." Nate pointed to a smallish net, like the ones sold in aquarium stores. "Maybe if you have to catch that spider, you know?"

"Not a bad idea, thanks. I was wondering how I was going to clean inside that tank." Kendra accepted the net and shrugged. "I'm looking for someone to take that spider off my hands, but I don't want to give the thing to someone who just wants to see if a tarantula will crunch when they step on it." Kendra paused in front of a women's bathroom and optimistically tried the door.

"Can't say I'd go to that much trouble for a spider, myself." Nate pointed at the door. "Want me to open this for you? Here you go." He took one of his keys and swiftly unlocked the door. "Well, I have to get on with my work, have a good evening and don't be calling me if that spider gets loose." Nate grinned and moved off down the hall.

12.

Tuesday

"You don't sound very excited to hear my voice. Remember me? Brian, the love of your life?"

"I'm thrilled, you've made my day. Happy now? What's up?"

"I called you at home and then your cell, but I should have known you'd already be at work. Are you guys raising farm animals at school that you have to feed at the crack of dawn? Second thought, maybe a herd of the school mascot bulls would make a good safety barrier around your portable. And their leavings would sure fit in with the—never mind, sorry, but what time did you get there?

Kendra parried. "First period starts in about half an hour." She wasn't going to tell him she'd been there for ninety minutes. "I wasn't expecting calls—especially from you—until later."

"Like you say, it's not that early," said Brian. "Listen, I was thinking we could go to the gym together this afternoon. I'll meet you there at 3:30 and we'll avoid the crowds."

"That sounds good—no, damn, I can't—I have a department meeting." Kendra frowned at the note on her calendar. "I can meet you later, though."

"Why don't you skip the meeting? I'll be going out of town again in a couple days. Let's spend as much time together as we can. Anyhow, you're always telling me what a waste of time those meetings are."

"But I have to talk to Tamra about my classes. I really need to go, Brian."

"All right. But we can have dinner tonight? You'll be free by then, I assume? No evening workshop or a visit to a student's home?"

"Don't be mad, please."

"I'm not mad, but don't blame me when I tell you about all the cute chicks that were bothering me at the gym. I'll be at your place around 6, then. See you."

Kendra replaced the receiver and let out a loud wail of frustration. She momentarily feared that someone might have heard. No, the teacher next door wasn't in yet and the kids outside were making too much of their own noise to hear anything else.

Damn, where had the time gone? Even if she moved fast, there was barely enough time to set up for the demonstration she was going to do for her first period science class.

***

"Mr. Favor, I hope I'm not disturbing you. I just have a teensy little favor to ask you," said Allana with careful politeness. She made herself comfortable on one of his office chairs.

"What's that?" asked Ray, without looking up from his BlackBerry.

"I know it's a lot to ask, but could I switch my prep to first period next semester?"

Ray's shoulders tensed, making it clear her request was not welcome. "Can I ask why, Mrs. Jarney?"

"I'd like to be able to check on the kids' attendance right at the start of the day, to make sure they're coming to school and going to their first period classes. That way there won't be any question about whether I'm monitoring their attendance."

"And is there a question about that?"

"Um, no, not from this end. What I meant is I have a few parents who want me to call them every day and let them know if their kids actually arrived at school. It's hard for me to do that when I'm teaching a first period class," lied Allana.

"It's good to see that you're concerned about attendance, but I can't have more than one Special Ed. teacher with a prep first period, Mrs. Jarney. At least three of you have to be teaching to make the overall schedule work."

"Then switch me with someone else, whoever you gave first period to."

Unexpectedly, Ray didn't challenge her. Without looking up he said, "Fine, let's do that. You can switch with Jack Sermon. Is that all? Have a lovely day." He scribbled notes on a sticky pad.

Allana was surprised at his easy acquiescence. Before he could change his mind, she got up and left. She was familiar enough with Ray's capricious moods to know she'd best not stick around to verify that she'd gotten her way.

* * *

Tamra ostentatiously bent her wrist to check the time on her new and very expensive wristwatch. She especially loved the white gold band. Having nice things was important to her. From time to time she met someone who told her that her priorities were upside down, but why was it they usually were people who had plenty of money themselves? After her childhood in a trailer park, she'd learned early on what it was like being poor, and she was going to do whatever it took to protect the life she'd made for herself.

For heaven's sake, she'd been waiting in Zant's office for over ten minutes while Julia dealt with a series of stupid parents, a clerk from the registrar's office and a TA from the counseling office. The secretary was devoting her full attention to these people as if Tamra wasn't even there. She'd love to take that secretary down a few notches.

Finally, the waiting area was clear and Julia acted like she'd just noticed Tamra's presence. "Mrs. Helens, I hope you haven't been waiting too long."

"Not at all, Mrs. Chatin."

"It's crazy here. Until we get a new VP, I have to send everyone to other offices, and that seems to involve a lot of arguing. Now, what can I do for you?"

"I've been asked to look through Mr. Zant's Special Ed. files. Some of the files should be taken downtown for safekeeping. If you can just show me where they are, I won't take up any more of your time." Tamra lifted her briefcase and took a step toward Zant's office, clearly expecting Julia's immediate cooperation. Instead, the secretary turned to her phone.

"Uh, I don't know anything about that. Maybe I better check with Mrs. Prescott."

"Special Ed. files are not under the jurisdiction of the school site; surely, you know that after working in this of-fice, Mrs. Chatin. If you'd like to speak to someone from the Super's office,

125

I can get one of them on the line for you."

The secretary hesitated only a second. "Never mind, I guess you know your business. I'll just ask you to sign the files out, if you don't mind."

"Fine," agreed Tamra.

With most of the clutter gone, the VP's office looked larger, though not much improved. Apparently, the room still hadn't been dusted. A clearly demarked rectangle showed the spot formerly occupied by the tarantula tank.

"They haven't cleaned the room yet," Julia needlessly explained. She pointed to a file cabinet. "The files are all in there now. They should be in alphabetical order, but I wouldn't take that for granted. I didn't go through every-thing."

"What about his desk? Or did the detectives empty it out?"

"As far as I know, they didn't. Anything special you're looking for?"

Tamra wasn't sure what Julia knew about Zant's past activities, but this was no time to arouse suspicion. Allana said she'd been unable to find the BlackBerry. That meant Julia might even have it herself, or the cops might have found it. But Julia might think it was odd if Tamra asked about it. To hell with it.

"Zant wasn't very organized. Did you find any unmarked folders, or loose papers?"

"Oh, there were tons of those. I did the best I could to put things back together. The ones I wasn't sure about are in that box."

Julia saw the look on Tamra's face and hastened to explain before Tamra accused her of incompetence. "Mr. Zant never threw anything out and sometimes I can't tell ..."

"Thank you, Mrs. Chatin, I'll manage. Please close the door after you, to keep the noise out."

***

"He keeps bothering me! You seen that, Ms. D?"

A boy and a girl stood in a rigid face off. Kendra knew that what had begun with insults could quickly grow into a physical confrontation. At least there was no audience, the lunch bell had taken care of that.

Kendra shook her head. "Actually, Misty, I saw you trying to

126

trip him when he got out of his seat and I heard what you both said after that."

"Chris started it!" The girl pushed out her lips in a pout.

"She's a retard," said Chris, choosing a word that was a popular put down, second only to calling someone "gay." The boy saw the look on his teacher's face and was re-minded that Kendra told them not to use such words. He mumbled, "Sorry, but she's talking trash. You heard her."

"I heard both of you, but Chris, didn't you agree that you weren't going to respond?"

The boy looked down as he remembered the conflict mediation session that had taken place only one week earlier. He picked up his backpack and mumbled, "I said I was sorry. Can I go?"

Kendra hoped she was making the right decision. "This is your last reminder, Chris. Go to lunch. Misty stay here a minute."

The girl glared at Kendra. "How come he gets to go?"

"Misty, you're getting way too much of my attention and not for a good reason. You were interrupting my class and now you'll just have to be late for lunch. You said the con-flict mediation helped you look at your behavior, that you'd make some changes."

"But Ms. Desola, Chris says stuff about me and I get mad."

"We discussed that. You are the one who controls the way you act, not Chris. You're giving him power over you. Do you think what he says really hurts you?" Kendra saw the girl's head shake and took the opportunity to go the next step.

"Maybe you need some more time," said Kendra. "Look, I have an idea, are you up for a little contest? The prize will be pizza from that place on the corner."

"Huh? Pizza?" Misty gave the teacher her full attention.

"Let's have a contest to see how long you can sit here quietly in my class. If you want to get the prize, you can't talk unless I call on you. That means if Chris says something you don't like, you can't respond, and you can't start any-thing either. So, if you agree, you won't be able to talk un-less you raise your hand and I call on you."

"What about Chris?" Misty wasn't about to let Chris off the hook.

"This isn't about Chris, it's to help you learn some self-control, help you stay out of trouble. This name-calling is a habit, the way smoking is a habit. Do you want to try or not?" Kendra knew that although Misty was a high school freshmen, her emotional development was that of a 4th grader.

"Okay."

Kendra dug around in a drawer and came up with a container of small bingo chips. "Pick a color."

Misty unrolled her hands from the hem of her oversized jersey and picked out a red chip.

"I'm putting a cup on the desk, see? For the classes you have with me, every ten minutes that you go without speaking out of turn, you earn one chip. Understand? If you interrupt the class, you don't get one. To give you an advantage, if someone else calls you a name and you ignore them, I will give you an extra chip for a bonus. That way the meaner they are, the more they end up helping you." Kendra dropped chips in the cup as if to demonstrate her point.

"What if someone lies and says I talked, but I didn't?" asked Misty, always ready to find a flaw.

"If I don't notice, I won't do anything either way. We can't set this up so it's perfect. Are you willing to try this or not?" Kendra was running low on patience.

"How do I win?"

"At the end of a week we can count up and see." Kendra did a quick calculation. "The first week you need to get 15 chips, okay? I don't expect you to be perfect, especially in the beginning. I know you'll have a hard time being quiet."

"How come I have to wait a week?"

"Like I said, you have a bad habit, and bad habits take time to kick. And, look, pizza's expensive and I'm paying. You don't expect me to buy you pizza every day do you?"

The student acknowledged the truth of that with a smile.

"You ready to try this?" Kendra waited.

"Pizza, right? From off campus, any kind?"

"Yes. Make up your mind. Are we doing this or not?"

"Okay, but I don't want anyone else to know."

"That's fine with me, but I can't promise that other kids won't figure out what's going on," said Kendra. "If they do, so what? There's no shame in trying to stop a bad habit. This is not much different than the class point competitions we have."

Misty said, "They might even want to try. They like pizza, too."

***

"Let's get started. I'd like to get out of here sometime today," complained Allana, who had commandeered Maretta's desk chair without a second thought.

Maretta's tiny classroom was cleverly arranged for teaching efficiency, but wasn't a comfortable place for a meeting. Regardless, this was the only Special Ed. classroom in the main building, a convenient location for Tamra. So there they were.

"Make yourself comfortable, said Maretta."

"I see Jack's not here to yak on about everything, so we can finish our business a lot faster," said Allana, ignoring Maretta's sarcasm.

"Where is Jack?" asked Kendra, settling on a low book-case instead of an uncomfortable student desk/chair.

"We don't need to wait," said Tamra.

"My students told me Sermon was out sick today," said Maretta, who traded students regularly with Jack. Unless she was certain they couldn't handle the regular classes, Kendra mainstreamed her students to avoid having to place them with Allana or Jack.

"He's out sick? I'm not surprised. He hasn't looked healthy lately," observed Kendra.

"Who cares," said Allana, leaning back farther in the chair. "Can we get going?"

"Yes, let's." Tamra held up a paper. "This is an update of the meeting timetable for the Individualized Student Plans. As you can see, the chart has three columns. The first lists meetings that were held on time with everything complete. The second column shows documents that still need signatures; either the parents or someone else hasn't signed off on them. The third column lists the meetings that haven't been held, that are overdue."

"Uh, yea. Well, we know about this already," said Allana, covering up a yawn.

"Yes, I'm sure you know because I've reminded all of you time and time again. How can you be so lackadaisical? The state's coming and there are legal issues involved with these meetings. They absolutely have to be held on time. The reason I bring this up again is that Mr. Zant was furious about your delays. He accused me of being too lenient and went right over my head. Now the big shots downtown know you're out of compliance. They are the ones who gave me this chart, and told me to fix the problem before the state review. And I intend to."

Tamra raised a hand to forestall interruptions and continued, "Originally, I cut you all some slack because I know it's ten times harder to teach here than anywhere else. But see where that got me? I've been made the fall guy. If you don't get your act together, after the review I will make sure your teaching placements are reviewed."

That remark brought Maretta to her feet. "That's not fair! I'm only overdue on three meetings; I just got late on the files. For god's sake, you know before we can even hold a meeting we have to do a lot more than just compute test scores. We have to fill out the eight-page goal sheets with goals that were written by the state. You think it's easy to select anything decent from that esoteric gibberish? Then there's that two-page sheet of codes we have to look up to cross-reference to the goal sheets. Then, even if we turn in the paperwork before the due date, you always send it back, rejected, because we forgot to fill in one stupid box, or we didn't use the correct codes."

Kendra added, "As far as the meetings go, half the time the parent or guardian doesn't show up, so what are we supposed to do? We can't finish the process without a parent signature. Do you know how much time we spend just trying to hunt the parents down? How can you blame us for having unfinished paperwork?"

Allana joined the complaint party. "I'm only late on a few students. You know I turned in the records, but I postponed some meetings because I didn't get the psych reports on time."

Tamra held up a hand. "Enough! I don't really care to hear any more excuses. All I can say is that I regret you haven't put the same energy into your teaching duties as you devoted toward trying to get Zant fired. At least you don't have that distraction anymore."

"I don't think that's fair—" started Kendra.

Tamra cut her off. "Fair, you want fair? You were calling me three times a week to complain about something Zant was doing to one of your students but you didn't seem to have the time to hold their meetings. Maybe you'd have more time if you didn't try to play Mary Poppins."

Allana covered her mouth and coughed to cover a laugh. There was an uncomfortable moment of silence until Tamra spoke again. "All right, enough. The past is the past. I've been covering your butts for months, but don't expect that to continue."

"We are grateful for all you've done," said Maretta.

Kendra was quick to say, "Yeah, we appreciate how understanding you've been."

Tamra didn't soften. "Unfortunately, your appreciation doesn't help. Now that Zant isn't around, I'm the scapegoat. The Superintendent is holding me accountable for your performance, as if my job is to be at Standard High every day to supervise, in spite of the fact that I'm responsible for a total of five schools."

"That does suck," said Allana, blatantly looking at the clock.

"If there's anything we can do to help? We could—" Maretta's offer was brushed aside.

"No, please, don't go there." Tamra shook her high-lighted ringlets. "Trust me, any word that comes from your department only aggravates the Super even more. The only way to help things along is to do what you're supposed to do. Get those meetings done and send in the signed documents before the end of the month."

Tamra looked at her notes. "Okay, other issues now. Kendra, I got a message from you about a problem with the master schedule."

"That's right. Mr. Favor has me scheduled to teach five different subjects next semester. How can it be legal for me to teach things that I'm not credentialed for? And anyhow, the union contract says we can't teach more than four subjects, right?"

"Well, as far as the first point, since you teach Special Ed. kids, they can assign you to teach any subject, but on the second, you're correct and I will send Mr. Favor a memo. I doubt if he wants to get the union involved, so wait a few days and check. I bet he backs off," said Tamra.

"Sounds great, thanks so much," said Kendra with relief. I already come to work at least one hour early every day. I don't know what hours I'd have to work with five subjects to teach."

"You amaze me," said Allana. "Who wants to be here at 7 a.m.? Speaking of that, I lucked out big time. I got Jack's first period prep. So, next semester, I don't have to show up until 9."

"He gave up his first period prep?" Kendra was so shocked by the switch she didn't react to Allana's stated intention.

"For heaven's sake, Allana," said Maretta angrily. "Prep. period is not supposed to be a sleep-in opportunity. You still have to be on campus, just like everyone else, by at least 8."

"Just kidding, just kidding," laughed Allana, happy that Maretta was riled up.

"Are we done here?" Kendra was tired of all the inevitable quibbling.

"Just a few more items of business, I'm afraid," said Tamra. The counseling office has some scheduling requests. And you did want to discuss the applicants for the VP's job, I assume? I just happen to have a good idea who will make the final cut."

* * *

Maretta rolled her chair back to its normal location. "Nothing like a friendly meeting at the end of a long day."

"Hah, you can say that again," replied Kendra, stretching her back. "No offense, Maretta, but you could use a few decent chairs in here. Okay, sorry, I guess, there's really no place to put them. I'm just grouchy from Tamra's browbeating. The only thing worthwhile was hearing who's on the list of candidates for the VP's job. A real bunch of winners. Well, I guess whoever is hired, none of them will be worse than Zant."

"You're such an optimist. Allana and Tamra sure acted like they don't care. I kind of wonder how Jack would have reacted to those names, though. Almost too bad he wasn't here."

"I hope he's okay. He's got diabetes and heart problems, did you know? But I have to admit I was glad not to have to watch him argue with Allana. I'm sick of the constant bickering that goes on between those two," said Kendra.

Maretta crossed her legs and sat back. "That's one thing you need to learn, how to take things in stride."

"Now you sound like Brian," said Kendra, listlessly wandering the room.

"I don't mean that you shouldn't take your teaching responsibilities seriously, just downplay some of the other stuff. All the petty quarreling and the politics—who cares? Take it as entertainment, kind of like a soap opera."

"You took the politics plenty serious when Zant went after our department," Kendra pointed out. "Anyway, that chapter is closed, and aren't we glad."

"Definitely. I really hope the new VP is a semi-normal person and we can coast through the rest of the year. I know a few of the people who are going to be on the final interview panel. I think they'll weed out any nut cases. I can't wait to hear about the interviews."

Kendra came to perch on a corner of Maretta's desk. "Well, look at this! And you make fun of my computer games?" Kendra held up a small figurine.

"Oh, please! That's not mine. That little wizard came off a girl's backpack, caused a disturbance. I took it away and it's been sitting there for a few days. Maybe it's true that Clarice stole it, or wouldn't she be screaming to have it back?"

Kendra turned the figure in her hand. "I saw some similar ones recently. If I'm not mistaken, this matches a set I saw in the custodian's break room. Did you know Mr. Ken collects fantasy figures? This little wizard is great." She saw Maretta's grin and countered, "Don't laugh at me. Well, go ahead, I don't care. Anyway, this could be Ken's. Can I take it?"

"Sure, ask him if he's lost a wizard. But, according to the story I got, Clarice found it in the girls' bathroom near the auditorium." Maretta made a funny face and giggled. "You think Mr. Ken was playing with toys in the girls' bathroom?"

"Now that's an image I hope doesn't come to mind the next time I see him."

"Me too!" The two women burst into laughter.

Maretta wove a path around the student desks, bending to pick up stray pens and pencils. "Seriously, if Clarice is stealing, we should report that. "

Kendra frowned. "What good will come out of reporting this as a theft? The wizard isn't valuable, but she'll surely get suspended, which to her is a five-day vacation—a reward, not a punishment. Meanwhile, she gets farther behind in class. We should address her behavior instead of just trying to punish her. I mean, Clarice needs a consequence, but..."

"You're way too soft on these kids." Maretta spoke with resignation.

"Now you sound like Zant. Okay, sorry, you know what I mean. There are no clear-cut rules about what's right or wrong; you have to know the circumstances."

Maretta's mouth gaped in exasperation. "You think there's a circumstance when it would be okay for Clarice to steal something?"

"Okay, for example, what if she really didn't believe she was stealing, or maybe someone else stole the wizard and gave it to Clarice."

"Okay, sure, there can always be extenuating circumstances, I see that. But let's stick to the concrete situation at hand. If you find out that Clarice was stealing and she knew she was stealing, let me know, okay?"

Kendra brought the tiny wizard closer to her myopic eyes. "We're not even sure if this thing belongs to Mr. Ken. I'll turn it into the lost and found if I can't find the owner."

13.

Wednesday

Kendra dangled the string just out of reach of Bobbin's flailing paw. With her other hand she popped the last bite of toast into her mouth.

Brian shuffled into the kitchen in his usual morning fog. "Is there any coffee left?"

"About a cup. If you need more, you know where to find everything. Maid service is offline. I have to leave soon."

"Grouchy, grouchy. I didn't have to get up this early, but I got up to keep you company and even brushed my teeth." He pouted to demonstrate that he'd made a major sacrifice.

"And that's appreciated," said Kendra who took the hint, ruffling his hair and giving him a kiss. The cat took this for an opportunity to run off with the string. She broke away from Brian to chase down Bobbins. Kendra was always care-ful not to leave string around because Bobbins might get entangled, or even eat it if he wasn't being supervised.

"I'm putting his string away. If he wants to play, use Mousie, okay?"

Brian grunted. He was already installed at the table, drinking coffee with the sports page under his nose. Kendra suspected that at this time of day he probably wouldn't notice even if Bobbins dropped Mousie into his coffee mug.

"Brian. Earth to Brian!"

"What?" Brian kept his eyes on the paper.

"You going to hang out here, or are you working this morning?"

Now he looked at the kitchen clock. "I'll be leaving pretty soon. I have to go back to my place and put on a suit to show the clients how professional I am. That way they can trust me when I'm out of their sight." He sighed. "If you'd let me move in with you, instead of me spending time driving back and forth, I could be here, playing with the cat," he said with extra drama.

"Give me a break." She opened the fridge and searched for something to take to work.

"Here's the section with the job ads." Brian slid the paper across the table. Kendra tactfully came over and feigned interest.

"I'll look at the ads later, promise. How can you multi-task even when you're half asleep? I thought you were locked in on the sports statistics."

"Heh. Speaking of that, I have a game tonight at the gym. Gonna see your favorite VP Favor there. You can always come and watch, you know. Maybe you could pick up some brownie points that way."

"My favorite VP? Sure, in a field of one. Favorite Vice Principals don't exist in my world. You'd think that a big school like Standard High would keep more than two VPs on staff—all the better to spread the aggravation around."

Brian laughed. "VPs are a rare, no make that an endan-gered species, at your school. And, speaking of endangered, if this cat doesn't stop chewing on my toes, he might be en-dangered soon."

"He's just trying to get you to play with him. And he's all yours because I have to get going now. Make sure everything's locked tight when you leave, okay?"

After receiving the Megan's Law email, Kendra realized she couldn't predict how far her adversary would go. She stifled a twinge of guilt about keeping Brian in the dark and asked if he knew anyone that installed alarm systems. She didn't own the house so she didn't want to do anything elaborate, although Mr. Pacholik wouldn't mind. The landlord wouldn't pay for the alarm system, but he loved tenant-funded upgrades.

When he asked her why she wanted the system, she told him that there had been a rash of burglaries in the neighborhood. It wasn't a lie. Two homes on the next street really had been robbed in the not too distant past. Brian didn't have to know the rest.

"With this ferocious lion you have for a pet, I don't think you have to worry about a break-in, but I will definitely lock up." Brian rattled the newspaper at the excited feline.

As she went to collect her bag from her tiny office, she heard the unmistakable sounds of cat fighting with news-print. Kendra hoped Bobbins was shredding the classified section.

When Kendra came over to Brian and nuzzled a goodbye on

the side of his neck, he was already back in the land of sports analysis. Bobbins was under the table with the ad section of the paper. Go Bobbins!

Brian gave her a one-armed squeeze. "I'll meet you at the Italian place at 6, okay?"

"Okay. You're not going to Dallas until Friday morning, right?

"Yeah, so I expect you to treat me well before I leave."

"Well, that depends on the report I get from Bobbins." She bent and picked up Mousie, and dropped the toy on the article he was reading. "Someone needs you," she said.

Bobbins eagerly leapt to the tabletop, shirring the Sports Section. Brian groaned and snatched the toy mouse, throwing it for the cat to chase. "I guess I know who counts around here."

***

Julia obviously wasn't taking any time off. There she stood at the attendance counter, carefully arranging silk plants she was removing from a big plastic bag. Kendra noticed all the baby photos had been replaced with tiny stuffed animals.

"How are you?" said Julia without warmth.

"Never a dull moment," said Kendra, coming to a stop near Julia's desk.

"Thanks again for the other day." The secretary folded the empty bag and stored it.

Kendra prepared herself for the unexpected. After the detectives' visit, she was uncomfortable talking to Julia, but if she handled things right the conversation would be over quickly. Kendra only had to find out if Clarice was a thief.

"I'm glad to see that you're in better spirits." Kendra pulled the wizard figurine from the pocket of her sweater and asked, "Did you lose this by any chance?"

"Huh. Where did you get that? There were some wizards like that in the batch I bought for Ken's birthday."

"That's what I thought. I saw what you put together; it was so creative."

The secretary flushed with the praise.

Encouraged, Kendra kept going. "Did any of the figurines go missing?"

137

"I have no idea. There were a few extra I didn't use, but I took them home. Why do you ask?"

"Last Friday, Mrs. Edwards took this one away from a girl, Clarice, who claimed she found it, but another student accused Clarice of stealing it. Mrs. Edwards and I would like to know the truth."

Julia asked, "Other than the fact it matches the ones I bought, I couldn't say. I suppose she could have taken it from the custodial room if nobody was around. The table was set up like that for a few days because we had to put off the party."

Kendra passed the figurine to Julia, who held it as if it was a spiny sea urchin. "Clarice said she found this in the girls' bathroom near the auditorium."

"Well, I did go into that bathroom after Mr. Ken's birthday party. After it broke up, I stayed for quite a while to clean up. I was so exhausted and I really had to pee, and the girls' bathroom was right on my way out. I was gonna pop in and use it, but God, it was so filthy, I walked in and right on out. I was carrying the leftover figurines in a bag and one could have fallen out, I guess. I didn't count them." Julia frowned, and looked like she regretted talking so much.

Julia dropped the wizard into a drawer. "Isn't this a big fuss over nothing? You do seem to love asking questions, though. I'm not stupid, you know, I can see what you're really interested in."

"Huh? I'm just trying to check Clarice's story, ask Maretta if—"

Julia stopped her with an angry look. "You want to know if I was over near the auditorium. And yes, I was in that bathroom, right down the hall from Zant's accident. But I didn't go near the north stairs. I was planning to go out that way—that was the reason I passed by the bathroom—but when I headed toward the stairs, I saw a mess of liquid soap on the floor. I didn't want to slip and break my neck, so I turned around and used the west exit instead."

Kendra attempted to lighten the mood. "We all do a lot of extra walking, the way bathrooms are so scarce here."

"That's true. We've all had our moments of desperation," said Julia with a tiny smile.

Kendra took the woman's improved mood for an opportunity to pursue a point. This was the second time she'd heard that something was on the hall floor near where Zant fell.

"There was soap on the floor? Interesting!"

"No, stinky is more like it. The stuff went right up my nose. That's the cheap crap the District supplies. I'd know it blindfolded. But who cares about that? You want something really interesting to chew on? I heard that the investigation is now officially closed."

Satisfied that she'd interrupted Kendra's train of thought, Julia picked up a notepad and strode away.

***

Shouts of "You stupid!" "DOH!" "You crazy, man." volleyed between the tables in the classroom.

"No, no, dinosaur bones are not faked," said Kendra in her most didactic voice. A student had just announced that it was a fact that scientists dug up chicken bones and passed them off as being fossils. Most of the class was tittering. Kendra knew this remark was intended to cause a disruption.

"All right kids, that's enough! I know that the photos of bone fragments on this page don't look like much, but if you turn to page 338, you'll see the complete dinosaur skeletons along with other fossilized bones. Scientists make careful examinations of fossils. They don't just dig something from the ground and make a bunch of wild guesses about what they've found."

Kendra didn't bother to ask the students if they'd seen any dinosaur or earth science exhibits. She knew that her students didn't visit museums. In recent years, school budgets for field trips had gone the way of—yes, dinosaurs—and these kids would never visit a museum on their own. Kendra also knew that they weren't likely to be watching educational TV channels.

"This one looks like Rogelio," sang out a student, trying for a laugh. Even though no one else picked up the insult, Rogelio threw a sharp look at the speaker.

"Shayla, we'll talk later," said Kendra. The girl shrugged. Kendra still worried that the girl's comment would lead to a fight after school.

"Stay after class a minute," Kendra told Rogelio, to the delight of his classmates.

Kendra pointed to the projection screen, where a diagram

showed various layers of soil and rock. "Back to work! Look at this chart. Figure out which of those layers is sandstone and which are igneous rock. Then label the ones that would contain fossilized materials. Write your answers on the sheet I handed out. Check your books if you get stuck."

There was low level grumbling at being handed such an arduous task, even though this chart wasn't new to them. High school subject matter was supposed to build on prior knowledge. Sometimes the students complained, "We already had this." Yet, when she probed a little bit she generally found they recalled next to nothing.

Kendra's students were not the only students at Standard High with gaping holes in their knowledge base, but the lags were more pronounced in the Special Ed. population. Al-though the kids had attitudes and disabilities that made learning more difficult, another reality, seldom discussed, was that the teachers who worked with challenging kids often gave up and took the easy way out. Her colleagues, Allana and Jack, were examples of that. Kendra, on the other hand, put a lot of extra effort and creativity into her job.

The silence in the room was broken by a comment. "My aunt said that there aren't any fossils in the Bible," piped up a female student.

Before Kendra was forced to address that pronouncement, the bell rang. "Your packets are due tomorrow," shouted Kendra above the din. "Rogelio, get over here. Now!"

But Rogelio ran out the door.

Kendra stacked notebooks to the rhythm of an unintentional mantra, "It never, never, ever, ever, stops."

***

Second lunch was underway when Kendra made her way to Mr. Favor's office. Now that the police investigation was closed, she was in less of a panic to unmask the emailer. She still intended to find out who was slandering her, but today she needed to make time for another quest as well.

She paused at the nurse's alcove. The little room was littered with folding chairs and a retired coffeemaker, behind which sat some cardboard boxes that appeared to have been there forever.

This was a junk room, to be sure, but still seemed an odd place for Nate to find an aquarium net.

Because of the location, Kendra thought of Ray Favor right away. Brian, who knew Ray on a social basis, had given Kendra some insight into the VP's frat-boy person-ality. Kendra suspected that Ray might have stolen Zant's lizard to play some kind of prank. Ray frequently went off campus for meetings and she wanted to find out if he was at school during the timeframe the lizard disappeared. She'd found some students who'd seen the animal alive and well as late as Wednesday lunch. Since Ray would surely lie if he was guilty, she'd thought of another plan.

Ginny was taking a bite out of a frosted cupcake. She nodded at Kendra and slid a telephone headset over her puffy hair.

"Hey, Ginny, how are you?" Kendra used her friendliest voice.

"What can I do for you?" asked Ginny. Her expression showed that she'd rather do nothing. She took another bite and licked frosting from her fingers.

"Ray here?"

"Nope." The secretary opened a large binder to signal how busy she was.

"Well, no matter. I'm sure you can help. I just wanted to ask if that meeting with George Brackston's parents went off on schedule. If they came in, could you see if they signed the permission for a psych evaluation? I have to follow up if they did."

"I don't know. When was that meeting? Doesn't sound familiar to me," said Ginny.

Kendra wasn't surprised, because she'd invented the meeting. She tried to sound forthright as she replied, "I think it was Wednesday afternoon."

Ginny flipped through a thick planner and said, "You must have the day wrong. According to this, Mr. Favor was off campus most of the day. He left around noon for a grant writing session downtown, and I remember now he complained he was stuck there until almost 8 p.m."

"Oh, well, I'm mistaken then. Hey, do you mind if I take a peek at the master schedule?"

"Doesn't bother me, but if he finds you in his office, I'll say I didn't see you sneak in." The phone rang and Ginny gave it her attention.

Kendra stood in the small office and reevaluated her conclusions. The little net was a perfect tool for lizard-napping, but Ray was not the lizard thief—unless she was wrong about the timing of the theft. Or, maybe there was no connection between the small net and the disappearance of Zant's lizard.

She should really drop the whole issue. After all, the reptile wasn't even her pet. Brian would go crazy if he knew she was worried about a lizard. But Kendra didn't like people messing around with animals. She wanted to know what had happened, and find the animal if she could.

Music blared from the hall. She heard Ginny's angry words followed by youthful laughter. This wasn't the place to stand around and think. The master schedule board was leaning against the wall in front of her, back facing out. She flipped it around.

Tamra was too optimistic about Ray's cooperation. The same five courses were still listed after Kendra's name. Oh well, maybe Favor would make the change in the next few days. Before she turned the schedule board back around, she noticed that the row that had held Jack Sermon's name and class assignments was now totally blank.

***

Kendra viciously stomped on the parking brake. Mr. Pacholik was at her front steps, kneeling next to a bucket. The landlord must be on "crack patrol" again. He was irritating at the best of times and right now, she didn't have any patience to deal with him. It was too late to drive away, as he'd already seen her.

"You're home late. They keep you after school for de-tention?"

Unwillingly, she walked over to the man, who was patching tiny cracks in the cement with some sort of compound. Instead of landscaping, the entire front of the house was paved. Concrete was one of the man's many obsessions; each crack had been patched a million times. She was certain that, like other homes on the block, her house was designed to have a front lawn, but Mr. Pacholik thought lawns were dirty. It was a miracle he'd left the small patch of grass in the back.

"I think you just got a package," he said.

"I wasn't expecting anything."

"Well, look around back. I was just driving up when I saw a car pull away and your side gate was open. I spent a lot of time rehanging that gate last summer. You didn't break it again, did you?" He stopped his work long enough to look her up and down appraisingly. "You've lost more weight, haven't you? I keep telling you, men like women with meat on their bones."

"It's been a long day; I'm going in. See you." Kendra fantasized upending the bucket over the old lecher's head as she went to get the package. She supposed that it had been delivered by the regular mail, since they were using fuel-efficient station wagons instead of trucks these days.

A piece of paper was taped to her back door. It was one of the missing pet notices that frequently popped up on telephone poles in the neighborhood. Printed at the top in large letters was the word "MISSING." Below was a photo of a cat that was a dead ringer for Bobbins and under it, a line of smaller type read: "Unless You Mind Your Own Business." Kendra dropped the note and charged inside, frantically calling out for Bobbins. She found him on her TV chair, safe. She scooped the cat into her arms and cried.

14.

Thursday morning

Two students were laminated together in a hot embrace. Jack didn't admonish them and they didn't notice him as he went by. Maybe when the first bell sounded they would peel themselves apart. Wasn't his problem. In fact, in his present mood, if the two started going at each other with knives he still would look the other way.

Jack reached his car and lowered the box he carried to rest on the hood. The last few yards had been a challenge. When his dizziness subsided, he stashed the box in the back seat. He regretted not eating breakfast, but he wasn't hungry.

Jack's car was sitting at the end of the lot closest to his room, to make the trips back and forth as short as possible. After an hour's labor his car was fully packed. The new teacher, his replacement, could have what was left.

There were a lot more kids around now. A girl twirled in a circle, spraying her friends with perfume. Three neatly dressed students walked by proudly carrying bits and pieces of a complicated mechanical contraption.

The staff would be arriving soon and he really didn't wish to be seen with a fully loaded car. To his chagrin, he saw Kendra approaching. Her arms were burdened with the fruits of an early morning session at the copy machine. With luck, she wouldn't notice the boxes on the back seat of his car.

"Hey, Jack, heard you've been sick. You coming back to work today?"

"I just came to get something from my room," said Jack, who, in truth, didn't feel well at all.

"I think you dropped something," said Kendra, gesturing toward the ground.

Jack looked where she indicated. A thin notebook lay on the ground, half hidden by a tire. He bent and retrieved the book, but started to sway as he straightened up. Kendra reached out to grab his arm, but Jack put a supporting hand on his car.

"Thanks. Got a bit lightheaded there for a second."

"You should be at home resting," suggested Kendra. "You okay to drive?"

"Yeah, I'll be fine in a minute or two. I'll just sit here till I feel okay. You can be on your way. I don't want to take up your time."

"If you're sure, then, I'll be going. Take care."

Jack watched her walk toward the portables. She was still young enough to be taken for a student at this distance, at least in his old eyes. He supposed that the kids thought Kendra was an old hag, or something worse. He knew what they thought of him.

He slouched against his car and surveyed the campus, from the portables to the main building. This could be his last visit to Standard High. Knowing that, the place some-how looked different, as an outsider might see it, sadder and yet more innocent.

The landscape blurred. Jack fished for his thermos and gulped. As soon as he finished his business here, he'd get some breakfast. There she was, walking toward the side of the parking lot. Jack got out and came up behind her. "Good morning," he said.

The woman spun around, keys jingling in her hand.

"You look unhappy—not because of me, I hope," said Jack.

"You're on time for a change."

"Yes, come along to my coach, ma'am, we can talk in there," said Jack, giving a theatrical bow. This flourish proved to be a mistake; he came out of the gesture in a dizzy wobble. He opened the passenger door for her. "Have a seat," he said.

"You look like the one that needs to sit down. I missed the CPR refresher course, so you're on your own," said Tamra, reluctantly moving into the car. She was about to let her shoulder bag slide to the floor, but changed her mind after a glance at the less than pristine carpet.

"You're worried about me? That's really touching."

"I know what you think of me, but I'm not all bad. I asked you to meet me so I could warn you. Detective Tapia interviewed me the other day and he asked a lot of questions about you."

"That was your big opportunity, wasn't it? Did you make up evidence about how I killed Zant just like you concocted stories to get me fired?"

"Let's not mix up two different things. The truth is, I didn't tell the detective anything about you except that you were one of many teachers Zant didn't like. But I thought you should know, and I didn't feel secure talking about it on the phone. Of course, now I guess the investigation's closed."

"Yea, that was then and this—" Jack held up a small envelope.

"—is now. I think I have something you want."

"What could you possibly have that I want?" Her lips curled.

"Okay, fine. I'll just pass on what I have to my contacts at the newspaper, or maybe your friend the detective would be interested."

"All right, I'll play. What have you got?"

Jack meaningfully extracted a snapshot from the envelope. "Before I give this to you, I just want you to know I have copies." He shoved the photo under her nose.

Tamra grimaced and pushed the photo away. The movement caused her hand to hit the dash and her key ring opened and slipped from her hand. She cursed and bent, fumbling for the keys and key ring ornaments. "What do you intend to do?" she asked.

"I have to say, I really wasn't out to get you. I was out shopping one day and just happened to see you and Zant, and you made such an odd couple, I wanted to record the moment for posterity. You know how they sell those disposable cameras at the checkout stand? Little did I know the photo would not only be a memento of our dear, departed colleague, it provides a beautiful motive for murder," laughed Jack.

"Asshole!" Her exclamation was virulent but somewhat deadened by her bent posture as she grappled for her keys.

"That's not fair. I wasn't going to do anything with the pictures, except tease you with them. But things are different now that I've entered the ranks of the unemployed. You and Zant screwed me good, and I'm not going to just lay down and take it, no pun intended. The next step depends on you. I need my job back and I know you can help, especially now that Zant is dead. For instance, you can say you found out your sources relative to my workday weren't accurate."

Tamra snapped the key ring shut and shoved it into her shoulder bag. "You're asking me to trust you. For all I know, you've already shown the photos to someone else."

"No, of course not. Here, to show my good faith, we'll make an exchange. Hand me my thermos and I'll hand over this photo." He pointed to the floor on her side of the car. "I'd get the thermos myself, but I won't feel around for it with you sitting there; I'm a gentleman."

Tamra lifted the battered bottle out from under her seat and thrust it at Jack. Her eyes widened as Jack removed the stopper and gulped directly from the thermos.

"That's just disgusting; how can you even drink out of that thing? You know, the students make fun of you every time they see it. Tell you what, I'll even buy you a new bottle in exchange for the photo and all the negatives."

Jack set the thermos on the dash. "Look Tamra, I'm not a monster. Just get me my job back, and I won't bother you again." Jack held out the photo.

Tamra snatched up the print and swung her legs out of the car. Then she looked back and snarled, "I wouldn't get heavily into photography, Mr. Sermon. You don't have the income anymore to support an expensive hobby. Of course, maybe you could return all your empty bottles and cans. That should keep you going for a while." In one move, she snatched up his thermos, spun out of her seat, and slammed the car door with all the force she could muster.

"Bitch!" yelled Jack. His car screeched out of the parking lot, scattering students and provoking angry shouts from a campus monitor.

***

Kendra shooed out a lingering student and went down the rows to collect the inevitable array of discarded paper. Her aide came back from a computer class where she'd been placed to help the Special Ed. kids.

"How was class?" asked Kendra.

"A little better today. One of the girls finally let me help," said the assistant, wearily lowering herself to a chair.

"That's progress. We can only try our best, and the rest is up to the kids," said Kendra. She knew that in theory, when an aide or teacher accompanied Special Ed. students to a regular class, that adult was there to help everyone in the class, but the "regular" students believed you were there only to keep an eye on the "special" kids. Unsurprisingly, the Special Ed. students would rather flunk the class than call attention to themselves by accepting help.

"I don't blame the kids, Ms. Desola. By the time they get to high school the Special Ed. stigma is too much for them to deal with. So, what do you want me to do during prep?"

Can you bring out their projects for next period and the supplies? I'm gonna go get my mail. Want me to get you a snack from the machines?" offered Kendra, fastening the ties on a brown envelope.

"No, thanks. I brought a drink from home, and stocked more sodas in the fridge for the kids, too."

Kendra had purchased a small fridge for the classroom so she could give cold sodas to her students for rewards. A can of cold soda was a useful motivator, but sodas didn't come cheap. The need for that out of pocket expenditure was another thing she and Brian disagreed about.

"Thanks, I forgot to check the soda supply myself. I might give some out this afternoon," said Kendra. "Okay, I'm going. See you in a while.

To the south of the portables, a female custodian was wheeling a flatbed cart. The cart bore a trashcan, a plastic bag filled with cans for recycling and a pile of objects destined for the lost and found. Kendra's students were constantly wailing over lost possessions, so she decided to have a look. There was silvery makeup bag, a padlock, two three-ring binders, a disc player, and a small thermos. The last got her full attention.

"Morning," said Kendra, walking beside the cart. She couldn't recall the woman's name and she wasn't up close enough to be able to read the name on the woman's school ID.

"How you doing," said the custodian without stopping. One of the wheels caught on a break in the pavement. They both slowed while the custodian yanked the cart free.

"That thermos, where'd you find it? I think I know the owner." Kendra picked up the bottle.

The custodian looked rather surprised. "Oh, the way she threw that thermos away, I don't think she wants it back. She heaved it at the dumpster like it was her own worst enemy."

"She?"

"Yeah, her aim was lousy, missed the dumpster by a mile. I went over to finish the job for her, but then I thought what a waste, I can use a thermos that size. It was probably too beat up for somebody like her to keep, with those nice clothes of hers and that big, fat ring on her hand."

"I don't think the thermos belongs to the woman you saw; she probably saw it lying around and thought it was trash. But, like I said, I know the real owner," said Kendra.

"Take it, then. I don't really need it." The custodian dry washed her hands in embarrassment.

"Thanks."

The custodian shrugged. "Well, I have to get this stuff up front. Have a good one." She pushed off toward the main building.

The bottle truly was a sorry sight. Kendra absently ran a finger over a scratch beside the frayed, mascot decal. Kendra doubled back to her room the way she'd come. Her aide looked up in surprise at the quick return.

"I ran into someone. Never made it to the mailroom." she said to her aide.

The phone chose that instant to ring. The damn thing always knew when she was in a hurry. She dropped the thermos into a drawer and took the call. "This is Ms. Desola."

"Hi, Kendra, Paul here. Good news, I have an answer for you about the computer."

Kendra turned so her aide couldn't see her face. She said lightly, "Oh good, I hope it wasn't too much trouble."

"Not a bit. Turns out, it's a school computer. It's one of those outside Mr. Favor's office," said Paul.

"Ah, okay. Have you, by chance, seen anyone use either of those machines recently?"

"I'm not really in a position to keep track of what goes on over there."

"That's okay. Thanks again, Paul. Bye."

Kendra had to restrain herself from running straight over to Favor's office. That trip would take more time than she had right now.

Instead, she found her cell phone and went outside. Happy to see that the signal was adequate, she punched in Favor's extension.

Several rings later, Ginny answered.

"Hey, Ginny, this is Kendra Desola. Can I ask you a quick question?"

"Go ahead," came the terse reply.

"Do you know who uses those computers outside of your office?"

"Not a clue. I don't even know if they work. You could ask Paul. Is that all, I'm busy." The clacking of a keyboard came over the line.

"Okay. Um, I need to talk to Ray. Is he there?"

Ginny admitted that her boss was there, but she didn't want to disturb him. After some back and forth, Ginny finally agreed to put Mr. Favor on the line.

"What do you want, Ms. Desola? I said I wasn't taking calls; I'm in the middle of something."

"Sorry, just a quick question. Who's been using those computers outside of your office?"

"Huh? I don't think anyone uses them. Why, do you want them? That might be okay, but you have to ask Mrs. Prescott if you want to have them moved to your classroom."

"So you're positive nobody used them recently?"

"I said I don't know. Try asking Ginny or Paul, or even my TA, Nicole Penniman." He cut the line without a goodbye.

***

Even though the school scheduled two separate lunch periods, there were still about 800 teens on the loose during each lunch. Kendra had been searching for Nicole for twenty minutes and was about to give up when she ran into Jessica, who suggested that Nicole might be in the office wing.

Nicole, Monique and a third girl Kendra didn't know were eating at a small table normally used for holding bins of mail. Ginny wasn't there, which explained how the girls were using the space in such a carefree way. They were laughing and chatting happily. Kendra's own stomach growled. This would be another lunch she wouldn't have. Kendra needed to talk to Nicole and this was the best time to do that. She'd have to separate her from her friends, first.

"Hi, girls. Hey Nicole, Jessica told me I might find you here," said Kendra, trying to act as if she met with Nicole on a regular basis. Kendra wasn't happy to see Monique there, but hopefully, the referral from Jessica would have a strong influence on Nicole.

"What's up?" Nicole asked between mouthfuls of fries. She delicately wiped a trace of ketchup from her lower lip.

"If you wouldn't mind, I need your help with something, just for a minute or two," said Kendra, hoping that she wasn't going to have to get pushy.

"What do you want with Nicole? Isn't Jessica your little TA now?" Monique's question was more than an observation. There was considerable animosity in her voice.

Fortunately, Monique's bad manners worked in Kendra's favor. Jessica was Nicole's best friend. Nicole threw Monique a look of disapproval, picked up her backpack and rose from the table. She turned to her lunch mates, "If I don't get back before the bell, be sure to put back the chairs or I'll be in trouble."

"Maybe you'll get spanked," giggled the third girl, who quickly sobered when she saw Nicole's angry expression.

Kendra led Nicole to the building's front entrance, where the broad staircase was enclosed by two, separate sets of doors. At this hour there wouldn't be much foot traffic coming through.

"What are we doing here, Ms. Desola? I thought you wanted me to help you with something," said Nicole, looking uneasy.

"Actually, I just need to talk to you and I didn't think you would want anyone to hear."

Nicole looked both anxious and interested. "Talk about what?"

"How should I say this—we're fortunate to have a Media Academy at school, but technology has to be used responsibly. We've discovered that someone has used school equipment to create slanderous material," said Kendra in an attempt to lead into the subject without directly accusing the girl. At this point there was no proof.

To Kendra's surprise, Nicole's immediately took her arm and said in a pleading manner, "I know I should never have made that tape, Ms. Desola. I know it was wrong, I'm sorry, really!"

Kendra was confounded by this confession, which didn't sound related to the emails; a reference to a tape made no sense. She hoped that she could lead Nicole into a full explanation. She led with, "I know that you're enrolled in the Media Arts Academy. You know the rules about using the equipment. Remember, a student was expelled last year, and wound up in court."

The girl's voice was pleading. "It's not what you think. I didn't mean to do it, but you and the other teachers were talking so loud, I couldn't help hearing you, and I already was set up to record an interview for the school paper." Nicole paused, and changed her tone.

"How can I get you guys to forgive me? Maybe Mrs. Jarney won't care, but I know that Mr. Sermon and Mrs. Edwards will be really mad if it comes out the way they ranted about Mr. Zant. I mean, like, you did too—I mean, you all were saying how . . ."

Kendra was definitely interested now and wanted to draw out the whole story. "Eavesdropping is bad enough, but why record it?"

"I know I shouldn't have and I really did a bad thing when I gave the tape to Zant."

The girl went mute and began to cry. Kendra decided to take a gamble. "I don't know if you decided to tape the meeting on your own, or if Mr. Zant put you up to it, but either way, taping without permission is probably illegal. Mr. Zant isn't around anymore, but you can be held accountable."

"I know. Our teacher warned us. Are you going to get me kicked out of the Media Academy?" Nicole's voice cracked.

Kendra ignored the question. "Who else knows what went on in that meeting except you, me and the other teachers you just named?"

"I don't think anyone does. I gave it to Zant, but then, a few days later, he, he . . . " Her voice trailed off.

"If you don't mind me asking, why did you tape our meeting? Have you got a problem with me, or with one of the other Special Ed. teachers? Did you want to make us look bad, write some kind of an article?" Kendra felt Nicole's apologies were contrived; the girl was mostly sorry that she'd been caught.

"No, I've got nothing against you guys, really. I just, like, I just wanted—I thought Zant might help me if I gave the tape to him. I was trying to get on his good side cause he didn't want to let me run for office, so when I overheard the things you were saying about him, how you were writing a letter against him, I knew he'd be interested.

Kendra was so amazed she could hardly get her next question out. "You used the tape to make a deal with Mr. Zant?"

Nicole's pout showed that the deal had not been a fair one. "I just have to be class president! Coming from a dump of a school like this, I need everything I can get to beef up my college applications. But as it turned out, he didn't put my name back on the ballot after all. I should have known better—I mean, I do know better, now. Please, don't tell anyone else. I don't want to be expelled before graduation. I've had time to think about what I did and I'm really sorry." New tears streamed down her cheeks.

"I'm not promising anything. I could get in trouble for not reporting you."

Kendra knew that even if she could get a hold of the tape she wouldn't use it against Nicole. She'd destroy it instantly. The wholly metaphorical expressions of murderous intent toward Mr. Zant along with all the other, angry words on that tape would be viewed in a different light now that Zant was dead. Even a closed investigation might be reopened. Fortunately that concern was way over the girl's head. Clearly, though, Nicole had an evil side. Kendra expected she might well know something about the email. The trick was asking the right question. Time for another try.

Kendra said, "All right, let's drop the subject for the time being, but I want to ask about something else."

Nicole was visibly relieved and assumed a cooperative expression.

"Have you or your friends been using the computers next to Mr. Favor's office?"

"Huh? No, aren't they, like, password protected? When I started being his TA, Mr. Favor told me not to even think about playing around on them. Anyhow, why would I want to use those old things? There are much better ones in the labs and the library."

"You sure they're password protected?" Kendra shot her a concentrated glare.

Nicole met her eyes without flinching. "I think you should ask Mr. Favor or Ginny about that."

"All right. I think we're done here, Nicole. In the future, I hope you're more respectful of other people's privacy. Right now I'm not planning on saying anything, but you gave the tape to Zant and we don't know who has it now."

15.

Thursday Afternoon

"Paul, you there?" Kendra poked her head into the labyrinth of audiovisual gear that appeared to pre-date the invention of the transistor. Paul came around a shelving unit, intently marking an inventory sheet.

"Hi. What brings you into my den of antique wonders?" asked Paul. His smile faded when he registered the indignant look on Kendra's face.

"I think you lied to me," she declared without preamble.

"What do you mean?"

"Like you suggested, I talked to people who might know about those two computers, and everything leads right back to you. To begin with, you never told me they're password protected."

The inventory list crinkled as Paul nervously waved it like a fan. "I don't understand. You said the email was a joke. Now, all of a sudden, you're angry? I think you should tell me what's really going on."

"You know more than I do—like who sent me that email!"

"You accusing me of lying? If the email was only a joke, how come you're so upset?"

Kendra grimaced. "All right, maybe I didn't tell you everything either, but . . . " Kendra removed her glasses and rubbed her eyes before any tears could come out.

"I'd like to help if you'll let me."

"I didn't want anyone to know. Someone faked a photo and a web page to make me look like a child molester, and sent them to me in emails, along with threats to spread them around." She replaced her glasses in time to see his horrified expression.

"God, that's awful. I didn't have any idea. If you said in the first place what was going on—Look, here's what happened. Mr. Favor told me to set up some guy on the network, and that computer was handy so I used it. I didn't want to violate the rule that no one but school staff can access the system, but Favor is a VP. What was I supposed to do? Now, I don't care if I get into trouble. I won't shield a guy who sends that kind of email." Paul pulled out some gum, offering the packet to Kendra before cramming two sticks into his mouth.

"So, who was this guy?"

"Sorry, never saw him before. I don't remember the guy's name. I'm better with computers than I am with people."

"What did he look like?"

Paul shrugged. "Just a guy. Young. Ordinary. I don't remember anything else about him. I was really busy that day because of a software glitch. My mind was on other things."

Paul went to his desk. "Because I ended up having to call in some help that day, I can check my records and give you the date." He sifted through a mass of paper until he found his electronic planner. He recited a date and apologized again, "You gonna ask Mr. Favor who the guy is?"

"Yes, and I'll tell Mr. Favor that you didn't offer me the information until I badgered you."

Paul gave her a concerned look. "Kendra, have you thought of going to the police?"

"I'd rather not have to. And, please, don't tell anybody else, okay?"

"All right. This makes me think, if something like that could be done right under my nose, right on campus, what else is going on I don't know about? You know, if you let me have a look at those emails, maybe I could find out something more helpful."

"I'll let you know on that. I have to go now."

Kendra hurried down the hall. Her class was being taught under the supervision of her adult aide, which was completely legal for brief spans of time, no matter what the ex-VP had tried to rule. The kids were supposed to be watching a video, but there was no guarantee things were going smoothly. What she wanted to do was talk to Favor, but all she could do was to return to her classroom instead.

Damn it, whoever sent that mail was going to be held accountable. She anxiously rubbed her hands together and stopped in her tracks. Her fingers were greasy with some black substance. She must have inadvertently touched something dirty in Paul's storage room. She veered from her path and went into the girls' room a few yards ahead.

She turned on the water but instead of a soap dispenser, she saw only its footprint on the scarred wall. Of course! How could she have been so stupid? What was she thinking? But that was a thought for another time. Kendra raced toward her classroom, wiping her hands dry on her pants.

***

"Five more minutes and then we're going to discuss your work," announced Kendra to the class. She was pleased to see that today's project was catching their interest. Jessica was helping a slower group at a table to one side. Everyone was working quietly for the time being. It really was a blessing that her 6th period class was relatively well behaved, since any self-discipline her freshman students possessed tended to wear away as the day progressed.

The kids looked up at the sound of heavy footsteps and the rustle of shopping bags. A female student shrank into her chair and with a deeply mortified face gasped, "Ma!"

All eyes took in the woman's garish outfit and bouffant hairdo. The kids stared in captivated silence as the woman purposefully walked over to Kendra. "Ms. Desola, I hope I'm not bothering you in class."

Politely, Kendra answered, "Of course not, Mrs. Borghesi."

"I don't mean to interrupt," she said, pulling Kendra to a relatively secluded area. All the surrounding young ears attempted to tune in. "I just wanted to thank you for helping out with that problem Crystal had. The bastard is locked up now and won't be putting a gun to another girl's head for a long, long time."

Kendra looked over the woman's broad shoulder to make sure their conversation wasn't being overheard. Crystal's tablemates were giggling, but they didn't seem to have heard anything. Students at the other tables were refocusing their energy on the assignment.

"Mrs. Borghesi, all I did was to help Crystal tell her story to the counselors," said Kendra, backing still farther into the corner. The woman pushed three bulging plastic bags at Kendra, who quickly set them on a table.

"No, no, I thank you so much, Ms. Desola. You were the only one who believed my daughter. Mrs. Jarney just told her to go to the campus policeman, but he didn't take my daughter seriously because she's in Special Ed."

Kendra had spent hours deciphering the story told by a hysterical girl with a language disability, so she did appreciate the thank you from the parent, but the timing wasn't the best. Hoping to send the woman on her way, she said, "Well, you should really be thanking the counselors, because the officer didn't listen to me either, not until the counselors convinced him."

She didn't add what a hard sell that had been to the counselors. Kendra knew from experience that in the eyes of most counselors, she also fell into the "Special Ed.: Do Not Take Seriously" category.

"But that's their job, Ms. Desola. You went out of your way, like you always do. Crystal likes you so much. That's why she went to you."

"Well, it's all over with now," she said with the hope that this conversation was also at an end.

The girl's mother, however, showed no signs of having a language impediment and launched into a description of the home cooked foods just given to Kendra.

"Ms. Desola, do you want us to wait, or should we just pack up 'til next time?" called out Jessica. This fortunately broke the tide of gratitude that surged from Mrs. Borghesi.

Kendra seized on the moment. "We really need to start the presentations now," she said to her TA.

"I've taken enough of your time," said the woman.

"Thanks for all the food," said Kendra.

The woman gave her embarrassed daughter a kiss and left.

Kendra turned to her class. "Which would like to be first?"

***

Nate was sitting in the custodians' room, reading a newspaper and drinking a soda.

"Hi, Nate. I don't mean to bother you. I wasn't sure what time you got here."

157

"Howdy, Ms. Desola. I got here a little early. What's up?

"I hope you don't think I'm insane, well, I'm sure you will think I'm insane for asking…" Kendra hesitated.

The custodian smiled and said, "We're all insane or we wouldn't be here."

"This is going to sound kind of funny, but I was in one of the girls' rooms today, and I saw that there wasn't any soap."

Nate showed only mild surprise. "How come you didn't use a staff bathroom?" he asked.

"The only soap I ever see in the women's restroom is what teachers bring in. I always assumed they don't like the school soap, so they bring their own?"

"Why are you so interested in bathroom soap all of a sudden? You going to make some kind of complaint?" Nate testily folded some pages of newsprint.

Kendra was taken aback by the intensity of the custodian's reaction. "No, this isn't about complaints. I told you that you'd think I'm crazy for asking." Seeing Nate relax, she hurriedly added to this question, "It's true then—the bathrooms never have soap?"

There was a protracted silence. The custodian contem-plated his boot-clad feet. Finally he stood and said, "Come with me."

Nate led her to the nearest boys' bathroom. Although it was past the hour when any students would be using the facility, he banged on the door before going inside. "You can't be too careful," he said, opening the boys' room door and leading the way inside.

There were crunching sounds beneath their feet. The scene in front of her was worse than she could have imagined. And after a full day's use, the stench was almost unbearable. The floor was strewn with what looked like sand. An upturned trash can, overflowing toilets and a garbage filled sink completed the picture.

"This is awful." Kendra stepped back, more than ready to leave.

"See this?" Nate gestured at the wall above the sink, where several rows of bolts protruded.

"Yeah, I see."

"This is what happens to soap and towel holders. We used to put 'em up, but the kids kept tearing 'em down. And if one or two of the soap holders ever stayed in one piece long enough for us to

158

fill, then the kids would go and empty all the soap out—squirt it, pour it on the floors, into the sinks and toilets."

"Ahhh." Unable to take another breath of bathroom air, Kendra backed out to the hallway and sucked in a few, deep fresh breaths. The custodian came to join her.

Kendra said, "Okay, I get the picture. The bottom line is that you stopped putting soap in the kid's bathrooms—" She held up a hand to stop Nate from interrupting. "I understand your reason and I'm in no position to argue. I just feel sorry that a few bad kids are able to dictate what happens to everyone else."

"We're sorry too, but nobody says the kids can't carry their own soap if they want. The stuff they bring themselves is much nicer, anyhow. That's why the faculty has always brought in their own. The only member of the staff who ever used the school soap was the nurse who used to work here, so we gave her a supply and she refilled her dispensers herself."

Nate clearly misinterpreted the troubled look on Kendra's face, because he quickly explained, "The custodians can't get anything nicer. We're not the ones that buy the soap. Someone takes care of that Downtown."

"Is any of the nurse's soap left on campus anymore?" asked Kendra.

Nate gave Kendra the same look he gave his youngest son when the boy spent five minutes cutting up his peanut butter sandwich into tiny squares, and spacing the pieces in orderly rows on his plate before eating it. "I have no idea."

Kendra said slowly, "Then what you mopped up from the hallway floor on the day you found Zant; was that soap?" She watched his face closely.

This last remark seemed to catch Nate off guard. "Probably."

"Liquid soap is slimy. Someone could easily fall if they walked in it," said Kendra, maintaining an even tone. "How do you suppose it got there?"

"The whole boys' bathroom was soaped. I guess some kid did it. That's their idea of fun. I don't try to look for reasons anymore. I try not to think about it. You just saw—would you want to think about what you were cleaning in there?" When Kendra nodded in agreement, he went on, "I have to do this every day, you know. One mess after the next. I don't go wasting time on why or how.

Mickey Hoffman

And speaking of work, I have to start my shift."

"Just a sec. So, the stuff on the hall floor—that could have come from the bathroom, right? Like someone tracked it?"

"Yeah, you know, the detectives asked about footprints, too."

"Did you see more than one line of tracks, maybe from more than one person?"

"Well, I was kind of interrupted when I saw Mr. Zant lying there, didn't stop to look at anything after that. I just backed out of the hall real quick." Nate thought some more. "Now that you mention it, I wouldn't call it one straight line of tracks, I think it was more like a few of them. But hey, I just clean, I don't do research on the dirt. You're awfully interested in this. Are you trying to get at something?"

"Did you tell the cops any of this?"

"Yeah, sure. I told the cops I mopped up some soap in the hall. They didn't seem as interested in the soap as you are, that's for sure. I'm sure they know their business." The custodian was tired of the topic.

Well, thought Kendra, the cops couldn't be faulted. They wouldn't even think to question the presence of soap near a messy kids' bathroom. Most people would assume that soap and bathrooms went together.

"I don't mean to be rude, Ms. Desola, but I have to get going."

"Sorry to make you late," she called after him.

***

Kendra walked slowly toward the front offices to get her mail. She felt depressed and tired. Her email problem remained unsolved and with every day that passed, she felt less comfortable at Standard High. Did anyone in this place ever tell the truth?

Deep in her worries, Kendra hardly noticed the mailroom was busy for that hour. She reached into her box and blindly pulled out the contents. She was half way to the workroom when she heard someone say, "Condolences, dear, for one of your colleagues."

Another whispered, "She doesn't even act like she's upset."

A third voice said, "I bet she doesn't know yet."

That brought Kendra to a halt. A music teacher pointed to a memo sticking out of her handful of mail. She plucked it out and

160

read: "We are sorry to inform the staff that Jack Sermon had a fatal car accident this morning. His only living relative, his sister, has asked that you do not contact her at this time. I am sure that our entire faculty deeply regrets the loss of such a wonderful colleague. Our Friendship Committee will be making suitable arrangements."

Through her tears, Kendra saw Jack—the way she'd seen him that very morning, tired and unsteady on his feet.

***

Brian came into the kitchen with Bobbins at his ankles. "You're not having any of this mu-shu shrimp, Mr. Cat," he said, holding the bag higher. Bobbins jumped to the table, anticipating Brian's next act. A fork and spoon clattered to the floor.

Kendra carried the unwilling cat to the bedroom. "Bob-bins just wanted to help us clear the table," she said. She went up to Brian and gave him a hug.

"Is that all the greeting I get?"

"I'm starving!"

Brian put the plastic bag of food on the counter and made a face at the small thermos that was nestled between two rubber-banded stacks of mail.

"Where did you get this thermos? No offense, but you don't drink out of that thing, do you?" He picked it up. "It's got a decal of your school mascot, for god's sake. Are you going all 'rah rah' on me now, too?"

Kendra sat down heavily, and burst into tears.

Brian squatted next to her. "Hey, I'm just kidding. Did I say something wrong?"

"It's not your fault. The thermos bottle belonged to Jack Sermon, and he died in a car accident today."

"God, that's awful. Wow, I'm sorry." He put his arms around her. "Are you okay?"

She wiped her eyes. "Yeah, I'm okay. Jack and I weren't close or anything, but we worked together, and he wasn't such a bad guy, you know? I'm just sort of in shock."

Brian set two dishes on the table and went back for the food.

161

"At least he didn't die at school. Sorry, I didn't mean that. So, what are you doing with his thermos, if you don't mind my asking?"

"Oh, I have a use for it"

"Please, not another home decorating project. You've been watching that channel too much. Well, this is your house, so go for it. I can't wait to see how a thermos bottle blossoms into a light fixture or—ouch!" He jumped at Kendra's pinch. "I'll be good. I promise. Let's eat before Bobbins breaks the bedroom door down." He opened the cardboard containers.

"That's right, this is my house to do with as I see fit. You can do whatever you want in your house, and I will do what I want in mine."

"We'll see about that," said Brian, flicking his eyebrows.

She said, "Maybe we should move to the dining room, give Mrs. Ireland something to watch."

"Only if you want to dine in the nude." Brian gave her a suggestive look.

"That's funny, but I'm here every day. I have to live with her next door so I don't think we should make the situation any weirder," said Kendra, helping herself to a generous portion of Sichuan style eggplant.

Brian gave a mischievous look. "At least I know someone's gonna miss me for a week."

"A week? I thought you were coming back Tuesday."

"The client changed the timeline for the exhibit."

"Talk about people changing jobs." She winced at her ill-advised remark. "Never mind, forget I said that."

Brian reached over and rumpled her hair affectionately. "You and poor Mrs. Ireland. I have to make sure I keep at least one of you satisfied."

***

The door chimes rang as Kendra stepped out of the shower. She yelled, "Just a minute!"

She grabbed a towel, dried herself enough to slip on one of Brian's t-shirts, and wrapped the towel around her hips for extra coverage.

Kendra opened the door for Maretta. "I thought you were going to call. How did you know I'd be home alone?"

Maretta gave a sardonic grin. "Isn't this basketball night?" Her question was rhetorical.

If Brian had been here, Maretta wouldn't have come. For some reason, the two had taken an instant dislike to one another. "Give me a minute to change, make yourself at home."

Kendra shouted from the bedroom, "Did you hear about Jack?"

"Yes, and I'm very upset. Can we not talk about him? I've been on the phone for hours with different people and I'm all cried out.

"Sure. I know how you feel."

"Anyway, I didn't come over to talk about him. You said you found out something."

"Do you want anything to drink?" Kendra appeared, now fully dressed, but still combing out her hair. She took a seat on a footstool.

"Your hair dripped water on the hall floor."

"That's what I was gonna tell you, about the floor. Guess what?"

"That's not a trivia category I'm good with," said Maretta rolling her eyes.

"When's the last time you saw any soap in a bathroom at school?"

"What? I came over because you said there have been important developments," complained Maretta.

"I'm almost positive Zant fell down the stairs because he slipped on liquid soap that was on the floor up there."

Maretta's voice didn't carry Kendra's level of enthusiasm for this purported clue. "That doesn't seem so mysterious to me. Soap isn't a rare commodity, you know. How does this change what happened to Zant in any meaningful way?"

"I happen to know that the soap wasn't the stuff that you or I would buy. The stuff on the hallway floor was school hand soap. Except the point is, the school doesn't stock hand soap anymore." Kendra waved her comb emphatically. "Nate told me that the custodians haven't supplied the bathrooms with soap in years because the students misused it and the staff prefers to bring their own. At least we know the women do."

"Give me a minute here. As usual, I'm a step behind you.

Okay, your real question is, if Zant slipped on soap, where did the soap come from?"

"Precisely!" Kendra pointed her comb for emphasis.

"All right, I see. That makes the situation more unusual. So where do you think the soap came from?"

"From the nurse's bathroom, or maybe from those boxes that are stored in the nurse's room. Nate told me the nurse was the only one who used it—back in the days when there was a school nurse."

"Okay, so let's say a soapy floor caused the accident. I see there could be something fishy about that, but Zant had to have a reason to go up there in the first place, or he wouldn't have slipped and fallen. If you ask me, the real mystery is why he went over to that hallway in the first place," said Maretta, putting in her objections.

"Yes, that's a big question, and one that didn't seem to bother the cops. And of course, the cops didn't see anything odd about a mess of soap in a hall near the bathrooms. But if I report what I know, the cops might start looking for murder suspects again, and I want to stay under their radar—unless I need their help to take care of the emailer."

"You don't think Zant's death was an accident." Maretta said slowly.

"What do you think? Doesn't it strike you there are too many coincidences?"

"I think coincidences do happen. And I also think that if what happened to Zant was truly by design, you shouldn't be playing detective like this. Anyone involved in causing his death would want to kill your interest in the matter, to use a verb you should worry about. Hasn't that occurred to you?" She gave Kendra a pointed look. "Just remember, it's best for all of us if Zant *wasn't* murdered. You should just stick to finding out who sent those emails before anything else happens."

Kendra moved to her couch and sat back wearily. "Point taken. I'll focus on my own problem."

"I wish I could believe you."

"I really have been working on the email problem. I found out which computer they came from and I know it was a man that sent them."

"Fantastic! Who?"

"Don't know the man's identity yet, but the emails came from a computer near Ray Favor's office. And this afternoon I found out that Favor actually knows the person!

"So why didn't he tell you who the man is?" Maretta was bursting with excitement.

"No. That's the hold up. Paul was the one who told me. Ray left campus before I could talk to him."

"Well, don't let it go," urged Maretta. "And the minute you do find out, go right to the cops! They'll be able to see you're the victim. Then, if you just have to, tell them about Zant too. After that, you've got to stop poking around. Promise?"

"I'm going to get a beer, want one?" Kendra sidestepped the question and headed for the back of the house.

"You're not going to change the subject that easily," said Maretta, following in hot pursuit.

"On the contrary, take a look at this." Kendra pulled the Missing Cat notice from a drawer in the hutch. "Just one more thing for me to keep from Brian."

16.

Friday Morning

On this rainy Friday morning the campus lay before her veiled in fog, a monochromatic expanse of cement, sooty stucco and puddles. Kendra hunched deeper into the hood of her raincoat. She gloomily predicted that her classroom would be flooded.

As she entered the quad between the portables, Kendra saw that Jack's classroom door was wide open. A frail, elderly woman stepped out, unfurled an umbrella, and picked up a canvas bag. Struggling under the weight of the bag, she tottered down the wooden steps. Kendra cut across the pavement and came up beside her.

"Can I help you carry that?" Kendra lowered her head to peer under the umbrella.

"How nice of you. That's my car over there. You're Ms. Desola, aren't you. I think we met once at Open House or something." She handed the heavy bag to Kendra and continued toward the parking lot.

"Yes, I remember. I know you're Jack's sister, but I'm embarrassed to admit that I don't remember your name."

"I'm Renee. Jack's only living relative." The woman blinked rapidly.

"I'm so sorry," blurted Kendra. "We all are. Jack was a good man. We're all sad about losing him. If there's something—the principal said you didn't want anything, but if there's—"

"Jack always said that word travels fast around this place. But I don't think anyone here will miss him."

Kendra offered, "Don't say that. I'll miss him. Really, if there's anything I can do?"

"Oh, it won't be easy, but I'm sure everything will all work out in the end." Renee blinked back tears.

This was very awkward. This woman was a total stranger but Kendra wished she could help, somehow. What could she do or say? She blurted out, "I could make you some tea in my classroom. It's just across the way here."

"Thanks for offering, but I'm fine. I hate to say, but Jack's death was probably more of a shock to you than it was to me. The mood Jack was in lately, I knew something bad was going to happen. He neglected his health even worse than usual." Renee paused as her plastic rain hat fluttered in a gust of wind. She righted it with her free hand and added, "I begged him over and over to watch his diabetes, eat right. Of course, Jack never was one to take my advice."

"But Mrs. Prescott said that Jack died in a car crash!" The words were out of Kendra's mouth before was able to stop them. She gave herself a mental kick for, once again, being inappropriately inquisitive.

"That's more or less true," said Renee, fortunately not taking umbrage at Kendra's remark. "In my opinion, it was the crash that killed him. The cops assumed he had a heart attack while driving. That doesn't sit right with me. The autopsy will prove them wrong, wait and see. Jack had a bit of blood pressure, true, but I'm sure that the accident had nothing to do with his heart."

"Eh?"

Renee explained, "His diabetes. Jack wasn't eating right. Jack had already had a few near misses before on the road. That's why I bought him a little thermos to keep in his car. That way if he felt light-headed he could pull over and have some juice to raise his blood sugar." Her voice faded with the last words.

Kendra recalled her last meeting with Jack. "You know, yesterday I talked to him before school and he did seem kind of dizzy."

Renee gave Kendra a hard look. "Before school? Yesterday? You might be the last person that saw him alive."

"He wasn't driving when I saw him," mumbled Kendra, who felt a guilty need to clarify the situation.

The old woman seemed not to hear, and explained, "He ran his car right into the side of that self-storage warehouse a few blocks from here. The cops said an eyewitness thought Jack tried to pull off the road, but lost control of the car." Renee unlocked the door of her ancient hatchback.

Horrified, Kendra felt an irrational desire to prove herself blameless. "I actually did ask him if he felt good enough to drive, and he said he'd sit in his car until he felt okay. I never thought of blood sugar; I just thought since he'd been out sick lately—"

Renee stepped back and shrieked, "Out sick? He was on unpaid leave after a disciplinary hearing. He was going to be fired. How can you pretend you don't know? Fine bunch you are!" Renee snatched the bag from Kendra and heaved it into her car.

Kendra didn't want to be one of that "bunch," but maybe she was. She knew anything more she could say to Renee would only aggravate the woman further. Maybe she couldn't do anything for Renee, but there might be something she could do for Jack, and that was to make sure justice was served.

She said, "Sorry," and ran to her classroom, planning her next step.

***

Ray set the computer monitor on a chair and went back for the components. Where was that custodian who was supposed to show up before the first bell? Yeah, right. The man wasn't on walkie-talkie either. And Ginny was late; that woman possessed a natural warning system that kept her from any contact with manual labor.

Ray had waited fifteen minutes before deciding to tackle the job himself. If he'd any idea how filthy those computers were, he wouldn't have touched the damn equipment. Now his white shirt was soiled, maybe ruined. He stormed back to his office to call the custodian again.

Ray didn't know why Kendra was interested in those two computers, but he was glad she'd brought them to his attention. They'd been there as long as he could remember, but he'd never given them any thought. Recently, though, he'd been paying more attention to potential security problems, and he realized unsupervised computers could lead to problems, password protected or not. Many hackers were of high school age. Standard High might have some students who were savvy enough to hack into the system.

The unsightly storage dump in the old nurse's room was another potential trouble spot. He wasn't sure what was in some of those cartons. What if they contained some toxic cleaning products? Ray didn't want to test his luck to see whether some dumb kid would sniff something to get high.

The custodian was supposed to remove the computers and computer desks and then go ahead and clear out all the boxes and other junk from the nurse's room. Ray had already done the first part, expedited the situation by moving it all in to one place. That way, when the custodian did show up, he couldn't pretend to be confused about what needed to be moved. What was left was a simple "clear out the whole room" plan.

He dialed the custodian's line and left another testy voice mail message. He knew why no one came. The custodians had been the ones who co-opted that room for storage in the first place, to avoid having to walk back to the main storeroom to get supplies. From there the room went downhill until it became a public dump.

His eyes rested on an iridescent pink ballpoint pen that lay next to his phone. That was another hazard to take care of, the sooner the better. Again, he dialed and when the counselor's voice mail instructed him to leave his message, he said,

"Hello, this is Ray Favor. I'd like you to reassign my TA, Nicole Penniman. I don't need a TA right now and Julia Chatin has been complaining that she's completely bogged down with errands. I'd like to help her out by giving her my TA. Let me know when you've done it. Thanks." Ray hung up.

He was certain that he was providing a morning's entertainment for, at minimum, the entire counseling staff, but hell with it, there was nothing that could be done about that. For a second, he even thought he heard laughter coming from the counseling office and was greatly relieved to find that the squeaks came from a custodial cart, which came to a rolling stop at his office.

***

"Hey, guess who?"

"I knew it was you, or someone doing a very good imitation," said Maretta, unlocking her door to admit Kendra.

"I'm here to ask you a big favor. I thought I better ask in person, in case I have to get down on my knees. Can you take 5th period class for me later today if I need you to?"

169

Maretta checked her scheduling book. "I can, but you'll owe me big time."

"So that's how you treat a friend?" Kendra shrugged out of her raincoat and stepped over to the tiny electric heater behind Maretta's desk.

"Well, consider what you're asking. If you wanted something small like one of my kidneys there would be no problem, but taking one of your classes during my prep, that's huge."

"You're so funny, you know? Seriously, now, I'll need you 5th period unless I call you before then and cancel. Okay?" Kendra raised her hands in supplication.

"Fine, I'll be there. Mind telling me why, though? You didn't say anything about this last night."

"After I talk to a few more people I'll tell you everything. Hey, this heat feels good. I wonder if the circuits in my room would handle one of these."

"Don't try to distract me. Are you going to see Ray Favor? We agreed last night you'd focus on the emails," said Maretta in a disapproving tone.

Kendra pulled at a stray lock of damp hair, deliberately avoiding her friend's gaze.

"Well, after more consideration, I think that if I can tie up a few more loose ends I'll be at the point where I can safely go to the cops and tell them what I know about Zant."

"Okay, okay, I know I won't change your mind, but why don't you wait until after school to do whatever it is you want to do, and I'll go with you."

"Relax, I'm just talking to a few people on campus."

"Zant was on campus, too, and look what happened to him." Maretta anxiously fingered an earring.

"I see your point," admitted Kendra. In spite of her pro-testations, she valued Maretta's opinion. "Don't worry. I'll be careful. And, not to change the subject, but I just ran into Jack's sister and she told me Jack was going to be fired."

"No way! So, that's why he didn't come to the last department meeting. And Tamra never said a word." Maretta hissed her disgust.

"Yeah, she must have known. I feel even worse now about poor Jack. We can talk about that later. I have to get back to my room."

Kendra zipped her raincoat.

"You're sure I can't I convince you to wait until after school?"

Kendra laughed. "You'd be a lot of protection."

"You're too stubborn. Look, I hate to do this, but I won't watch your class unless you call one of those detectives right now and make an appointment to talk to them." Maretta pointed to the phone on her desk."

Kendra frowned. "That's not fair."

"If you don't like my bargain, maybe Allana will agree to watch your kids this afternoon?" Maretta knew how to get Kendra's attention.

"Now you're really threatening me. All right. I'll call the cops, but I don't have the number on me."

Maretta opened a small leather case and with an evil smile passed a business card to Kendra. "Detective Tapia left a stack in the staff room. Perhaps he's psychic."

"Let's hope not."

Kendra was relieved when the call went to a voice mail center. She left a message asking Detective Tapia to call her.

"Satisfied, Ms. Edwards?"

"I guess I have to be."

"Glad to know you're happy, dear. I'm really running late now. There will be a lesson plan waiting for you on my desk, 5th period."

***

The harsh fluorescent ceiling lights glanced off the old Formica tables. Kendra wondered if the yellow, orange and blue plastic chairs were meant to be cheerful. Perhaps, those colors were appealing to very young children, but they didn't seem to cheer up high school kids and the colors gave her a headache. After all her efforts to beautify the room, even painting the walls at her own expense, that hideous furniture squatted there like a metaphorical finger of defiance.

Why did she always take on impossible tasks? Kendra reflected that Maretta was probably right. She habitually made things harder for herself by overstepping her limits, being too compulsive, too analytical. Perhaps she did have a character flaw.

Mickey Hoffman

In spite of the lecture she'd just given herself, Kendra picked up the phone.

"You have reached the office of Special Education, Site Supervisors," the voice mail started. Kendra was trying to decide whether to leave a message when the recording cut off and a woman's voice inquired, "Who's calling?"

"This is Kendra Desola, from Standard High—"

"It's me, Kendra. I forgot to shut the machine off when I got here. I was planning to call you, actually," said Tamra.

Kendra said, "I finished the behavior plans."

"That's exactly why I was going to call you. Everything has to be last minute with you people."

"You could have picked them up from me while you were at school yesterday morning." Kendra held her breath.

"Damn, you're right, but I didn't know they were ready. I'll have to come get them." Tamra gave a sigh of distaste. "Please leave them for me in the mailroom."

Unable to control her voice any longer, Kendra mumbled an affirmative and hung up quickly. Tamra did not realize she had just volunteered the information that she'd most likely been the last person to come in contact with Jack Sermon before his death.

Kendra grabbed the nearest object, fortunately an eraser, and threw it at the wall. She wanted to do something physical before she burst. A short sprint out the door and she could be jogging across the field. No, what good was a run when what she really wanted to do was to pack her stuff, walk out and never come back to this place.

The warning bell blasted. The school day was about to begin. She heard one of her students shouting words to some hip hop song. How could she desert the kids? They didn't deserve that. Well, most of them didn't. She pulled her comforting, thick sweater in closer to her chest and sat at her desk. She would grab another few minutes to talk herself down, and make the kids wait outside until the last possible second.

***

The sun was breaking through, making her walk more pleasant, even if her destination was not. Ray might refuse to talk to her or

172

he could continue to lie, and she'd end up with nothing.

When Kendra arrived at Ray's office, she saw that the computer tables were gone from the nearby hall. There were lines like skid marks on the floor. Her eyes followed the black markings. They led to the Nurse's alcove, which, to her surprise, was completely empty. She felt her heart race.

Ginny was talking on her headset. For her to be that engrossed in a conversation, she must be trading gossip. The secretary pointed at the VP's door to indicate Ray was in, for once not giving Kendra the third degree.

Kendra was losing courage. What if Ray was personally involved with the emails? That would be too freaky. Maybe she should have handed this over to Detective Tapia. But he hadn't called her back. Too late, here she was.

Ray was pouring over a desk strewn with work and didn't look happy to see her. He didn't look at all threatening either. That was reassuring.

"Ms. Desola, how nice of you to spend your precious lunch period visiting me,"

"If you'd told me the truth, I wouldn't be here wasting *your* precious time," she sniped back. "I know you let someone use one of the computers I asked about. And don't blame Paul—I made him tell me."

Ray countered cautiously, "Why is this an issue?"

Kendra closed the office door. "If you don't already know, I've received two anonymous emails and they were sent from one of those computers. Someone's been threat-ening me with a slander that could cost me my career and make my life hell for years to come." Before he could protest, she raised her palm to stop him. "Before you ask, I won't give you any details. The point is, you know who sent them to me."

Favor stood up and uttered a few words of disbelief, but Kendra insisted. "Who's the guy that Paul set up on that computer?"

The VP stumbled to explain. "A friend told me he wanted to play a joke on you from inside the system. He knew you'd find out the email was in-house, and he wanted you to think it came from one of the other teachers. That's all I know about it."

"Who was it?"

"Brian. It was Brian."

Kendra felt the room go cold. It was all she could do to say, "No."

Ray didn't reply. A sneeze could be heard on the other side of the partition, reminding Kendra that she couldn't scream the way she wanted to. Instead, she stood rooted and silent.

Ray spoke first. "I know this looks bad, but even if Brian used that computer, he would never threaten you. There must be another explanation." Seeing tears in Kendra's eyes, Ray quickly explained, "Look, I think there's been a mistake. Brian said he was going to play a trick on you, that he wanted to send you mushy letters and make you think someone nerdy at work had a crush on you, a joke, that's all. You're telling me he did something that I can't believe Brian would ever do. You can't think that either!"

"Okay, then who else could it be?"

"I don't know."

Kendra wanted to believe Brian was innocent, but she'd always thought the emailer might be trying to get her to quit, and the timing was right. The Megan's Law page had arrived after Brian found out Zant was dead.

Maybe Ray was still lying to her? She felt like grabbing his tie and yanking it, real hard. "Except for Brian, did Paul put anyone else on those machines? They're password protected."

"I don't know." The VP switched to professional brisk-ness. "It's impossible for me to know if Brian was the only one who used that machine. I'd hate to think Paul lied to you. Maybe some kid hacked the computer. I bet you don't have to be a genius to break into our network."

She said, "I can't be sure it was Brian, but don't pretend you have no involvement in what happened. Regardless of who sent the emails, those computers were your responsibility."

"Now, you're not going to make a big deal out of this, are you? Look outside. I've already had those machines removed. So it's all taken care of."

Kendra fumed at the way he trivialized the situation. "It's not taken care of until I know for sure that those emails will stop!"

"Ray returned to his chair with a dramatic sigh. "Just don't be piling blame on me! You should be grateful to me; I saved your butt big time with that tape Zant had."

Kendra did a double take. "You've got the tape?"

Ray saw Kendra's expression and grinned. "You know about the tape, eh? Well, don't make waves about my com-puter oversight because I made sure the tape never got to an audience."

"You took the tape from Zant's desk! Do you know the detectives were really interested in that busted desk drawer?" She was shocked to hear Ray laugh.

"Well, it's none of their business, is it?"

"They were trying to make it my business."

"Sorry about that. I had to do something after Zant went out of his way to tell me that Nicole had given him a present. He implied that he'd use it to bring down my career—you know how he was—so I went to have a look."

"And you found the tape."

"I saw the envelope and I knew right away it had to come from Nicole. When I opened it and found a homemade tape, locked away like that, I got worried. I took it away to play it, see what it was." Ray looked apologetic and embarrassed at the same time.

This was getting into territory both of them wanted to avoid. Kendra was familiar with some of the gossip, but she'd always deemed it unlikely that Ray Favor would get on such familiar terms with a female student. There was no real reason to believe school gossip, to think that anything inappropriate was going on between Ray and Nicole.

Kendra, herself, was experiencing a taste of what malicious slander could do. She didn't know what other people would think of her if they saw the faked web page or the altered photo, but she hoped they wouldn't jump to judgment. After all that had happened recently Kendra was beyond being able to worry about Ray's conduct.

"I don't care about what's on the tape. I only care about making sure I don't get any more of those emails." On the contrary, she thought, the tape could be used to her advantage, especially the fact that Favor was the one who stole it from Zant's desk.

"Just don't jump to any conclusions" Ray added in a softer tone, "When Brian gets back, I'll take you guys out to dinner."

"I don't think so," she replied on her way out.

***

175

During lunch, a certain clique of senior girls habitually roosted along the fence near the soccer field. Today, Kendra found Nicole there with a small group of friends.

"Sorry to interrupt your lunch, Nicole, but I need you to come with me," said Kendra.

"Now?" whined Nicole. She took a huge bite out of her sandwich, as if to demonstrate she couldn't walk and eat at the same time.

"Is there a problem?" asked one of Nicole's friends. The girl's tone said that if there was a problem, Kendra was causing it. The girl's body language was patterned after the afternoon talk shows where guests routinely spring at each other's throats.

This isn't going well, Kendra thought. She tried to ignore the possibility the situation could get ugly and focused on her target. "Nicole, I'm sure you'd prefer to have our conversation in private."

To the obvious amazement of her friends, Nicole handed her drink to a companion and gathered up her things. Kendra headed for her classroom with Nicole unwillingly trailing behind. When they reached the portables, a couple of students ran over, pleading to gain entry to the classroom. Kendra sent them away and led an unhappy Nicole inside.

The girl threw down her backpack and stood just inside the door. There must have been something in Nicole's upbringing that had conditioned her to acquiesce to adult authority, or she'd never have agreed to come with Kendra, but defiance was implicit in her posture.

Nicole opened, "Why don't you leave me alone!"

For an answer, Kendra reached into a cabinet and brought out the small net. Nicole's chin jerked, but she said nothing. "I'd like my lizard back," said Kendra looking straight into the girl's narrowed eyes.

"Lizard."

"The one that you stole from Zant's tank," appended Kendra.

Nicole raised her chin. "I don't know what you're talking about. You're crazy." The girl started to leave.

Kendra knew that she must handle this just right. Nicole wasn't going to be cooperative unless it was in her own self-interest to do so. Given Ray's recent admission, Kendra had a better hand to play.

"Then, let's change the subject. The cops found out that there was a theft in Mr. Zant's office right around the time of his accident."

Nicole feigned disinterest. "So?"

"The cops might be interested to know that Ray Favor was the one who broke into Mr. Zant's desk. And stole a cassette tape."

Nicole gazed fixedly at a chart of the Periodic Table as if determined to commit the elements to memory.

Kendra continued, "The cops would be even more interested to know that Mr. Favor stole the tape only because you made it, and Ray worried he might be on it." Kendra let her voice rise suggestively, hating herself for what she was doing.

Nicole roused from her contemplation of the elements. She grumbled, "Why would Mr. Favor think I'd do some-thing like that?"

Under other circumstances, Kendra would have found Nicole's question quite interesting. Maybe the girl was so amazed that Ray didn't trust her that she wasn't thinking about the bigger picture. Kendra wasn't about to waste time puzzling that out.

"Actually, Mr. Zant went and told Mr. Favor that you'd given him a gift. He didn't say what sort of gift it was. Ask Mr. Favor if you don't believe me."

Nicole went still. Kendra let her stew. The girl played with her thin braids. At last, Nicole looked up and asked, "Are you going to say something to the cops about the tape, or about me and Ray? We haven't done anything wrong, I swear."

"I'd like to talk about the lizard. If you won't answer my questions, I'll have to let the cops ask them. I'm giving you the benefit of the doubt, here."

"All right. Ask me, then." Nicole spoke so softly Kendra moved closer to hear.

"First, I want to know about the lizard. You were on campus the afternoon of Zant's accident, weren't you? And you took the poor thing."

"Yes, all right, yes. I took the stupid lizard. I wanted to get back at Zant after he didn't put me back on the ballot, you know?" Her voice was filled with self-justification but she looked scared, trapped.

"You took the animal, and then what?"

"My idea was to put the thing in one of the gross boys' rooms and then make Zant have to hunt through every one of them until he found it." She gave an anxious look at Kendra.

"Like the bathroom behind the auditorium?"

"Yeah. Monique said we should pick one bathroom and, like, do something to really mess up the room, so Zant would get all stinky dirty." Nicole spoke without guilt, merely describing what was, to her, a mundane gag.

Kendra shook off her revulsion and said, "You used hand soap to make the mess."

"Yeah, I remembered from my freshman year how the kids used to pour the soap all over. I knew there was some in a carton in the old nurse's room. So, we dumped a ton on the boys' room floor, and then we let the lizard loose in there." She stopped as if that was enough explanation.

Kendra thought of several questions, but only said, "And then?"

"Then, I used my cell phone to call Zant's office. When he answered, I disguised my voice and told him if he wanted his lizard, he should look in that boys' room. Then, me and Monique, we ran like hell."

Kendra studied the girl carefully, trying to discern if there was still more to be told. "You didn't stick around to see what happened?"

"No." Nicole didn't seem to think that an explanation was needed.

Kendra choked down her disgust. "So, you and Monique ran off—which way did you go out?"

"We were going to the bus stop, so we went out the side, by the driveway."

"You're sure that neither of you went over to the north stairs, the ones between the auditorium and the gym?" Kendra was thinking about the tracks on the hall floor. The girls might have gone that way and Nicole was lying.

"No."

One last try. "You girls didn't get any soap on your-selves?"

"No way. That stuff is gross. We were careful, just leaned into the bathroom and squirted the soap in. What difference does that

178

make? You can ask Monique, too. I know you have reasons not to believe me but it's the truth."

Kendra wasn't at all sure how to proceed. The details of Zant's accident had never been made public, especially the detail of the soap. Could Nicole really have thought Zant might have fallen down the stairs for some totally unrelated reason? If she was telling the truth, perhaps the girl believed Zant could have walked in and out of the bathroom without tracking anything. But the evidence didn't support that. Soap had been tracked down the hall by more than one set of shoes.

"Nicole, you're not stupid. You knew that this was the same area where Zant fell, but you never came forward."

"What do you mean? Why would I? I didn't have any-thing to do with that."

Although Kendra was fairly certain that the two girls had played a part in what had happened, she didn't know if they were legally to blame. Morally—it was almost a certainty. In her mind's eye she saw the VP run into the bathroom to get his pet, slipping and sliding as he tried to capture it. She visualized the terrified lizard running out of the bathroom, down the hallway with its owner giving chase. Toward the stairway.

Kendra was still unsatisfied with how this information fit with some other facts. There were still details to explore.

"You can go. We'll talk about this again." Kendra didn't attempt to hide her dislike for the student in front of her.

"You don't believe me!" Nicole seemed genuinely sur-prised Kendra wasn't willing to completely drop the issue.

The girl angrily swept up her pack and burst out of the room. A chill came in through the gaping door. The sky had clouded over again. Kendra watched Nicole slice through the crowd until she disappeared from view. The warning bell sounded. Lunch was over.

Kendra pulled a can of soda from the fridge and grabbed a whiteboard pen with her other hand. She wrote: "5th period will be taught by Mrs. Edwards. Behave!!!"

17.

Friday afternoon

Kendra couldn't take her eyes off Julia's tartan plaid hair bow, an unfortunate accessory to the pink blouse that draped the secretary's ample torso like a deflated balloon. Kendra felt guilty about the blatant examination, but she kept her eyes fixed on Julia all the same. Julia was obviously trying to avoid Kendra so she was taking her time, time Kendra didn't have, to deal with a clerk from the registrar's office. Hopefully, Julia would sense Kendra's stare and would want to deal with her just to be rid of her. Apparently, the tactic was working because Julia glanced back and self-consciously tucked her blouse firmly under her belt.

How many hours had she sat, stewing in this very chair, waiting to see Mr. Zant? But today, the twist in her gut came from the revelation about Brian. Her mission with Julia was a good way to keep busy so she wouldn't think about him. Also, a conversation with Julia would fill in the final gaps in the Zant story.

Finally seeing an opportunity, Kendra darted to the counter. "Julia, have you got time for a break?"

Julia said tartly, "Aren't you supposed to be teaching? This is fifth period."

"I have my room covered. I'd like to talk. If you're in the middle of something, I'll wait." Kendra made it look like she was going to hover there for as long as it took. Without a VP on board, the little waiting area was empty. Kendra would be the only one there, and counted on the fact that her long-term presence would make Julia uncomfortable.

Reluctantly the secretary said, "I can take a few minutes." She took a step toward the break room.

"Why don't we step into the office instead. It's more private."

The secretary stiffened. "Is this work related?" she asked sharply.

This wasn't going well. To hell with it, Julia wasn't exactly her friend. "I'll go ahead and say what I have to say right here, then. I don't care if anyone overhears. Or, if you prefer, we can go straight to the police."

"About what? They're done with this place. What are you after me for? Leave me alone!"

Kendra stood fast. "I'd prefer to be left alone also. You're a fine one to talk when you deliberately put the detectives on to me. They came out to my house. Just because I asked a few, ordinary questions and pointed to the desk drawer? I don't know why you played that up so much for the cops unless there was something you wanted to steer them away from yourself. That sound about right?"

"No, of course not."

In spite of her threat to broadcast the conversation, Kendra lowered her voice. "And then, if putting me in the line of fire wasn't enough to scare me off, you dropped a note at my house. That was a bit over the top, don't you think?"

"You're crazy! I don't know what you're talking about," said Julia stepping back.

Kendra walked to a nearby phone. "Have it your way." Kendra reached into a pocket and pulled out Detective Tapia's card.

Julia hustled over and put a hand over the receiver before Kendra could pick it up. "What are you going to do?"

"I'm going to tell the cops that you and Zant were walking in the same hallway the afternoon of his accident," said Kendra in a slightly louder voice than was necessary.

The secretary looked around fearfully. She pulled Kendra by the wrist into Zant's empty office, shut the door, and said, "Happy now? I don't know anything about Zant. Your threats are way off base. I didn't set the detectives on you. All I did was show them Zant's broken drawer."

Kendra rubbed her aching wrist. "Don't try to deny you've been after me. I can't believe a word you say, because I know for a fact you've told me a whole string of lies."

"Like what?"

"Like what you really did the afternoon Zant had the accident. The evidence doesn't support what you told me."

"Evidence? What do you know about evidence?" Julia gave Kendra a dismissive look.

Kendra decided to go for it. "You claim that you didn't go near

the stairway, but the custodian saw more than one set of footprints tracking over there. I think some of them belonged to you."
Kendra felt rewarded as she watched Julia's composure break.
"Okay, maybe I did go over there, but I didn't do anything to Zant, I swear! He was already dead!"
Kendra was encouraged by her deductive success and quickly challenged, "He couldn't have been dead. He died in the hospital."
"He looked dead," Julia whimpered. "I saw him and ran. How could I know he was still alive?"
The answer hung in the silence between them; Julia would have known if she'd bothered to check. Kendra didn't have enough forgiveness to deal with such cold inhumanity.
Julia dropped to the wooden bench and started to cry. To Kendra's mind, the scene resembled one from a 1950s courtroom drama at the moment of denouement, the witness astonishingly revealed to be the real murderess. The TV judge had no trouble deciding who was guilty. Unfortunately, this was real, and was she, herself, sure that she'd have done something different if she'd been in Julia's position?
Julia took a deep breath and said, "I don't know what happened to Zant. Like I told you before, when I left the girls' room I intended to go out the north stairs."
"But you didn't turn around to avoid the soap like you told me before. You kept going," said Kendra. "All the way to the stairs." Her words sounded like an indictment.
Julia flicked a look up at Kendra, who stood solidly before her. "By the time I noticed that there was something on the hall floor, I'd already stepped in it. I thought about doubling back, but I was already so close to the staircase I kept going. I was just real careful how I walked, so I wouldn't slip. When I got to the top of the stairs, I saw a man's body lying at the bottom."
"You knew who it was." Kendra ground the words out.
"Of course I knew." Julia spoke as if this was of no particular consequence.
And you didn't care, thought Kendra, for once not vocalizing her opinion. She shook her head in total disbelief and said, "You left him there. Just like that."
Julia's nose wrinkled and she whined, "I told you. I thought he was dead, and I was scared. Maybe I should have done something,

but he wasn't moving. I was sure he was dead, so what did it matter?"

Kendra was repulsed at the woman's coldness—even though she was convinced she was telling the truth this time.

Julia squared her jaw and added, "I was afraid people would think I pushed him. Everyone knew the way Zant treated me and how much I hated him. Who would have believed me?"

Kendra's voice was reflective as she spoke. "You behaved like everyone else does in this damn school. All you thought about was yourself."

"Don't you judge me! Do you know what he did to me? The bastard deliberately interfered and ruined my adoption! After what he did, I will never, ever, be able to adopt. He knew that adopting that baby meant everything to me, so he interfered on purpose."

The secretary's face knotted with anguish as the words came. "He was an evil man. Nobody misses him and nobody cares how he died. He hurt a lot of people around here—more than you know. Even if they don't say so, everyone's glad he's dead. Just in your department alone, he was doing something to Mrs. Jarney, and I'm positive he got Jack Sermon fired, too."

She rose from the bench and finished, "Maybe someone did kill Zant, but the killer wasn't me."

Kendra was so overwhelmed by the secretary's testimony she hardly noticed as the woman stomped away. She was lost in a vision of Julia stepping cautiously down the empty hallway, pulling up short at the sight of Zant's body. Then what? Did Julia cry out? Stand over him and gloat? Run away? Or did she—A figure materialized in the doorway, breaking Kendra's reverie. The clerk was back. "Where's Julia?" she asked.

"Not sure," said Kendra. She glanced at her watch, grimaced, and headed for the nearest exit.

She tried to recall what lesson she was supposed to teach next period. Instead, her overloaded brain flashed back to a discussion in her college philosophy class. One day there had been a heated debate over a "what if" situation the professor posited. The more she thought about the example, the more relevant it became:

A man named George had a very obnoxious neighbor, Mike, who didn't clean up after his two big dogs. One day George decided to get revenge. He set up a hidden camera so he could watch the front of his house while standing in back at his sprinkler system controls. Then he chose a very cold day and waited for Mike to come out with his dogs. Mike and the dogs appeared and at the right time, George turned on the sprinklers. Mike backed up at full speed to get out of the strong spray of icy water. In a span of seconds, the unexpected and unimaginable happened. The dogs jumped wildly and pushed at Mike. In his panic, Mike forgot about the four steps that led down to the sidewalk. He tripped and wound up with a broken back. As a result, Mike became a paraplegic. Soon after, in combination with some existing medical conditions, Mike died. Was George guilty of manslaughter?

Before Kendra could decide if her flashback was useful, a mob of unruly adolescents stampeded across her path. Fifth period must have ended. She saw that she'd reached the portables on autopilot. Maretta was coming toward her. "You owe me double," she said.

"That bad?" Kendra asked.

"Tell you after school. Come over!"

***

"Well, you sure can pick 'em," said Maretta with resignation. She settled Kendra in a chair, a box of tissues within easy reach. The door to Maretta's classroom was locked to prevent interruptions. The last thing Kendra wanted was to see other teachers in her present state.

Kendra set her glasses back on her nose. "I'm still not 100% sure that it was Brian. Why would he do something like that to me?"

"If Brian did send those emails, what will you do?"

"Break up, what else?" Kendra's voice wavered. "And another relationship goes down the drain." She blew her nose and added, "Oh well, I was starting to feel that we weren't going to make it anyway. He was too critical, too demanding."

Maretta hugged her and said softly, "You might not want to hear this, but maybe you should report Brian to the police. If you confront him alone, who knows what he'll do? He's got to have some serious issues, you know? Maybe he's even done things like this to other people. You did talk to the detectives, right?"

"They still haven't called me back, but that's just as well

because of what I learned this afternoon. Detective Tapia will be more likely to take me seriously now. Wait till I tell you what else I found out about Zant. I'm just not sure what to tell the police."

Kendra thought that this was one instance where telling the whole truth might not be the best course of action. Poor old Standard High would make the news again. And Zant's death really was an accident. She decided not to share this particular train of thought.

Maretta looked annoyed. "The truth would work, no?" She went to a small, concealed fridge and pulled out two cans, handing one to her friend.

Kendra's throat was parched from crying, and in her exhausted state, nothing could have sounded better than the brittle, "crackle-fizz" that came when she opened the cold can of soda. She took a few sips.

Maretta pushed the phone toward her. "You should try calling the police again—but not before you tell me every-thing first."

"*Everything* might take longer than I have the energy for right now. Okay, don't give me that look. I'll give you a summary, okay?" Kendra's index finger traced random patterns in the condensation on her soda can while she considered where to begin.

"The whole thing started because a student, Nicole Penniman, wanted to get back at Zant. With a friend's help, she stole his lizard, and they threw the poor thing into a boy's john—the one near the auditorium. Then they called Zant and told him where his pet was."

"So that's why he went up to that end of the building." Maretta clapped her hands as if she'd just caught a tangible truth between her palms.

"Yep, and to make their little prank nastier they dumped liquid soap all over the bathroom floor to make sure that Zant would get good and dirty when he tried to catch the lizard."

Maretta's shocked response came out as a squeak. "My god, they're responsible then!"

"In a way, yes, they are. I certainly don't believe that Nicole expected Zant to end up dead. She couldn't predict exactly what would happen after she set up the prank. In fact, it seems as if nobody does know exactly what happened. Maybe the lizard ran out to the hall and went for the stairs with Zant chasing behind.

But it's also possible Zant decided to use the stairs for some other reason and the fact that he fell wasn't even related to anything the girls did." Kendra stopped at Maretta's sour look. "I don't mean to sound like I'm defending the girls."

"They created a dangerous situation. Zant could have easily have hurt himself in the bathroom, without ever going near the stairs."

"I suppose that's true. But if a kid leaves a slice of pizza on the stairs, does he get arrested for someone slipping on the pepperoni?"

Maretta huffed, but shook her head. "I guess not, but what if the little bugger put the pizza slice there on purpose?"

"That's my point. Nicole didn't soap the stairs, if you see what I mean. She didn't intend for Zant to fall down twelve steps and die. Anyhow, if you're upset over what Nicole did, wait till you hear the rest of what's been happening around here."

"No, you're kidding. There's more?"

"Jack—" Kendra only got out one word before Maretta burst in.

"Nicole and Jack?"

"Down girl, give me a chance. Remember Jack's little thermos he always carried around? I know, we thought it held vodka or something, but Jack's sister told me that the thermos contained grape juice. Remember, Jack was dia-betic? I saw him the morning he died, and he was weaving around like a drunk. Well, he wasn't drunk. He was light headed from low blood sugar. And a short while later he ran his car into a wall."

"So, you're saying he was dizzy and lost control of his car?" As if on cue, an engine roared to life in the school auto shop beyond Maretta's window.

"He lost control all right, but I think that happened with Tamra's help. She somehow got possession of his thermos. She was seen throwing it away right around the time Jack was crashing his car."

"How did Tamra get Jack's thermos, and what would she want with it?"

"I can't say how she got it, but that thermos was a safety thing for Jack, a necessity. According to Jack's sister, he took the thermos along in his car, so that if he felt lightheaded while

186

driving he could pull over and drink some juice. But he didn't have it in his car that morning. I think maybe low blood sugar caused his accident. And why was Tamra throwing it away? That's kind of weird, isn't it?"

Maretta got up and cracked a window. "I follow what you're saying. Only, if Jack had had the juice in his car, how do you know that he would have stopped to have a drink anyway?"

"I don't, but if Tamra did take the thermos, she took away Jack's opportunity to make that decision. There was an eyewitness who said Jack might have been trying to pull off the road. And there's another possibility. Maybe Tamra knew there was something in the thermos besides juice, maybe something she put in there. Then he drinks it and—"

"Whoa! But you said she had the thermos, not Jack. So how did she dope his juice, get him to drink it and take his beloved bottle away from him? I just can't buy any of your wild suppositions. You've sure developed a very low opinion of our coworkers. After what's happened with Brian, maybe your emotions are affecting your judgment, Kendra. I refuse to believe that a person we see all the time—Tamra of all people—would try to kill someone. What possible motive could she have?"

Kendra smiled at her friend's skepticism. "A 'low opinion' of our coworkers? I guess you haven't found any Special Ed. documents with *your* signature forged on them? I couldn't understand why Tamra didn't catch the discrepancies. Now I realize she's involved. And don't forget, Tamra had to have a hand in getting Jack fired. And also, Jack warned me to be careful about asking questions, but he didn't tell me why. Maybe he was worried about Tamra."

"I understand why you've been hesitant about going to the police. What you've told me puts a lot of people in a bad light. But they could easily regard what you call evidence as just a lot of guesswork."

"Yeah, I'm afraid of that, although you got the short version. Some of the other details help a little." Kendra scrunched her empty can.

Maretta narrowed her eyes and sighed in resignation. "Fine, I can live with that for now. Still, I think you should go right to the police station and stay there until you talk to them. You'll be safer that way, especially if you're right about Tamra. And God knows what else you've stirred up. I'm not even sure I like knowing what you've told me. This puts me in a bit of a spot too, doesn't it?"

Kendra got up. "I promise that if the detectives don't call me back by tomorrow, I'll go over to the police station." She hugged Maretta. "Thanks for the soda and for listening to my wild stories. Talk to you tomorrow."

After Kendra left, Maretta pulled out a phone list and scanned the columns. The number of the local police department was prominently figured in bold type. She adjusted the paper so the bottom edge was neatly aligned with the rim of her desk and considered her options.

***

When Kendra got home, she turned off the ringers on the two house phones, and turned her cell off as well. She knew Maretta would kill her if she knew, but Kendra just couldn't talk to anyone until she got her thinking straight—something she felt might never happen.

The display on her answering machine seemed to glow with a new magnitude of brightness, taunting her resolve to ignore the waiting message. Kendra roamed about and did anything and everything except play back the message. The kitchen was made spotless and Bobbins became tired of playing. Finally, she decided to get it over with and hit the play button.

Brian's voice pleaded, "Kendra, listen, don't hang up on this! Please! Ray called me—I'm so sorry about the emails. I just wanted to make you see how vulnerable you are working at Standard High so you'd quit working in that hellhole around those lowlifes and nutcases. Then, when Zant died, I stepped it up 'cause I was really afraid for you. I had to get you out of there, and you weren't listening to reason. I know you're mad at me, but call me, please? I love you."

She viciously jabbed the erase button and stopped a breath short of hurling the blameless machine to the floor. Instead, she shuffled robot-like from room to room, stuffing Brian's belongings into a trash bag, which she dumped outside. As she relocked the back door, she realized her hands were shaking.

188

The doorbell rang before she was halfway through a box of her favorite comfort food. With the chime, Bobbins abandoned his plans to capture the cheese crackers and went to investigate. Kendra swooped him up and closed him in the bedroom so he couldn't run out, even though she doubted she'd be letting anyone in the way she felt.

But when she got to the front, no one was there. She heard voices coming from the side of the house, moving toward the back. There were at least two people. Maybe the detectives were responding to her message by coming out to see her? Kendra made it to the kitchen in time to see Tamra and Allana through the side window.

Damn it, what were those two doing at her house? She could pretend she wasn't home—an obvious lie given that they must have gotten a glimpse of her through the window—or she could find out what they wanted. Their determined knocking demanded a response. She cracked open the back door.

The two women pushed past her, through the tiny utility room into the kitchen. Kendra followed but kept her distance.

Tamra spoke first. "Avoiding us?"

Kendra shot back, "What is this—what do you want?"

Allana walked toward Kendra. "I warned you to mind your own business, but nothing gets you to stop."

Oh god, thought Kendra. That note was from Allana? Kendra readied herself to run past the women in case she needed to. She'd die before she let Allana get near the bedroom.

Allana held out a hand. "Give us Zant's BlackBerry and we'll leave."

"Huh? I don't have his BlackBerry!"

"Bullshit! You've been sneaking around, asking all those questions. We know you broke into his desk."

Tamra said, "Just hand it over and we won't tell anyone you stole it. Since you shouldn't have it in the first place, you can't really show it around anyway, now can you?"

"I don't have it—so you can leave now," said Kendra without much hope. She didn't have the strength to deal with this confrontation, let alone to ask them why they were so gung ho to get the device.

"We're not leaving without it, so either you give it to us or we'll search the place," said Allana. I'll start in the bedroom. Tamra, why don't you start in the kitchen."

Kendra's first thought was to protect Bobbins. She started for the hall when suddenly, Tamra cut across her path, grabbed Jack's thermos bottle from where it lay near the sink, and made a beeline for Kendra shouting, "Who have you told about this?"

Allana didn't like the digression. She tried to take the thermos from Tamra's hand. "What are you doing with that skanky thing? We're here to get the BlackBerry."

"To hell with that. It was your idea to come here and I thought it might be amusing, but we've gone far enough."

"I'm not leaving here empty-handed," countered Allana.

Tamra gave a dry laugh and with a belittling tone said, "It's true what Zant told me; you really are too dumb to be a teacher." Before Allana could recover from her shock, Tamra added, "To be honest, I'm not even sure Kendra has the BlackBerry. You were so worried about it, and I wanted to make you sweat, to pay you back for your disloyalty."

Allana screamed, "How dare you!" Her face cycled through anger and disbelief, ending with her gaze fixed hard on Kendra.

Kendra responded by raising her hands in an expressive "I don't have what you want" gesture.

For a moment, tension arced between the three women, Allana and Tamra mere inches apart, and Kendra a few feet away, ready to fight, or flee. A heartbeat later, Allana expelled a violent breath and regaining a semblance of her usual confidence snapped, "I don't know what game you're playing, but to hell with you, Tamra!" Muttering a final string of curses, Allana ran through to the front and out the door.

Tamra shot a victory smile in that direction, but, in a blink, tossed the thermos aside, jumped at Kendra and shoved her against a wall. Before Kendra could recover her balance, Tamra wrapped strong fingers around Kendra's thin upper arms.

"What are you doing with the thermos? What did Jack tell you?

Kendra twisted to squirm free, crying, "You're crazy! Let me go!" She could not escape Tamra, who was larger, stronger and fueled by malevolent purpose.

"You little bitch! You're into everything, aren't you? Maybe you really do have the BlackBerry. She tightened her grip on

Kendra's arms until Kendra gasped with pain. "I'm asking you again. I know you two were friends. What did Jack tell you?"

In response, Kendra kicked at her, but Tamra twisted her hip and pinned Kendra more firmly to the wall. Still struggling to break free, Kendra panted, "I can ask you the same thing. What were *you* doing with Jack's thermos. Why did you throw it away?"

"Mind your own business, you bitch. I've had it with you."

"You killed him didn't you! Why? What did he ever do to you?" Kendra half sobbed the question.

"Now who's the crazy one." Tamra laughed.

"You're hurting me! Let me go!"

"Not until you answer my question."

Another voice, strong, masculine and calm spoke out. "What question would that be, Mrs. Helens?"

Detective Tapia stepped into the kitchen. Tamra froze, dropped her hands and backed away. Kendra slumped against the wall and watched as Detective Howard and Allana came into the kitchen behind Tapia. Allana must have left the front door open during her dramatic departure.

Tamra wasn't quite finished. She took a quick step toward the thermos. Detective Tapia interpreted her movement as an intention to run, and he deftly cut her off. "Not so fast. You're not going anywhere."

"What's going on here, Ms. Desola?" said Detective Howard. She pointed at Allana. "We found her running out the front door in a rage, so we collared her. She told us she's a teacher friend of yours, and something was going on in your house."

Kendra collected her thoughts. How could she explain? "This thermos bottle belonged to Jack Sermon, a teacher who died when he drove his car into a wall. Tamra somehow got hold of Jack's thermos and she threw it away right around the time he died."

Tamra shouted, "I told you, damn it. Jack gave it to me. I was going to buy him a new one. So I threw the old one away. End of story."

Kendra rubbed her bruised arms. "Then why did you attack me when you saw I had it?"

"That's my business, but it's not a police matter. I had nothing to do with Jack's death and you can't prove that I did."

Detective Howard looked exasperated. "You're fighting over a thermos bottle?"

"I found it by chance, and brought it home. When Tamra saw it here just now, she attacked me. It's a long story. . . ."

Tapia listened to her theory about the last hours of Jack's life. His only response in the end was to nod and to ask her one question. Pointing his notepad at Tamra he said, "You want to press assault charges against this one, Ms. Desola?"

Kendra nodded.

"Take her in," he instructed his partner. "I'll take care of the thermos."

Howard escorted Tamra from the room. Allana took this as a cue to leave too, but Tapia stopped her and asked Kendra, "She involved?"

Kendra said, "I don't know." She couldn't prove that Allana was guilty of anything except connivance. That being said, under normal circumstances, the fact that Allana had called her a "teacher friend" would have had her in stitches.

Allana was at the point of tears. "Can I go?"

Tapia hesitated. "For the moment, Mrs. Jarney, but I advise you not to get too far away. There are certain business transactions that took place between you and Mr. Zant that we need to clear up.

This time, Allana went quietly.

Detective Tapia wasn't ready to leave. He turned his full attention on Kendra, who was standing at the wall, hugging herself. Unexpectedly, he took a sweater from a chair back and held it out to her. Kendra gratefully drew it over her shoulders. Sensing the danger was past, she sagged into a chair.

"Better?" Tapia asked. "You'll need to come to the station soon to press charges. Before that though, you and I need to talk over a few things."

She eyed him warily. "Like?"

Tapia took a chair to join her at the table and gave her a long look. "I always had a feeling we'd talk again, Kendra. By the way, your friend Maretta really cares about you. She phoned us with concerns about things you discovered. Seems as if we made the right decision to respond to your message and her phone call in person."

Kendra wasn't sure what to say. Something inside her fought against her learned distrust of police officers. Tapia did not seem to be trying to entrap her. She said, "I guess things got out of hand."

"You could have avoided this by coming forward. By the way, it didn't take us long to discover why you were so resistant to our questioning. After what happened to your brother—the way he was locked up for a crime he didn't commit—well, I might be reluctant to trust investigators too. Since I don't think you're about to spill your guts to me, I think the best way to proceed is I go ahead and tell you what I think happened and for now, you just listen, okay?"

She nodded, curious in spite of herself.

"We found a number of interesting things as we moved along in our investigation. Like Zant's BlackBerry. That was interesting in itself, but the people who were freaking out trying to find it—that really got our attention.

"Zant showed his dark side far beyond his choice of office pets. He coerced a number of women in the district into relationships and blackmailed them when he couldn't bed them. When I was a kid there were things called 'slam-books,' of malicious gossip and incriminating facts that students used to hurt and control one another. I guess you could say Zant kept a 'SlamBerry'."

He studied her face with an expression that approached sympathy. "The way Zant treated people, we didn't find too many people crying after he fell down the stairs. I'm not singling you out, don't worry. But here's what I have been able to piece together. Maybe you can tell me if I'm right?"

Tapia paused for a moment when Kendra shifted nervously and continued, "Someone who hated Zant stole the lizard out of his terrarium, and maybe taunted him so he'd run in a panic to get it and dive straight into that boys' room, which was slathered with industrial strength soap. You've been asking about footprints, so you probably know there were several sets of soapy footprints up and down the hall going toward the stairs."

Kendra started to say something, then pressed her lips closed. This is a ploy to get me to fill in the blanks, she thought.

"So, Zant went up there to get the lizard, and since his clothes were covered with soap, he must have fallen in it while attempting to grab the animal. The critter must have run for the stairway or maybe Zant had already captured it and in his frenzy didn't pay attention to the goo on his shoes. Either way, he was trying to go down the stairs when he slipped and fell to his death."

193

"That takes us to the second set of prints, those of a woman who wears a size eight—the same shoe size as Julia Chatin, Zant's secretary. We don't really know what she was doing there. We know she skidded a bit before she reached the stairs and circled above the body but didn't approach it. I'm guessing that she didn't stick around when she heard the third person to join the party— Nate the custodian. As you know, he saw Zant at the bottom of the steps and called for help immediately."

Kendra's pulse slowed a bit. *Julia's not on my conscience, then. What else does he know?*

Tapia gave her a measured look and flipped a page in his notebook. "There is a fourth set of prints, women's size nine and a half. Casual shoes, a popular brand the kids are wearing. These prints are partly tracked over and left a puzzling pattern. They come out from the bathroom and then track in two directions, toward the stairs and also back to the far end of the hall away from the stairs. Looks like she removed her shoes because the prints just stop suddenly. So, maybe this woman saw Zant, maybe not."

Nicole must have lied to me! She went over to the stairs, but when? Maybe she was hiding somewhere to watch how her little prank went down. Did she see Zant fall? My god, another silent witness! But if I say something to Tapia he'll arrest her for sure and Nicole as a murderess doesn't fit the facts. Unless...

She sensed that Tapia was expecting a response. Better give him one before he started asking questions. "Seems it was an accident like we all thought, but those people, they all just left the man lying there!"

Tapia shook his head. "With the kind of injury he sustained, I doubt that Mr. Zant could have been saved even if a neurosurgeon had been standing at the bottom of the stairs. That's how things go sometimes. Still, as it is, a lot of justice did come out of this.

On account of the criminal charges, both Tamra Helens and Allana Jarney will lose their jobs; your "friend" Allana has her own set of issues. I'd guess Mrs. Prescott won't get her big promotion and Mr. Favor's got some questions to answer." He gave her a half smile. "Even your boyfriend's nasty little email games surfaced and cost him."

She caught her breath. "You—"

"Yes. I was trying to figure out how to pass that little piece of information along to you, but I found out you discovered it on your own. If this teaching gig doesn't work out, you could become a detective. Speaking of which, you wouldn't have any insight about that fourth set of footprints, would you?"

The rattle of rain against the kitchen window was the only reply. The detective leaned back, his eyes casually roaming the kitchen as if he was in her home, kicking back, on a social visit. Kendra took this as a stand-off, half friendly, half intimidating. That would do just fine, for now. She counted breaths. When she got to 14, Tapia frowned and closed his notebook. "Well, I guess we're done for now. I'll be in touch. You got a paper bag I can have for this thermos?"

She helped him package the thermos and watched with relief as he tucked it under his arm and started to go. But suddenly, he turned back, and added, "By the way, when we were examining the lower hallway, we found a fancy looking lizard. One of our techs is an animal lover, wants to find it a good home."

To her own amazement, she smiled. Tapia saw an opportunity and pressed, "You're sure there's nothing else you want to tell me?"

"Not at the moment. Good night, Detective."

He shook his head and gave up the fight. Just as the front door shut, she shouted after him, "I'll call you."

www.ingramcontent.com/pod-product-compliance
Lightning Source LLC
Chambersburg PA
CBHW060218180626
46813CB00007B/2874